COLONEL FITZWILLIAM'S DILEMMA

Lady Catherine de Bourgh has invited herself to Pemberley, intent upon bringing about an engagement between her daughter Anne and Colonel Fitzwilliam. But her ladyship has failed to take into account the remarkable improvement in her daughter's health and spirits since the arrival of her new tutor, the charismatic Mr. Asquith. Meanwhile, enchanted by the widowed Celia Sheffield, Colonel Fitzwilliam is perturbed to learn that her fortune is being contested by an individual in Jamaica — from whence Mr. Asquith also hails. And when the obsequious Mr. Collins shares grave rumours concerning the tutor's character, further suspicions are raised . . .

Wendy Soliman was brought up on the Isle of Wight in southern England but now divides her time between Andorra and western Florida. She lives with her husband Andre and a rescued dog of indeterminate pedigree named Jake Bentley after the hunky hero in one of her books. When not writing she enjoys reading other people's books, walking miles with her dog whilst plotting her next scene, dining out and generally making the most out of life.

WENDY SOLIMAN

COLONEL FITZWILLIAM'S DILEMMA

Complete and Unabridged

ULVERSCROFT
Leicester

First published in Great Britain in 2013

First Large Print Edition
published 2015

A catalogue record for this book is available
from the British Library.

ISBN 978–1–4448–2403–2

Published by
F. A. Thorpe (Publishing)
Anstey, Leicestershire

Set by Words & Graphics Ltd.
Anstey, Leicestershire
Printed and bound in Great Britain by
T. J. International Ltd., Padstow, Cornwall

This book is printed on acid-free paper

1

'How surprising.' Fitzwilliam Darcy looked up from reading his letter and smiled across the breakfast table at his wife. 'It seems we are restored to favour.'

'With whom are we out of favour?' Lizzy asked, returning her husband's smile.

'Lady Catherine is to pay us a visit.'

Lizzy arched a brow. 'Even if I am disobliging and selfish, unworthy of her notice?'

'No!' Georgiana cried, sharing a horrified glance with Kitty. 'Never. Not you, Lizzy.'

'Unfortunately your aunt doesn't share your good opinion of me.'

'Lady Catherine wanted Fitzwilliam for her daughter.' Georgiana wrinkled her nose. 'It was the silliest notion in the world. But Lady Catherine has always been blinded by her determination to have her own way.'

'It sounds as though Lady Catherine has come to her senses,' Kitty Bennet, Lizzy's younger sister, said as she buttered a second slice of toast.

'Does she give a reason for her visit?' Lizzy asked.

'She is in raptures over your condition, and

wishes to heal the breach between us.'

Lizzy tossed her head. 'That is very generous of her, considering it was her who created the breach.'

'Yes, but I cannot refuse to let her come.'

'I would not have you do so.' Lizzy paused. 'She heard about the forthcoming addition to our family from Charlotte Collins, presumably.'

'No, I wrote to inform her of it myself.'

'Oh, you didn't mention it.' Probably because if Lady Catherine continued to cut Lizzy, Will would prefer her not to know his olive branch had been repulsed. Will never said as much, but Lizzy knew he was disturbed by the rift with his aunt. 'When can we expect her?'

'In about a week.'

'My cousin Anne will accompany her?' Georgiana asked. 'And Mrs. Jenkinson too, I presume. Anne can never go anywhere without her faithful companion to fuss over her.'

'Georgie! That was almost a discourteous remark. Lady Catherine will say my bad influence is rubbing off on you.' Lizzy sent the younger woman a warm smile. 'I, on the other hand, am very pleased with you.'

'I didn't mean anything by it. It's just that I sometimes think Anne is stifled by the constant attention she receives.' Georgiana sighed. 'Poor Anne. Being an heiress to such an extensive estate as Rosings must be a terrible burden.'

'Mrs. Jenkinson will not form part of their party.' Will waved Lady Catherine's letter across the table. 'My aunt dedicates a considerable part of her missive to complaining about her ill-usage at that lady's hands.'

'Good heavens,' Lizzy said. 'Has there been a falling out?'

'One of Mrs. Jenkinson's nieces has married well and required a governess for her growing family. Mrs. Jenkinson felt duty bound to take the position.'

'From which one must surmise the niece didn't marry *that* well and played upon her aunt's strong family values to acquire a good governess at no cost.'

'Oh dear.' Georgiana's eyes danced with mirth. 'That idea would not have occurred to me.'

'It has occurred to our aunt,' Will replied, 'and she had a very great deal to say about undutiful servants who have no sense of loyalty.'

'Shall Lady Catherine and her daughter travel alone, Mr. Darcy?' Kitty asked.

'No, they are to be accompanied by a gentleman.'

Lizzy groaned. 'Not Mr. Collins, please.'

'No, my dear, not Mr. Collins but a Mr. Asquith.'

'Asquith?' Lizzy wrinkled her brow. 'That name came up in my correspondence with Charlotte Collins but I cannot think — '

'Lady Catherine says he is a gentleman in straitened circumstances. He applied to Mr. Collins for a position at the church school. Collins sought Lady Catherine's advice, naturally — '

'Oh, naturally,' Lizzy replied, sharing a smile with Kitty.

'Lady Catherine insisted upon meeting the young man. He had been recommended to her, although she does not say by whom, and was so taken with Asquith, she engaged him as Mrs. Jenkinson's replacement.'

'Anne de Bourgh has a male tutor.' Lizzy was shocked. 'It will do her the world of good.'

'According to my aunt, Asquith is well-educated, well-travelled, sensible, and deferential. He will travel with them and make all the necessary arrangements for their comfort at the various posting inns on their route.'

'And Lady Catherine's coachman could not have done that for her?' Lizzy lifted her shoulders. 'Still, I confess to a great curiosity and look forward to making Mr. Asquith's acquaintance. Any man who meets with Lady Catherine's approval will be meek and obsequious. Anne will be in no danger of corruption from contact with him.'

'Do you not find this departure on Lady Catherine's part intriguing?' Will asked.

Lizzy nodded. 'I recall now that Charlotte told me Mr. Collins was quite put out by Mr. Asquith's elevation to Lady Catherine's inner circle.'

'Ah, now this starts to make more sense.' Will frowned as he continued to read. 'Colonel Fitzwilliam can be spared from his duties, and Lady Catherine has asked us to invite him also.' He caught Lizzy's eye, and his frown gave way to a smile. 'He is now the favoured candidate for Anne's hand, and she needs our help to persuade Fitzwilliam.'

'She thinks you will encourage the colonel, I suppose,' Lizzy said.

'Then she is in for a disappointment. Fitzwilliam is his own man.'

'Invite the colonel by all means. I enjoy his society, even though I cannot help feeling sorry for his situation.'

'Save your sympathy, Lizzy. Fitzwilliam will not be coerced into a situation that doesn't suit him, no matter how desperate his circumstances.'

'In that case, I shall not interfere and will

allow true love to take its course. Speaking of which ... ' She turned towards Georgiana and Kitty with a mischievous smile. 'If Colonel Fitzwilliam can be spared, I dare say Major Halstead and Captain Turner can be too.'

Both girls brightened considerably. The officers had been guests at Lizzy's first house party as mistress of Pemberley, six weeks previously, and found great favour with Georgiana and Kitty.

'I shall write and invite Colonel Fitzwilliam, and extend the invitation to include his two friends,' Lizzy said. 'It will be so much easier to entertain Lady Catherine if others are present.'

'I will not have you over-exerting yourself,' Will replied, fixing Lizzy with a stern look.

'Oh, nonsense. I am as strong as an ox. Besides, since we are not to go to London for the season, it seems only fair the girls should have their share of entertainments.'

'And Jane and Mr. Bingley are now close by,' Kitty reminded them. 'They will not wish to leave Campton Park for long, having only just moved into their new estate. But since it is only ten miles away, I expect we shall see them.'

'Jane's condition is more advanced than mine, Kitty. We cannot expect her to gallivant all over the place just to oblige us.'

'Have you left your card with our new neighbours, yet?' Will asked Lizzy.

'Actually, Georgie and I planned to call this morning.'

'I know Lord Briar and am glad he will be living so close. By all means include him in our entertainments if you find their society congenial.'

'Thank you. Lady Catherine can hardly object to such eminent company.'

Will stood up, leaned over Lizzy, and kissed her brow. 'Excuse me, my dear. I have business with my steward.'

Georgiana sighed as she watched her brother leave the room. 'I still can't get over the way Fitzwilliam displays so much affection towards you in public,' she said. 'He always seemed so severe before his marriage. Now I see a very different side to him.'

Lizzy was tempted to say that if Will had shown even half as much public affection for her before their previous house party, then a very great deal of mischief on the part of Miss Bingley and Mr. Wickham could have been avoided.

'You won't let Lady Catherine interfere in my affairs, will you, Lizzy?' Georgiana seemed suddenly anxious. 'She will insist upon knowing what is best for me, and I don't have the courage to stand up to her.'

Lizzy patted her hand. 'Fear not. She already thinks so ill of me that the blame for anything you do to displease her will be lodged at my door.'

'Oh, but that would not be fair.'

'Perhaps not, but Lady Catherine's censure cannot harm me. Now come along, Georgie,' she said, sighing. 'If we are to call on Lady Briar, we ought to get ourselves ready.'

* * *

Anne de Bourgh barely noticed the discomfort when their carriage passed over a rough piece of road and the wheels caught in a deep rut, rocking the conveyance and jolting its occupants. She was completely taken up by the melodic timbre of Mr. Asquith's voice as he related tales about his adventures in the Indies. He had travelled to so many exciting places, seen so many things, and met so many interesting people. She, on the other hand, hadn't very often left Kent.

'Those people sound like savages, Mr. Asquith,' she said, gasping. 'Were you not afraid for your life?'

Mr. Asquith smiled his beautiful smile and Anne felt colour invade her face. He was such a handsome man, so charming, so well informed, so non-judgemental, and so tolerant of her many weaknesses. It would be so very easy to fall in love with him, and what a farrago that would cause.

'Not in the least. I was accompanying Master Harry back to his father's plantation. Sir Marius looks after his slaves well, and they have no reason to complain. I have always found if you treat people fairly, they react in like fashion. It is my opinion people are not born evil or deceitful, usually they become so out of severe necessity.'

'Do you really think so?' Anne sat forward, feeling none of the breathlessness this simple exertion would once have caused her. 'How extraordinary. I do not have your worldly experience, but have often thought the same thing. I don't suppose all poor people are thieves or malingerers, and they would much prefer to find honest work if they possibly could.'

'Quite so.' Mr. Asquith nodded as though she had made some remarkably deep, insightful statement. Earning his approval, even if she wasn't sure she deserved it, gave Anne a ridiculous amount of pleasure. 'Since talk of slavery being abolished has become so widespread, many informed people believe it will eventually happen, despite all the opposition. Sir Marius hopes to persuade his slaves to remain in paid positions, and I dare say they will wish to do so.'

'Because they are well off and have no cause for complaint,' Mama said briskly.

'That is certainly true in the case of Sir Marius's plantation, Lady Catherine.'

'Then perhaps he is too tolerant.'

Anne tried not to feel jealous when Mr. Asquith bestowed one of his dazzling smiles upon her mama. 'I believe a willing worker will always be more productive.'

'Hmm, perhaps.'

As the carriage rattled along, Anne glanced out the window. She was unsurprised that Mr. Asquith had the last word in this exchange. It was rather extraordinary when one thought about it. Mama was nothing if not forthright in the expression of her opinions, but Mr. Asquith made his point with such charm and deference that even Mama couldn't find fault with his manner. She appeared to respect his courage and intellect, just as Anne privately thought Mama respected Eliza Bennet, now Mrs. Darcy, for standing up to her during her visit to Rosings last year.

Mrs. Darcy. Anne briefly closed her eyes, revelling in her narrow escape. For years, she had known Mama intended that title for her. Frankly, Mr. Darcy terrified her. He was so severe, so . . . well, so everything she was not, but she had always supposed he wouldn't be able to resist having Rosings as well as Pemberley beneath his stewardship. She was heartily grateful to Mrs. Darcy for saving her from a situation that would have made her even more invisible than she already was.

But her relief had been short-lived. This visit to Pemberley, ostensibly to heal the rift between Mama and the Darcys, had actually been arranged so Colonel Fitzwilliam could admire her. Admire? Humiliation washed through Anne. She was no beauty, possessed few talents and even less conversation. People made her so nervous she never knew quite what to say to them. Besides, her mother seldom left her with an opportunity to speak for herself.

She wasn't supposed to be aware of her mother's efforts to bring her and the colonel together, but she had overheard Mama discussing it with Mrs. Collins. The colonel frightened her almost as much as Mr. Darcy did, but she knew he could not afford to turn his back on her, any more than Anne could refuse to do her duty.

Anne glanced across at Mr. Asquith, seated with his back to the horses, smiling at something her mother had just said. Oh, how

11

she wished things were different. She knew nothing of Mr. Asquith's family. He was very reticent on the subject, and strangely, Mama had not made too many enquiries in that respect. Not that any were necessary. He was obviously a gentleman without means. His education, his manners, his refined tone, and his elegant manner of conducting himself, all attested to that fact. If only Anne was free to please herself . . . Of course, she never would be and so there was little point in having regrets.

'Are you warm enough, Anne?'

Her mother's voice jolted Anne out of her reverie. Until recently, she had been asked that question all the time. When Mr. Asquith had first arrived at Rosings, she heard her mother explaining her frail state of health, emphasising that she was not to be over-exerted. Mr. Asquith had merely raised a brow, said he was sure that was a temporary situation and, as Miss de Bourgh grew older her health would most likely improve. How strange. No one had ever suggested she would outgrow her maladies before.

'How many more days shall we have on the road, Mr. Asquith?' she asked.

Enclosed in a comfortable carriage, with just her Mama and Mr. Asquith for company, she wished the journey could go on indefinitely. Better yet, she dared to pretend it was just her and Mr. Asquith making the journey and that his glamorous smiles were all for her.

'Two more nights should see us in Derbyshire, Miss de Bourgh.'

Only two nights? Anne sighed. It hardly seemed fair.

★ ★ ★

'How did you find the Briars?'

Lizzy lay on a settee in her private sitting room, her head resting in her husband's lap. 'I liked them very much.'

'I thought you would. Do they plan to stay in Derbyshire until after Christmas?'

'They have no plans to go to town for the season. One of their sons is in his final year at Cambridge, and the other is in Europe doing whatever young men do when they have need to let off steam.' Lizzy glanced up at Will. 'Presumably you had a Grand Tour.'

'I did.'

'Ah, so you will be able to satisfy my curiosity. What *do* young men of fortune and privilege do with themselves in Italy, and Greece, and all those other places that are considered *de rigeur*?'

Will chuckled. 'In your condition, I am

sure it's not a good idea to shock you. Suffice it to say that idle young men do need, as you so charmingly put it, to let off steam away from their own doorsteps.'

Lizzy sent him a speaking look. 'Your son needs to be informed.'

Will rested a warm hand possessively on her belly. 'What makes you so sure it's a boy?'

'I certainly hope he is.'

'Good heavens.' Will flexed a brow. 'Why?'

Lizzy lifted her head from its comfortable resting place, genuinely surprised. 'Of course you want a son to inherit and carry on the Darcy name. I know the angst my mother suffered each time she produced a girl and failed to cut off the Longbourne entail. I would prefer to know at the earliest opportunity that I have not inherited her inability to bear sons.'

'As far as I know, it is impossible to inherit such traits.' He pulled her onto his lap and kissed her brow. 'Besides, I have nothing against daughters. Pemberley isn't entailed, nor will it ever be. If we have no sons, our eldest daughter will inherit.'

'Thank you.' Lizzy felt a welling of deep love for her husband's consideration. She knew he couldn't possibly be telling the truth. All men secretly desired at least one son, did

14

they not? 'It is silly to worry about such things, but I feel rather sorry for your cousin Anne, having the future responsibility for Rosings resting upon her shoulders. Any woman in that position would be viewed as an easy target and taken advantage of.'

Will laughed. 'In Anne's case, not while there is still breath in Lady Catherine's body.'

'Quite, but Anne is not cut from the same cloth as her mother.'

'Which is why my aunt wishes to see her married. If not to Fitzwilliam then to someone equally suitable.'

'Of Lady Catherine's choosing?'

'Very likely, but we cannot interfere.'

'No, I suppose not.'

'Lady Catherine has many faults, but she does love her daughter and wants the best for her. She understands Anne's limitations and wants to ensure she, as well as the Rosings estate, prospers after she is gone.'

'Of course she does.'

'And we seem to have drifted a long way from the subject of the Briars.'

'That's because you very cleverly turned our conversation away from the subject of your infamous Grand Tour.'

Will sent her a smouldering smile. 'What makes you suppose it was infamous?'

'If it was not, you wouldn't be so keen to

avoid talking about it.' Lizzy reached up a hand and gently traced the line of her husband's face. 'However, I will not press you. And, as to the Briars, I saw Lord Briar only briefly but he seemed very affable. He sent you his compliments, by the way. As to Lady Briar, I thought her quite charming, although she is delicate and suffers with her nerves. I spent half an hour with her and her sister.'

'She has a sister residing with her?'

'Mrs. Sheffield is a lot younger than Lady Briar, but very charming. She cannot be more than five-and-twenty, but is already a widow. Her husband died over a year ago, somewhere abroad. She did not say where. Anyway, she had just returned to England and, at the moment, her home is with her sister.'

'What is she like?'

'Educated, well-bred, and very beautiful. She and Lady Briar seem close. Although Mrs. Sheffield is considerably younger, she seems to take care of her sister, rather than the other way around.' Lizzy canted her head, thinking the matter through. 'There was something slightly mysterious about that lady, but I couldn't say precisely what.'

'Well then, we shall invite them to dinner, and I dare say Mrs. Sheffield will have told you all her secrets by the time the first covers are removed.'

Lizzy punched her husband's arm. 'You make me sound like a busybody.'

'People tend to confide in you because they trust you to be discrete.'

'Hmm, perhaps.' Lizzy felt her eyelids dropping and stifled a yawn.

'Come, you need to rest before dinner.'

She was lifted by a strong pair of arms. The next thing she knew she was nestled between crisp cotton sheets. She had so much to do, so many arrangements to make, but they could wait. She would sleep, just for an hour, and then dress for dinner.

2

'Let battle commence,' Lizzy muttered as she stood with Will, Georgiana and Kitty beneath the entrance portico at Pemberley, watching Lady Catherine's barouche make its way up the long driveway.

'Did you say something?' Will asked.

Nothing that bears repeating. 'I was just remarking your relations have made good time. I had not expected seeing them until tomorrow at the earliest.'

Will sent her a droll look. 'Ah, is that what you said?' His lips twitched and she felt the muscles in his forearm strengthen beneath her fingers resting upon it. 'I must have misheard you.'

'Stop making fun of me,' she hissed. 'You know how nervous I am.'

This time, Will definitely smiled. 'If my aunt wishes to heal the rift between us then she would be wise to show the deference due to my wife.'

'Why do you always know exactly the right thing to say?'

He patted the hand still resting on his sleeve. 'Because you are my life and the only

18

thing that is truly important to me.' He paused, sending her a playful look. 'Apart from my estate, my sister, and my new horse, naturally.'

Lizzy bit her lip to prevent herself from laughing and did her very best to look severe. 'You will pay for that comment later.'

'Oh, I do hope so. I rather enjoy your chastisements.'

'Behave yourself, Mr. Darcy!'

'If I must, Mrs. Darcy.'

The carriage came to a smooth halt directly by the portico and Will's footmen ran forward to let the steps down. Unsurprisingly, Lady Catherine was the first to emerge from it. She looked up at Pemberley's façade and frowned, as though expecting to see signs of it having crumbled in protest at having Lizzy foisted upon it.

'Welcome, Lady Catherine,' Will said, stepping forward and bowing over her hand. 'I trust the journey was not too tedious.'

'A decent carriage made it bearable.'

When she could no longer avoid doing so, Lady Catherine turned her attention to Lizzy. 'Mrs. Darcy,' she said, her tone bordering on the uncivil.

'Lady Catherine.' Lizzy replied, bobbing the merest suggestion of a curtsey. 'Welcome to Pemberley.'

Lady Catherine's only response was to wrinkle her nose. She turned to Georgiana and her severe expression softened, just fractionally.

'Georgiana, you have grown since we last met.'

'Lady Catherine.' Georgiana curtsied. 'We are very pleased you have come.'

'I am anxious to learn of your progress on the pianoforte. You must not, under any circumstances, neglect your practise.'

'I can assure you, I do not do so.'

Lizzy interceded. 'May I bring my sister, Catherine Bennet, to your ladyship's attention?'

Kitty nervously curtsied, while Lady Catherine viewed her with a disinterested air. 'Miss Bennet,' she said distantly. 'I was unaware your sister resided at Pemberley, Mrs. Darcy.'

'Kitty divides her time between Pemberley and my sister, Mrs. Bingley, who now lives just ten miles from here. Kitty and Georgina are the greatest friends.'

'Are they indeed.' Lady Catherine seemed dissatisfied to hear it.

Lizzy felt her temper rising. Given they had not even entered the house yet, this was a sorry start indeed. She quelled the riposte that sprang to her lips and turned her attention to Anne de Bourgh, who had joined the party at the portico on the arm of a gentleman.

'Miss de Bourgh,' Lizzy said, offering her hand, surprised to see colour and a hint of animation in Anne's usually wan countenance. 'You are very welcome.'

'It is very pleasant to be here again, Mrs. Darcy. Of all seasons, I enjoy autumn the most. The colours of the leaves are spectacular.'

'And Pemberley has no shortage of trees to admire.'

Anne de Bourgh had just spoken more words to her in one sentence than she did the entire time Lizzy had been in Kent the previous year. Remarkable!

'This is Mr. Asquith,' Lady Catherine said, offering no further explanation.

Lizzy appraised him while he exchanged a few civil words with Will. Tall and lean, dressed in sombre yet elegant clothing that wasn't the first word in fashion, the man had an engaging air and exquisite manners. His disarming personality had survived several days in the close confines of a carriage with Lady Catherine, which said much for his disposition — or desperation. Lizzy was already starting to understand the cause of the differences in Anne de Bourgh and wondered why Lady Catherine had risked exposing her precious daughter to such a vital man.

Lizzy wondered if Lady Catherine meant to show Anne a little more of the ways of the world through contact with a man who had clearly seen much of it. If so, it was a risky strategy that did not allow for the romantic nature of even the most sensible of girls.

'Mrs. Darcy.' Mr. Asquith bowed over her hand, a charming smile gracing his lips. 'It is most gracious of you to welcome me into your house.'

'You are very welcome, sir,' Lizzy replied, meaning it. 'Shall we?'

She turned toward the entrance vestibule. Lady Catherine claimed Will's arm and preceded her into the house. With a wry lift of one brow, Lizzy fell in alongside her sister, while Georgiana lingered behind with Anne and Mr. Asquith.

Lady Catherine sailed into the drawing room and placed herself in a chair beside the fire.

'This room has been redecorated,' she said accusingly.

'Certainly it has,' Lizzy said evenly. 'It was long overdue.'

'My sister liked it the way it was. And the bronze figurine that was always on the mantelpiece is gone.'

'It has been sent away to be cleaned,' Lizzy replied.

Lady Catherine sniffed. 'What are you two girls giggling about?' she demanded, looking toward Georgiana and Kitty, seated together a little way apart from her.

'We were discussing sketching, Lady Catherine,' Georgiana replied. 'Kitty and I share an instructor.'

'I am astonished. I understood you Bennet girls had no particular skills other than a fortunate penchant for finding rich husbands.' A sharp, audible intake of breath on Kitty's part failed to quiet Lady Catherine. 'Is that not what you implied when you visited Kent last year, Mrs. Darcy?'

Lizzy silently counted to ten before responding. She noticed Will's expression darken and sensed he was about to spring to her defence. There was no need. Lady Catherine had deliberately thrown down a gauntlet Lizzy was quite ready to pick up. She was prepared to endure Lady Catherine's barbed tongue if it meant Will would be reconciled with his difficult relation, but she absolutely would not have her family insulted. She turned to Lady Catherine with an arch smile.

'Then let me hasten to reassure you on

both counts, ma'am. My sisters and I possess many talents, and Kitty is the perfect example of that. Her sketching is on a par with Georgiana's. I am sure she will be happy to show you examples of her work, should your ladyship be interested.' Lizzy paused. 'As to attracting rich husbands, I am unsure if that can be described as a talent. Whether or not we are worthy of them is a question for the husbands themselves to answer.'

'I am the fortunate one,' Will said, stepping forward to rest a proprietorial hand on Lizzy's shoulder.

'Unquestionably,' Mr. Asquith replied with a polite smile.

Now that was interesting. Mr. Asquith did not toady to his employer. Lizzy wondered, in that case, how long he would remain beneath Rosings' roof.

'Mr. Asquith happens to be a talented artist and has been instructing Anne. Her sketching is remarkable.'

Of course it is! Lady Catherine had conceded defeat by changing the subject back to sketching, and Lizzy was willing to keep the peace by following her example. 'Then perhaps you and Miss de Bourgh would care to join Georgie and Kitty in the morning?' she said to Mr. Asquith. 'They plan to capture the changing colours of the

Pemberley woods. I am sure they would appreciate the benefit of your advice.'

'Thank you, Mrs. Darcy. I should be delighted.'

'I am unsurprised to discover Anne has a natural talent for sketching, now that her health permits her to indulge,' Lady Catherine said to no one in particular.

'I am glad you have found an occupation to which you are so well suited,' Lizzy said in a quiet aside to Anne de Bourgh.

'Suited, perhaps. I certainly enjoy it. Talented . . . hardly that.'

'Nonsense!' Lady Catherine interceded. 'I hope I am not the sort of parent who is blind to her child's faults. Indeed, I am not, and if I say you have talent, then talent is what you have. You merely need to apply yourself and others will see it too.'

'With Georgiana and Miss Bennet to encourage me, Mama, I can safely promise to do so.'

Servants bearing refreshments caused a hitch in the conversation, but Lizzy was satisfied with the way she had defended herself. When Lady Catherine lifted a delicate cup to her lips, replaced it in its saucer and grudgingly offered her and Will her congratulations on the forthcoming addition to their family, Lizzy knew she had won this initial skirmish.

'I hope you left Mr. and Mrs. Collins in good health, Lady Catherine,' Lizzy said.

'Mrs. Collins is occupied with her baby daughter. No good will come from mollycoddling the child, and so I told them both in the strongest terms. You will do well to remember that, Mrs. Darcy.'

'I certainly shall.'

'Who else is to join us, Darcy?' Lady Catherine asked.

'Colonel Fitzwilliam and two other officers from his regiment will be with us tomorrow, along with Major Halstead and Captain Turner. We also have new neighbours, Lord and Lady Briar. And, of course, Mr. and Mrs. Bingley are now close enough to be intimate with us.'

'Briar? I knew a Lord Briar when I was younger. Did they not reside in Sloane Street?'

'That would be the present Lord Briar's father,' Lizzy replied. 'The current Lord Briar purchased his estate a few months ago and plans to reside mostly in the country. They have Lady Briar's sister, a young widowed lady, living with them.'

Lady Catherine accepted a cake. 'Has this widowed sister been left well provided for?'

'I believe Mrs. Sheffield inherited the bulk

of her late husband's estate.'

'Then why does she not live on her estate?'

'That is a question you must ask Mrs. Sheffield,' Lizzy replied.

'If estates are left unattended, workers take advantage.' Lady Catherine straightened her spine. 'That is why I never leave Rosings for long. No one takes advantage of my good nature.'

It was all Lizzy could do not to choke on her tea. 'I am sure they do not,' she managed to say.

Lady Catherine continued to hold court, firing random questions at one and all. By the time the new arrivals took themselves off to their chambers to rest before dinner, Lizzy was already feeling the strain.

'Did Lady Catherine mention how long she plans to stay?' she asked Will, leaning heavily on his arm as they went up together.

Will patted her hand. 'You did well to tolerate her unpardonable rudeness so calmly.'

'You expected me to be blunter?'

Will chuckled. 'You got it exactly right.'

'What did you make of Mr. Asquith? I rather liked him.'

Will quirked a brow. 'Every lady in the room appeared to, including my aunt.'

'Ah, so you noticed that, too. Your cousin has improved considerably, no doubt due to his influence. The changes in her appearance and willingness to speak up for herself are remarkable.'

'So I observed.'

'I can't believe how much latitude Lady Catherine affords him. I wonder why. What do we know about him?'

'Absolutely nothing, other than that he has received a gentleman's education. I shall quiz him on his background at the first opportunity, just to please you.'

Lizzy sent her husband a playful smile. 'But you are not the tiniest bit curious yourself?'

'He does seem to have got the measure of Lady Catherine. That is extraordinary enough to excite my interest.'

'He didn't come in for a single word of criticism from her the entire time we were taking tea, which is more than can be said for the rest of us.'

'I am willing to admit I am intrigued by the unorthodox arrangement.'

'Poor Mr. Collins.' Lizzy smiled as they entered her chamber. 'He must be feeling severely neglected. His company will no longer be so desirable at Rosings now Lady Catherine has a more acceptable alternative. I owe Charlotte a letter. I shall write to her in the morning and press her for more particulars regarding Mr. Asquith.'

Will kissed the back of her hand and headed for the adjoining door to his own room. 'Get some rest, my love. You will need it if you are to withstand my aunt's demanding company for a week or longer.'

'Longer?'

Lizzy sank onto a stool and surrendered herself to Jessie's capable hands, barely waiting for her maid to unfasten her hair and help her out of her gown before making her way to her bed and closing her eyes.

A week suddenly seemed like an eternity.

3

Anne sat on a stool beside Georgiana and Miss Bennet on the edge of Pemberley woods. Biting her lip, she concentrated upon capturing the slant of the mid-morning sunlight filtering through the leaves — a difficult ambition to achieve using charcoal.

She was distracted by the lively discourse between Georgiana and Miss Bennet, to which Mr. Asquith made frequent contributions. He walked behind them, looked at their drawings and offered suggestions and encouragement. Anne was included in everything that was said, but struggled to respond spontaneously. Spontaneity had never had a place in her life, and she found it hard to adapt. Supposing she expressed an opinion and everyone else disagreed with it or worse . . . laughed at her? It was much safer to concentrate on her drawing, and say as little as possible.

'Your perspective is not quite right, Miss de Bourgh.' Mr. Asquith peered over her shoulder and pointed to the area at fault. 'If you were to make those trees proportionately smaller, I think it would better serve.'

Anne resisted the urge to glance at her companions' sketches. She was convinced theirs would be better. Unlike her mother, she harboured no unrealistic ideas about her artistic abilities, but she did enjoy sketching enormously and wondered why she had not tried it before Mr. Asquith had made the suggestion. She had been told so frequently she was not well enough to do anything that required the slightest effort. Now she knew better.

She sighed. 'Perhaps I should start over.'

'That would be a shame since you have captured the leafy canopy perfectly. Just a few minor adjustments here,' he said, pointing, 'would set the matter right.'

She was conscious of robust strength and raw masculinity emanating from Mr. Asquith as he stood directly behind her and she breathed in the musky aroma she associated exclusively with him. She wondered if the delicious sensation that warmed her entire body could be desire. She had read a great deal on the subject, but had never thought to experience it first-hand.

And nor would she, she reminded herself, briskly reapplying herself to her drawing. If her mama even suspected the nature of her thoughts, Mr. Asquith would be blamed and dismissed without a character. That was a risk she could never take. Ensuring Mr. Asquith retained the employment he clearly needed was her way of repaying him for all the positive changes that had occurred in her life since his arrival at Rosings.

Part of her was jealous because he treated Georgiana and Miss Bennet in exactly the same friendly, slightly deferential manner he showed towards her. Georgiana and Miss Bennet were both prettier than she was. They were also livelier and, unlike her, not afraid to express their opinions and laugh at themselves. How dull she must appear by comparison.

'Ladies, I think we should return to the house,' Mr. Asquith said a short time later as he consulted his pocket watch. 'Mrs. Darcy will be expecting us for luncheon.'

'It looks like it might rain this afternoon,' Mama declared over luncheon. 'Oblige us by reading aloud this afternoon, Mr. Asquith.'

'With the greatest of pleasure, Lady Catherine.'

Anne noticed a shadow flit across Mrs. Darcy's features. It did not seem to occur to Mama that Mrs. Darcy might have made alternative arrangements. Not that Anne was complaining about Mama's suggestion. Mr. Asquith had a deep, velvety voice and managed to inject life and passion into even the dullest text, bringing it alive in ways the author probably never intended. Anne could have listened to him reading all day long. She loved the way his long, capable fingers curled around the side of the book, the way the colour of his eyes seemed to change in accordance with the words he read. She settled herself in the corner of a settee, with Kitty Bennet next to her, and a legitimate excuse to feast her eyes upon the man with whom she had become obsessed.

Mr. Darcy joined them when tea was served, and Mr. Asquith finally got to rest his voice. Anne watched him, hoping he would come to join her. He did not. Instead, he stood up and joined Mr. Darcy in front of the fireplace. They fell into easy conversation, but Anne was unable to hear what subject so enthralled them.

'Ah, here are the officers,' Mr. Darcy said, glancing out the window.

He and Mrs. Darcy hastened to greet the new arrivals. Anne glanced up and caught Mr. Asquith looking directly at her with a sympathetic expression. That he understood her agony was almost her undoing, and Anne looked away before it could affect her too much. A great many things had changed for the better in her life since Mr. Asquith came into it, but she would never find the strength to disregard her mother's wishes, and that was an end to the matter.

★   ★   ★

Joshua Fitzwilliam dressed slowly for dinner, thinking about the scene that had greeted him in Pemberley's drawing room a little earlier. He had not realised Mrs. Jenkinson had been replaced by a man, but had liked Asquith on sight. He possessed great sense and, apparently, considerable mystery. If Lady Catherine knew anything of his history, she was not saying. Joshua found it all rather extraordinary. He would have laughed in the face of anyone who suggested she would risk exposing her precious daughter to a man's continual company — and such an unusual man at that.

He noticed some differences in Anne, including improvements in her health, but felt nothing for her other than cousinly affection. Part of him wondered what was wrong with him. Marriage to Anne, procuring steward-ship of such a grand estate as Rosings, would see an end to his financial problems. The majority of men would grasp the opportunity with both hands.

Unfortunately, Joshua had an annoying habit of not following the majority.

He sighed and made his way downstairs, responding to a request from his aunt for a private interview before the others came down. He did not need to ask what it was she wished to say to him — nor could he think of a reason to delay the inevitable.

'Ah, there you are, Fitzwilliam,' Lady Catherine said when Joshua opened the door to the small sitting room. She annoyed him by making it sound as though he had kept her waiting, which he had not.

'You wished to see me, Lady Catherine.'

'Pray be seated.' Joshua swished the tails of his coat aside and took the chair beside his aunt. 'It's time to put Rosings' affairs in order,' she said without preamble. 'I am not getting any younger, and I wish to oversee a smooth transition.'

'I do not have the pleasure of understanding you, ma'am,' Joshua replied, understanding her perfectly well. 'Do you require a new estate manager?'

'Don't be so obtuse, Fitzwilliam. It does not become you. It is time for Anne to marry, so that her husband can get to grips with the management of the estate.'

'I see.'

'I had hopes of Darcy. To unite the great estates of Pemberley and Rosings had been his mother's greatest wish, as it was mine.

However, we will not talk of his wilful disregard for his duty. Instead, we will discuss yours.'

'Mine, ma'am?' Joshua elevated a brow, his temper in danger of erupting. The cavalier manner in which she appeared to think she could dictate the path of his entire life rankled. 'Whatever can you mean?'

'Anne's health has precluded her from seeing much of the world.'

'She appears a great deal better.'

'She is, but if I were to launch her upon society now, she would be inundated with fortune hunters.'

Joshua conceded the point with a nod. 'She does not know enough of the world to be able to make an informed choice.'

'Precisely. Asquith's appearance in Kent was opportune, and he has done much to bring Anne out of herself.'

'What do you know of Asquith's background? He seems gentlemanly enough, but I have never heard of his family.'

'He is not a gentleman, although he received a gentleman's education. His father was Sir Marius Glover's plantation master in Jamaica. Asquith was born there, and Glover paid for him to be educated alongside his own son at Harrow and then supported him at university.'

'That was remarkably generous.'

'Sir Marius is philanthropic, and I trust his judgement.'

What an exceedingly enigmatic statement.

'Asquith's father died when he was still a small boy, and Sir Marius took him under his wing. I have advised him not to advertise his background and to allow his achievements to speak for him. He would be looked down upon if the truth became public knowledge, and I need him to help me bring out the best in Anne without distractions of that nature.'

'It must be difficult for Asquith to have enjoyed a gentleman's education, but not be able to benefit from having a gentleman's background.'

'Enough of him.' Lady Catherine fixed Joshua with a gimlet gaze. 'I believe you know what I expect from you.'

'Indeed, ma'am, you are quite mistaken.' Joshua had no intention of making this easy for his aunt. 'I am unable to account for your wishing to speak privately with me.'

'Nonsense! I had hoped we could come to an agreement quickly and sensibly. However, if you insist upon making me speak plain, then I shall oblige you.' Lady Catherine squared her shoulders. 'You are the man I would see my daughter united with.'

'Me!'

'I am not taken in by your reticence. You must have been aware what I had in mind when Darcy failed to oblige me.'

'Ah, so I am second best.'

'That is not what I meant and well you know it.' Lady Catherine made it sound as though she was discussing nothing more permanent than a trip to the theatre. 'Anne suffers from a nervous disposition and is not strong. She needs a husband with whom she feels comfortable, and familiar. And I need her to be united with someone worthy of taking over the mantle of Rosings. Of course, you will need to resign your commission and dedicate your entire attention to the estate. There is much for you to learn, and when you are married you can — '

'Wait, if you please, Lady Catherine. You are being too hasty. I am very content with my military career and am not yet of a mind to marry.'

'Foolish boy! Think of Rosings and all the benefits you will enjoy from being master of that estate.'

'Marriage is an emotional commitment between people who hold one another in affection.'

'Nonsense, marriage is a business arrangement. I thought you had more sense than to be taken in by notions of true love.' Lady

38

Catherine flapped a hand in dismissal of such a preposterous idea. 'Such felicity never survives the first year. If you doubt my word, look no further than your brother and the way he was duped by a pretty face that disguised a calculating brain and social ambition.' There was nothing Joshua could say to that, and so he remained silent. His brother's calculating wife was determined to be the Countess of Braithwaite and, having achieved that ambition, almost bankrupted the Fitzwilliam clan with her extravagance. 'You need to marry for money, and we both know it.'

'Even if I were to agree, what does Anne have to say on the subject?'

'She does not need to know about it until you and I have reached an understanding. I will tell her when the time is right, and she will do as I ask. She is a dutiful child.'

'This has all come as a surprise, Lady Catherine. I am conscious of the honour, but you must grant me time to think about it.'

'Don't take too long. Spend some time in Anne's company here at Pemberley, get to know one another better, and think carefully about the advantages. The wealth and prosperity of the Rosings estate is quite on a par with Pemberley, you know.' Lady Catherine sounded a little desperate, presumably because she had expected immediate acquiescence rather than prevarication. 'Think of that.'

'I will readily give you my word to think about it.' Joshua stood up, and offered his aunt his arm. 'We should join the others. They will wonder what has become of us.'

Joshua brooded on his conversation with his aunt throughout the evening, restless and angry about the cold nature of his aunt's suggestion. He glanced across the table at his cousin, caught her eye, and smiled at her. She returned the gesture and quickly dropped her gaze again. It wouldn't be so very bad, he supposed. Anne would give him no trouble, but her mother was altogether another matter. Joshua had little choice but to do as Lady Catherine suggested and ought to count himself fortunate.

So why did he feel like a condemned man?

4

'You handled Lady Catherine well.' Will touched Lizzy's cheek as he removed himself from her bed the following morning. 'She was unpardonably rude when she expressed her dissatisfaction with the dinner you served.'

Lizzy smiled. 'She was testing me, hoping for a wild reaction so she could tell herself, and you no doubt, that she had been right about me all along. However, she did not get her way.'

Will laughed. 'So I observed.'

'Never mind Lady Catherine. Colonel Fitzwilliam seemed a little distracted. I assume Lady Catherine has already told him he is expected to marry Anne.'

'Undoubtedly.' Will tightened the belt on his robe and nodded. 'And I can understand why he hesitates. He is more accustomed to issuing orders than he is to obeying them.'

'The colonel does not strike me as the type to satisfy himself with a marriage of convenience, however dire his circumstances.'

'Possibly, but he does not have the pleasure of pleasing himself.'

'How very dispassionate of you.'

'Facts must be faced, my love.'

'Yes, I suppose they must.' Lizzy sighed. 'Still, the improvements in Anne are so very remarkable. She is more intelligent than I realised. I actually heard her contribute to a conversation voluntarily, *and* she expressed her opinion very sensibly.'

'She certainly talks more than she once did.'

Lizzy shook her head, marvelling at her husband's lack of perspicacity. Surely he had noticed how Anne's gaze seldom left Mr. Asquith and that she regarded him with total adoration? Jane and Mr. Bingley were due to arrive in the afternoon and for a short visit and Lizzy would value Jane's opinion about Mr. Asquith's character. It would be quite like old times when they had sequestered themselves in one of their bedchambers at Longbourne for hours at a time, discussing various gentlemen — specifically Jane's prospects of securing Mr. Bingley. The only difference this time would be that they were contemplating the suitability of gentlemen for women other than themselves. God forbid that they were turning into their mother.

Lizzy canted her head and looked up at her husband. 'It seems odd Lady Catherine would employ a man about whom she knows so little, and one who could so easily turn her daughter's head in directions Lady Catherine would not wish it to be directed.'

'Lady Catherine told Fitzwilliam he is the son of Sir Marius Glover's plantation manager in Jamaica. That gentleman paid for Asquith to be educated in England alongside his own boy.'

'Really?' Lizzy arched a brow. 'Well then, Mr. Asquith will have much to talk to Mrs. Sheffield about when she comes to dinner tonight with the Briars. Her late husband made his fortune in Jamaica.'

'Perhaps Mrs. Sheffield is known to him. That ought to make for interesting discourse.'

'Ah, so you think there is something about Mr. Asquith's background he doesn't wish to have commonly known?'

Will leaned over Lizzy and kissed her brow. 'I did not say that.'

'You didn't have to.' She reached up and stroked his jaw. 'My letter to Charlotte Collins, asking her what was known about him in Kent, has already been sent. Hopefully, Charlotte will satisfy my curiosity and reply by return.'

Will sent her a teasing smile. 'Which will do nothing to stop you from asking your own questions.'

Lizzy had no reply to make. She was too taken up with her husband's lovely smile to find the breath for words. Whenever he looked at her in that particular way, her insides melted, desire blossomed, and she fell in love with him all over again.

'I know that look.' He wagged a finger at her. 'And the answer is no. You have a houseful of guests, and you are in a delicate condition. I will not place added demands upon you.'

'I thought I was the one doing the demanding.'

'I have business to attend to and must leave you for the morning.' Lizzy pouted. 'Promise me you will not over-exert yourself.'

'The thought of a tedious lecture from your aunt about the responsibility I bear for the Pemberley heir will be enough to keep me in line.'

'Then, for once, I have reason to be obliged to Lady Catherine, provided you do not treat her lecture as a challenge and disregard it.' Will's expression darkened. 'Don't give me reason to worry about you, my love.'

Lizzy reached up and kissed his lips. 'You have just said the only thing that will make me obey you.'

'Thank you. Now I must go. I will see you at luncheon.'

Lizzy laid back and closed her eyes, breathing in the masculine aroma that lingered on Will's pillow. It was ridiculous really. They had been married long enough that she ought to be over her initial infatuation with him. Being mistress of Pemberley ensured she had plenty with which to occupy her time. She hugged Will's pillow to her breast, making a mental note to ask Jane if she still felt obsessed with her Mr. Bingley, and missed him the moment he left the room.

Laughing at her foolishness, Lizzy rang the bell. Jessie brought up her breakfast tray, and then helped her wash and dress. Lizzy went down, but none of her guests were anywhere to be seen. She glanced out of her sitting room window and noticed Anne de Bourgh sitting alone in the herb garden, a sketch pad on her lap. Anxious to speak with her alone, and equally anxious to avoid Lady Catherine, Lizzy slipped out a side door and joined her.

'I hope I am not disturbing you.'

'Not in the least, Mrs. Darcy.'

'Oh, please call me Lizzy. And I hope I may address you as Anne.'

'I would like that. So few people do. They are too afraid of what my mother will say if they presume to be familiar. Besides, I have never had any close friends.'

'Well, I am not afraid of your mother, and so Anne it is. And you now have a friend in me, if you will allow it.'

'With the greatest of pleasure.'

'That's settled then.' Lizzy smiled. 'What are you drawing?'

'I was trying to capture a likeness of those herbs growing against that fountain, but I think I am being too ambitious.'

'Let me see.'

Lizzy examined Anne's sketch. It was rudimentary, but still better than anything Lizzy could have achieved.

'What do you think? There's no need to be kind.'

'I am no expert, but there is a certain rustic charm in your image. I am sure Mr. Asquith will be able to tell you what to do to improve it, but I can offer no advice. I cannot draw to save my life, you see.'

Anne appeared surprised by the admission. 'I thought there was nothing you could not do.'

'Did you really?' Lizzy blinked. 'What a very strange image you have of me, but it's hardly deserved. I am very outspoken, I suppose, which people often mistake for confidence. It is just I never have been able to hold my tongue if I think someone has spoken out of turn or has been unjust. That trait has landed me in all manner of trouble.' Lizzy emitted an embarrassed little laugh.

'But it is hardly my fault if I have firm opinions upon every conceivable subject.'

'Whereas I never have anything to say that people wish to hear.'

'That once might have been true, but since your health has improved, I can see a vast difference in you.' Lizzy smiled. 'I believe Mr. Asquith must take some credit for that.'

Anne blushed. 'Yes. I was terrified of him when Mama first engaged him as my tutor.'

'We were surprised when we heard of his appointment.'

'He was very kind right from the start, very patient, and did not treat me like an invalid.' Anne paused, lost in reflection, her sketch abandoned. 'Mr. Asquith made no allowances for my supposed infirmities, and I gradually started to feel . . . well, normal I suppose. But I am still very dull and uninteresting.'

'No, you are not.' Lizzy patted her hand. 'Never think that way.'

'Mr. Asquith has taught me to aspire to things I had always supposed were beyond me, but now I . . . well, perhaps that wasn't such a good thing. If one does not have expectations, then one cannot be disappointed when they are not realised.'

'Because you cannot have your heart's desire?'

Anne's head shot up. 'Whatever do you mean?'

Lizzy smiled. 'Mr. Asquith is very elegant, very charming. Were you to have formed an attachment, I can quite understand how it would have happened.'

'Is it that obvious?' Anne shot Lizzy a startled look. 'Mama would dismiss him on the spot if she had the slightest notion. I am here because . . . well, I am not supposed to know, but I'm not quite the numbskull Mama supposes me to be.'

Lizzy's heart went out to the girl. 'Your mother has your best interests at heart.'

'Yes, I dare say.'

'You must not feel pressured to do things you would prefer not to.'

'I am not you, Lizzy. Besides, I have always known what is expected of me.'

Lizzy didn't quite know how to respond, but seeing Mr. Asquith approaching saved her from saying anything at all.

'We are friends now, Anne,' Lizzy said, standing. 'Please feel free to talk to me about anything, at any time.'

'That means a great deal to me.' Anne smiled. 'Having a friend, a confidante, for the first time is a comforting thought.'

Lizzy returned to the house, thinking that was one of the most poignant statements she had ever heard. Having grown up surrounded by four sisters, not having a confidante would have been unthinkable. Poor Anne. Born into all that money and privilege, and yet she was lonely and completely lacking in self-confidence.

★ ★ ★

Joshua spent the day with Darcy, which gave him a legitimate excuse to avoid squiring his cousin Anne. Seeing Darcy at his most efficient, handling the management of his estate with skill and intelligence, reminded Joshua that a similar future was his for the taking. Common sense told him to grasp the opportunity with both hands and thank Lady Catherine for her benevolence.

So why did he hesitate?

He sat astride his horse and surveyed Darcy's land, which stretched as far as the eye could see. So, too, did the land attaching to Rosings. Anne was no longer a timid church mouse, and occasionally offered up an opinion of her own when there was the least likelihood of it being heard. She made no effort to single Joshua out, and her response when he had addressed a remark to her the previous evening had been stilted, almost disinterested. It was evident the prospect of their union held no more joy for Anne than it did for Joshua. It had not previously occurred to him that she might be as averse to the idea, having assumed she would do as her mother asked because she always had in the past.

Joshua slid his arms into the coat his man held out for him and stood still as Cox brushed imaginary specks from the shoulders. His next move ought to be to speak candidly with Anne, discover how she felt about her mother's proposal, and then decide how to proceed. Anne looked a great deal better, and no longer hid beneath several layers of shawls for fear of catching a chill. She had altered in subtle ways, and as Joshua tripped lightly down the stairs, he determined to discover whom or what had wrought such changes in her. He was equally determined that Anne would speak honestly about her feelings. He understood Lady Catherine's determination to see the Rosings estate pass into capable hands, but those hands would not be Joshua's if they came at the expense of her daughter's happiness. He did not love Anne de Bourgh, but he did feel a duty of care towards her and would not force her into a loveless marriage against her will.

The Bingleys had arrived that afternoon and Darcy, Bingley, and Asquith were already in the drawing room. Joshua was received warmly and accepted a glass of whisky from Darcy with a nod of thanks. Turner and Halstead followed on his heels and were provided with refreshment, also.

'Our neighbours are joining us for dinner this evening,' Darcy told them. 'Lord and Lady Briar and Lady Briar's sister, Mrs. Sheffield. Did you happen to know Mrs. Sheffield's late husband, Asquith? I believe he made his fortune in Jamaica.'

'The name is not familiar,' Asquith replied, shaking his head. 'But then a lot of Englishmen have interests in Jamaica. I am acquainted with only a few of them.'

'It was just a thought. Sometimes these coincidences happen.'

Joshua's instincts told him Asquith had not answered Darcy's question honestly, but what possible reason would he have to lie about it?

'How are you enjoying your new estate, Bingley?' Joshua asked.

'Very much indeed,' Bingley replied with great enthusiasm. 'It is exactly right for us in all respects. I shall enjoy sharing it with my family, although my sisters seem quite determined to remain in London for the present time, which I own surprises me.'

'They probably want to give you time to adjust to married life,' Darcy said hastily. 'After all, they were always with you in

Hertfordshire, as was Mrs. Bennet.'

Bingley pulled a wry face. 'That is certainly true.'

Joshua said nothing, but knew the real reason why Bingley was denied his sisters' company. Miss Bingley had recruited Wickham to help her undermine Eliza's position during a house party at Pemberley a few weeks previously. Supposing Darcy to have come to regret marrying Eliza, she had convinced herself she was the true object of Darcy's affections. It was Darcy's contention she was quite mad, an opinion which was supported by the best medical brains in the business.

Darcy's price for not informing Bingley of his sister's treachery was that she undergo treatment for her condition. Mrs. Hurst had taken it upon herself to ensure that happened. Miss Bingley would never be invited to Pemberley again, but how that could be avoided if she returned to the north and resided with her brother was a problem Joshua didn't envy Darcy having to wrestle with. Joshua knew Eliza was especially keen for the Bingleys not to learn of the problem, at least until after her sister's confinement.

The ladies joined them, and the conversation became more general. Even before the neighbours arrived, they were a lively party.

Lady Catherine attempted to dominate proceedings, but was generally ignored as proper deference was shown to Mrs. Darcy. Joshua considered joining his cousin, but she was engaged in animated conversation with Asquith, causing Joshua to wonder if that gentleman could be the cause of the changes in Anne's demeanour. Indeed, looking up at him as she was at that moment, eyes sparkling, cheeks slightly flushed, she appeared almost pretty.

Joshua noticed Lady Catherine watching them, a slight frown marring her brow. He moved to join Anne and her tutor and engaged the pair in polite conversation. If that was the way the wind blew then Joshua would not stand in his cousin's way provided, of course, Asquith wasn't just a fortune hunter. He would make it his business to find out more about his circumstances.

His attention was drawn to Simpson, standing in the doorway to announce Lord and Lady Briar and Mrs. Sheffield. He had heard much about Darcy's new neighbours, but had not been warned to expect Mrs. Sheffield's quite extraordinary beauty. One look at her and the breath left his body in an audible whoosh. The lovely vision that captured his attention boasted a profusion of dark blonde curls, exceptionally blue eyes, and an adorable air of vulnerability that made

Joshua yearn to protect her, even though he was unsure if there was anything she needed protection from. Although no longer in mourning, she was modestly gowned in grey silk that clung to her svelte form and sent Joshua's mind spiralling in all sorts of inappropriate directions.

He could not have said why, but as he waited for his turn to be introduced, he felt as though his entire life had been leading up to that moment.

5

Anne usually found crowded drawing rooms daunting places. She was either dismissed as uninteresting, or people talked at her incessantly, ingratiating themselves for reasons of personal advancement. No one seemed interested in her for her own sake, and she could think of nothing clever to say if she was singled out. But this evening everyone appeared comfortable and in good spirits, not a sycophant in sight.

'Are you enjoying the change of scenery, Miss de Bourgh?' As though sensing her watching him, Mr. Asquith approached and instigated a conversation.

'Oh . . . er, yes.' She summoned up a smile, conscious of her mother observing them closely from across the room. She was simultaneously quizzing Georgiana about something, but that did not prevent her from also glaring at Anne. She must take better care not to allow her true feelings to show. Lizzy had already noticed, but if Mama had done so, surely she would have said something? Whatever happened here, her days with Mr. Asquith were numbered, and she was determined to make the most of every one of them before they were separated for good. 'It is a long time since I was last at Pemberley. Mr. Darcy seems so much less severe since his marriage.'

'From what little I know of Mrs. Darcy, it is my opinion he could not have chosen a more suitable wife.' Mr. Asquith fixed her with a probing glance. 'I am so very glad he found her.'

Was he aware that her mother had wanted Mr. Darcy to marry her and he was glad the match had not gone ahead? Her heart swelled with hope, even though such hope was . . . well, hopeless. 'Yes, as am I.'

'The countryside is very different to Kent,' Mr. Asquith remarked after a short pause.

'Indeed. The peaks are rugged, yet quite starkly beautiful.'

Anne's heart lurched when she noticed Colonel Fitzwilliam approaching them, even though it was unreasonable to suppose she could keep Mr. Asquith to herself for long. She assumed Mama had already spoken with him, and he was here to press his suit. Why would he not be? Rosings was a rich prize, well worth a little effort on his part. Anne was surprised and a little ashamed at the uncharitable turn her thoughts had taken. Were it not for Mr. Asquith, she would not have minded marriage to her cousin too much. He did not possess Mr. Darcy's taciturn disposition and had on one or two occasions during his annual visits to Rosings actually made Anne laugh. Even so, the thought of committing herself to such a man — to any man other than Mr. Asquith — abhorred her.

She had fallen deeply and passionately in love with a man her mother would never permit her to marry.

'Rain is expected tomorrow,' Colonel Fitzwilliam said, 'and Mrs. Darcy is proposing amateur dramatics to keep us all entertained.'

'A play?' Anne frowned. 'If you are suggesting I should take part, Colonel, please save your breath — '

'I have been asked to organise something, but we will not have enough players. Can I persuade you to take pity on me, Miss de Bourgh, and make up the numbers?' Mr. Asquith flashed a charming smile that caused Anne to go weak at the knees and sent colour flooding to her cheeks. When he looked at her in that particular manner, it was difficult to deny him anything. 'It would be a sorry way to repay Mrs. Darcy's hospitality if I failed to oblige her.'

'I have never tried anything like it.' Anne

shook her head, horrified at the thought of putting herself forward, even for Mr. Asquith's sake. 'I don't have any natural talent for acting.'

Colonel Fitzwilliam laughed. 'That doesn't stop half of those treading the boards in Drury Lane.'

'It's the greatest fun imaginable,' Mr. Asquith assured her. 'You get the opportunity to pretend to be someone else, which can be quite liberating.'

He spoke as though he appreciated the daily torment she felt at being herself, which should not have surprised Anne. Mr. Asquith understood her in a way no one else ever had, and nor would they — not ever.

'Well, perhaps a minor role, if it would help you.'

'Mr. Asquith!' Mama's voice cut through the hum of conversation and several heads turned in her direction. 'A word, if you please.'

'Excuse me.'

Mr. Asquith bowed and strolled across the room. If he felt annoyed to have their discourse interrupted by Mama's autocratic command, he gave no indication of it. Anne watched his retreating back, only tearing her gaze away when she realised Colonel Fitzwilliam had addressed a remark to her, and she had not responded.

'I beg your pardon,' she said, blushing again. 'I did not hear what you said.'

'I asked how long Asquith has been with you?'

'A little more than three months.' Anne's smile was probably less guarded than it ought to have been. 'He is very interesting and informative.'

'Then I am glad, for your sake.'

A commotion at the door caused all heads to turn in that direction. Lord and Lady Briars and Mrs. Sheffield were announced and Anne could sense she had lost Colonel Fitzwilliam's attention. Mr. Asquith, she noticed, glanced at the new arrivals and as quickly looked away again. Her mother dismissed him with a negligent wave of her hand because Mr. Bingley had joined her. Anne was pleased when Mr. Asquith returned to her side.

'I understand Mrs. Sheffield's late husband made his fortune in Jamaica,' she said. 'Did you know him, Mr. Asquith?'

'I do not recall the name.'

'I am sure you would not have forgotten Mrs. Sheffield, had you met before. She is very beautiful.'

Asquith inclined his head. 'I must take your word for that. I had not noticed.'

'It is hard for me to believe any gentleman would be blind to such beauty. Indeed, why should he be? Beauty in all its forms ought to be admired.'

'Then if you insist, I shall admire Mrs. Sheffield, but only after we have been introduced.'

★   ★   ★

Lizzy and Will greeted the new arrivals with the greatest of pleasure. Introductions were made, with sufficient deference shown to Lady Catherine to satisfy even her exacting standards.

With their relaxed manners and natural charm, Lord and Lady Briars were soon engaged in polite conversation. Lizzy, whose back was aching, felt justified in joining Jane, seated on a chaise beside the fire.

'You look hot, my dear. Are you quite comfortable?'

Jane winced. 'Not entirely, but I would not have missed this party for the world. I so enjoy seeing the improvements in Kitty. She really does seem quite taken with Captain Turner, and he with her.'

'We ought not to get our hopes up. The chances of the captain's father permitting such a match are slim.'

'Why? Because we are not good enough?' Jane smiled. 'That might once have been a valid argument but my marriage, and especially yours, have raised our status as a family.'

'True enough I suppose, but it might all come to naught.' Lizzy smiled. 'Let us leave Kitty and her captain to enjoy one another's company without interference from their old married sisters. What do you make of Lady Catherine?'

'You would do better to ask me what I make of Mr. Asquith. Now there is an interesting gentleman.'

'Yes, Anne de Bourgh is quite taken with him, and he is the best thing that could have happened to her. However, I believe Lady Catherine regrets engaging him.' They watched as Lady Catherine called Mr. Asquith to her side for the second time in five minutes so he could perform a menial task better suited to a footman. 'I sense trouble brewing.'

'Especially if Lady Catherine has settled upon Colonel Fitzwilliam for her daughter.' Jane hid a smile behind her hand. 'Have you observed that he hasn't been able to remove his gaze from Mrs. Sheffield since she entered the room?'

'Yes, I did notice that.' Lizzy grinned. 'Oh dear. Lady Catherine failed with Will, and now her second choice might rebel.'

'Only if Mrs. Sheffield is attracted to the colonel and has funds of her own.'

'I got the impression Mr. Sheffield left his widow well provided for, but, of course, I know nothing of the particulars.' Lizzy patted her sister's hand. 'Now, tell me about Campden Park. What did you decide about the small sitting room? Shall you change the décor?'

Jane spoke enthusiastically about her new home. Lizzy had viewed it shortly after Mr. Bingley decided to purchase it and liked what she saw. It was a fraction of the size of Pemberley, but still a substantial estate, albeit a trifle neglected. Jane was enjoying bringing it up to date.

'I shall take pleasure in showing it to Louisa and Caroline when they next join us.' Jane frowned. 'I cannot think what could have detained them in London for so long.'

'Perhaps they are being thoughtful and leaving you and your Charles to enjoy one another's company. Besides, I recall Mrs. Hurst telling me she and her sister planned a visit to Brighton.' Lizzy regretted the necessity to lie to Jane. 'And bear in mind, your purchase of Campden Park and removal north all happened very quickly.'

'That is how Charles does things. Once

he makes up his mind about something, he cannot wait to act upon his decision.' Jane grinned. 'Do you recall when he took Netherfield? One moment we heard rumours a gentleman was considering it, the next he was installed. He also quit it equally quickly when he thought I did not enjoy his society.'

Lizzy winced. 'No one can accuse your husband of not being a man of action.'

'I would not say this to anyone except you, Lizzy, but much as I enjoy Louisa and Caroline's society, I have also enjoyed making my own decisions at Campden Park. I know their opinions would most likely not have coincided with mine, but I would have felt duty bound to take them into account.'

'Well, there you are then. Did I mention I received a letter from our Aunt Gardiner?' Lizzy asked in a hasty change of subject.

'No. Do tell.' Jane sat forward. 'How are Lydia and Mr. Wickham managing in town? I dare say my uncle already regrets his generosity.'

Mr. and Mrs. Gardiner had come to the rescue following Wickham's attempt to manipulate Lizzy a few weeks previously. Having quit the army altogether, Wickham found himself without occupation, unable to support his wife. They had offered Wickham a position as manager of one of Mr. Gardiner's warehouses, which had a small apartment attached to it. Wickham had been scathing of the offer, but Lydia had shown great maturity and insisted upon her husband grasping the opportunity. Neither Lydia nor Jane knew the full particulars of Wickham's fall from grace, and Lizzy hoped it would remain that way. Even so, she had an uncomfortable feeling she had not heard the last of Wickham, and that he would find a way to interfere in her life again.

'Wickham is as idle as always, but Lydia has taken to the life with enthusiasm.'

'Ah, but will it last?' Jane looked concerned. 'You know Lydia. She has fads.'

'She understands this is their last chance and will ensure Wickham does as he is told. It will be harder for him to stray now that he is constantly in her company. Besides, Lydia enjoys all the fabrics that pass through the warehouse and is already becoming quite an expert upon the best establishments to sell them on to.'

'Well, I suppose fashion is the one subject guaranteed to hold our sister's interest.'

'It also helps that they are in London,' Lizzy added, smiling as Will and Mr. Bingley approached them.

'Are you here to scold me for gossiping

with my sister and neglecting our guests?'
Lizzy asked Will.

'Actually, my suspicions were aroused by
your both sitting down, as you ought to be.'

'And why should that make you suspicious?'

'Since when did you ever do anything that
was expected of you?'

'That is grossly unfair!' Lizzy cried,
laughing.

'Dinner is about to be served. I must
attend to Lady Briars, and Bingley has kindly
offered to take Lady Catherine in. We shall
seek them out now, so that Lady Catherine
has no time to organise people the way she
wishes to.'

Lizzy shook her head. 'And you accuse me
of meddling.'

Will sent her an enticing smile. 'Indeed, my
love,' he said softly. 'I would not dare.'

Lizzy was still laughing when she entered
the dining room on Lord Briar's arm.

★ ★ ★

'Allow me to serve you a small portion of
roast pigeon, Anne.'

'Thank you, Colonel.'

Joshua did so and then passed the platter
further down the table. He could not recall

the last time he had enjoyed a dinner more, or one at which the time had passed so quickly. He had dutifully escorted Anne to the table, ensured her needs were met, and kept her entertained with polite discourse. But his attention was focused on Mrs. Sheffield, seated directly across from him between Halstead and Turner. It was a pleasure to feast his eyes on her lovely features whenever he glanced across the table, which was frequently, but he remained frustrated since he couldn't speak across the table.

Perhaps that wasn't such a bad thing, he decided as the meal progressed and the glances they shared became more probing and prolonged. Being unable to converse with her now gave him a legitimate excuse to seek her out in the drawing room after dinner. He knew something of Jamaica himself, having spent a few months there at his late father's behest before returning to England and purchasing a commission in the army. It gave them an interest in common that would be both natural and polite to discuss, given they had barely exchanged more than a handshake and a few words thus far. He listened to her lilting voice as she responded to questions put to her, keen to hear what subjects engaged her attention so he would know what else to talk to her about when their time came.

Anne's company was relatively undemanding, and Joshua was free to watch his fellow diners. The mood was elegantly relaxed, for which Joshua gave Eliza credit. She had a natural way about her — far less stiff and formal than Darcy's. It was playful almost, and put people at their ease. There was a marked difference in Darcy, too, since Joshua's last visit just a few short weeks ago, and he appeared less reticent than usual. He gave Eliza the credit for that change, too.

His fellow officers were taken up with Georgiana and Eliza's sister, but did not neglect Mrs. Sheffield. As their commanding officer, Joshua would have seen them cashiered had they done so. The only person who appeared less than delighted with the evening's progress was his aunt, presumably because Joshua had not yet given her an answer.

The other possibility was she disliked her daughter's growing interest in Asquith. Well, what the devil had she expected when she brought a male tutor — and such a charming and worldly one at that — into her sheltered daughter's life? Lady Catherine seldom did anything without a reason, but Joshua suspected on this occasion, matters had not gone the way she had hoped. She sat sour-faced on Darcy's left, not dominating the conversation because Darcy cut her off politely but firmly whenever she gave her opinion a little too forcibly.

Each time Joshua glanced up, he caught Mrs. Sheffield studying him. He was encouraged by her interest in him, until it occurred to him that the lady was not fascinated by him, but appeared to be avoiding looking in Asquith's direction. Now that was interesting. When Mrs. Sheffield first entered the room, Asquith had stiffened and muttered something unintelligible beneath his breath. He had denied knowing her, but Joshua was now convinced Mrs. Sheffield and Asquith were not strangers. A hot shaft of jealousy pierced Joshua when the possibility of their being secret lovers occurred to him. He as quickly dismissed the idea. If they were, Asquith would have had no reason to seek employment with Lady Catherine, keeping him separated from the object of his affections. He had no way of knowing he would come to Pemberley at the same time as Mrs. Sheffield was in the district. Satisfied on that score, Joshua pondered upon what other reasons there might be for the pair to deny they were acquainted.

'Have you decided what performance your players will entertain us with, Mr. Asquith?'

Mrs. Darcy asked.

'I have settled upon a light comedy, ma'am.'

'A comedy, Asquith,' Joshua said. 'That ought to be just the thing.'

'I hope you are not thinking of anything too modern,' Lady Catherine said, frowning. 'I do not hold with all these new-fangled ideas people find so amusing.'

'Indeed not, Lady Catherine. I have a particular piece in mind, but unfortunately I am one lady short.'

'You are planning theatricals?' Lady Briars asked.

'Yes, ma'am. The weather is supposed to deteriorate, and we thought it an amusing way to fill the time.'

'Perhaps my sister would oblige,' Lady Briars said. 'Did you not do that sort of thing in Jamaica, Celia?'

'No,' Mrs. Sheffield replied.

'I could not ask Mrs. Sheffield to inconvenience herself,' Asquith replied at the same time.

'Nonsense.' Lady Briars appeared determined. 'It is just what you need to bolster your spirits, my dear. I absolutely insist.'

Mrs. Sheffield's smile was brittle and did not trouble her lovely eyes. 'And I am equally determined not to spoil the production by having anything to do with it.'

An awkward silence ensured, broken by Mrs. Darcy when she glanced down the table to ensure everyone had finished, placed her napkin aside, and pushed back her chair. 'Come, ladies, let us leave the gentlemen to their port.'

Every male in the room was instantly on his feet helping the ladies with their chairs. Joshua flattened himself against the wall as the ladies filed past his position. He hoped for a look, a sign of interest of some sort, from Mrs. Sheffield. When she did not glance his way, he felt severely disappointed. His only reward was a waft of her light, floral perfume as she left the room.

The gentlemen did not linger over their port. When they returned to the drawing room and Joshua looked for Mrs. Sheffield, she was nowhere to be seen. Nor was Asquith. He had preceded Joshua from the dining room, Joshua himself having been detained by a question from Darcy. Where the devil were they both? It was beyond his imagination, given the tension he had sensed between them, they should be the only people missing and not be together. Joshua slipped back out of the drawing room before his aunt could demand his company for her daughter and sauntered over to the door of the small adjoining sitting room; the most obvious place for Asquith and Mrs. Sheffield to have taken refuge. He was rewarded by the sound of voices — a man's and a woman's — coming from within and didn't scruple to eavesdrop.

'It is most unfortunate we should meet in this way,' Mrs. Sheffield said. 'I had no idea you would be here, or I would have — '

'Indeed.' Asquith said the one word with a marked lack of civility.

'What do you intend to do?'

'I have not yet decided.'

A long pause, and then Mrs. Sheffield spoke again. 'Thank you, at least, for not making your suspicions public so far. I have told you many times they are unfounded, but if you do not choose to believe me, there is nothing I can do about it. Even so, such a slur, even if it is not supported by evidence, which it cannot be because there is none, would show me in a bad light.'

'We made a mistake in pretending we do not know one another.'

'I did not know what to do and followed your lead. I had no idea you were here, whereas you must have realised who I was when Mrs. Darcy mentioned my name.'

'Yes.'

'Please do me one kindness, even though I

have no right to ask it of you. If you do decide to voice your suspicions, at least warn me in advance and give me an opportunity to tell my sister myself. She suffers from a nervous disposition and such a slanderous allegation would make her condition worse. I would leave here, return to my husband's estate, but I am not free to do so. My husband's brother seeks to — '

'Yes, I heard something about that.' Perdition, why the devil did Asquith have to interrupt? Joshua wanted to know a great deal more about the slanderous allegations Asquith was considering levelling against Mrs. Sheffield. 'We ought to return to the drawing room before we are missed.'

Joshua was shocked by Asquith's abrupt tone and complete lack of sympathy when it was obvious Mrs. Sheffield was in some sort of trouble. Trouble that was visited upon her in Jamaica. He concealed himself when the two of them left the room and delayed his return to the drawing room, slipping into it virtually unseen.

His tardiness meant any opportunity to converse with Mrs. Sheffield was again denied to him. Music had been suggested, and it appeared Mrs. Sheffield played, as did Georgiana and Eliza. The three ladies conferred, and Mrs. Sheffield was persuaded to perform first. Joshua enjoyed music, and Mrs. Sheffield was a proficient pianist. It was apparent, but unsurprising given the conversation he had just overheard, that she was preoccupied and gave her performance less attention than it deserved. Even so, he joined in the warm applause at the end of her piece, when she gave way at the instrument to Georgiana.

Mrs. Sheffield found a seat at the side of the room, and Joshua strolled across to join her. People had got up and moved around when Mrs. Sheffield quit the instrument, so Joshua's movements went unnoticed by the rest of the gathering.

'May I?' He indicated the vacant seat beside Mrs. Sheffield.

'Please do, Colonel.'

Joshua swished the tails of his coat aside and seated himself. It was impossible for him to establish from her demeanour whether Mrs. Sheffield welcomed his company.

'You play very well.'

'You mistake the matter.' She flashed a rueful smile. 'My performance was unremarkable. These surroundings are rather daunting.'

'I cannot believe you are a stranger to elegant salons.'

'The salons in Jamaica are not on this scale, and since returning to England I have been in mourning. I am still reacquainting myself with society's mores.'

'Your absence has been society's loss.'

'It is very gallant of you to say so.' She lifted her gaze to his face and smiled. The effect that simple gesture had on Joshua sent desire spiralling through him in a disquieting manner. 'I am fully aware of my limitations as a musician.'

'You do yourself an injustice.' Joshua paused, sensing he was losing her attention. 'How do you find Derbyshire?' he asked.

'Cold,' she said with another smile.

'Quite, but rather beautiful also.'

'Yes, what I have seen of it so far. I enjoy riding very much. It is something I missed during my years in Jamaica. It was too hot and not safe enough. But now I am back, I am intent upon exploring the countryside here.'

'Then allow me to offer my services as a guide.'

'Oh, thank you, but I did not mention my plans in order to beg for a companion.'

'It would be my pleasure. I spent a lot of time here as a boy and know the area like the back of my hand. Really, I would enjoy the excuse to show off my local knowledge.'

'Well, if you are sure — '

'Absolutely sure. Would tomorrow morning be too soon?'

She raised a brow, and Joshua cursed his impatience. As a military tactician, he knew rushing an unplanned strategy through was a recipe for disaster, but the blame rested entirely with Mrs. Sheffield. There was something about her that caused him to act impulsively. 'Do you not have responsibilities to detain you at Pemberley?'

God's beard, did everyone know what his aunt expected of him? 'Not that I am aware of,' he replied casually.

'Even so, I — '

'You need not concern yourself with the proprieties, if that is what makes you hesitate. This is the country, not the *ton*, and if it would make you feel better, we could take a groom with us.'

'That particular difficulty had not occurred to me, but now that you mention it — '

'You are in need of a friend hereabouts, are you not, Mrs. Sheffield?'

She gasped. 'Whatever do you mean by that?'

Joshua glanced at Asquith, standing beside the piano and singing, accompanied by Mrs. Darcy. Joshua now had reason to review his opinion of Asquith and was annoyed that he appeared to do absolutely everything he attempted with consummate skill.

'I sense antagonism between you,' he said

softly, 'and would like nothing more than to be your friend. Do not suspect me of ulterior motives, madam, because I have none.'

She closed her eyes and then nodded. 'You are very perceptive.'

Or a damned good eavesdropper. 'I live to serve.'

'Really, it is nothing. I have no wish to visit my trifling problems upon you.'

'Not so very trifling, I think,' he replied softly, holding her captive with his eyes.

Mrs. Sheffield turned away, as though worried about what he might read from her expression. 'Very well, Colonel. Thank you. I shall be pleased to ride with you in the morning, but have we not been warned to expect bad weather?'

Perdition, so they had. 'Weather permitting, naturally.'

Her spontaneous laughter enchanted Joshua and drew curious glances from several others in the room. 'The elements do not answer to anyone, not even colonels, and will do as they please.'

Joshua responded with a wicked smile of his own. 'They would not dare to disappoint me.'

6

'Leave us.'

The sound of Mama's autocratic voice caused Anne's maid to bob a hasty curtsey and vacate the room.

'Mama, I did not expect to see you about so early.' Anne said, pushing her half-eaten breakfast aside and summoning up a smile.

'I thought you would still be sleeping.'

And yet you came to disturb me? 'I agreed to join the other ladies this morning. We are to start work on the play.'

'I did not give you leave to participate. I'm not sure I approve.'

'My role will be a minor one, and I would hate to disappoint everyone.'

Mama fixed Anne with a penetrating glare. 'Everyone or someone in particular?'

Anne swallowed, unsure what she had done to occasion her mother's suspicions, but for once she wanted something badly enough to stand up for herself. She had probably not chosen a good moment to act rebelliously. Mama had broken her self-imposed exile from Pemberley grudgingly, and now that she was here, she did not like seeing Mrs. Darcy as its mistress. She had been bad tempered and highly critical of that lady's conduct since her arrival.

'I feel so much stronger nowadays and look it too,' Anne said, avoiding a reply to her mother's question, mainly because there was nothing she could possibly say short of an outright untruth that would not condemn her. 'Everyone says as much.'

Mama narrowed her eyes. 'I miscalculated when I permitted Mr. Asquith into your life. He has turned your head and made you forget your duty.'

'Does that mean you plan to dismiss him?' Anne could hear the despair in her own voice.

'That rather depends upon you.'

'Me?' Anne opened her eyes very wide. 'I have a say?'

'You are old enough now to understand what is expected of you.'

'I have always known that, Mama,' Anne replied quietly.

'You have been protected and cossetted all your life, which is partly my fault, and partly a consequence of your fragile health.' Mama paced around the chamber, looking uncharacteristically flustered. 'You have never seen anything of the real world, nor do you understand its ways. I was hoping Mr. Asquith would give you some insights, make you understand just how privileged you are, and prepare you for what comes next.'

'He has taught me a great deal.'

'More than I anticipated, clearly.'

Anne had no idea how to respond. 'I do know how fortunate I am,' she said instead. 'How could I not?' *Especially when you constantly remind me.*

Mama fixed Anne with the full force of her determination. 'With privilege comes responsibility, Anne. Never lose sight of the fact that many people rely upon Rosings for their livelihoods. Since your papa died I have done my level best to maintain the estate and keep it profitable, but it is no easy task and has sapped my strength.'

Anne sat a little straighter. Her mother had always appeared indefatigable and never admitted to any weaknesses. 'Are you feeling unwell, Mama? You did not say anything before. Have you seen a doctor?'

'I am tired. It is time to start ceding my responsibilities to you, or rather to your husband. Which means, I must choose the right man to keep the Rosings estate running smoothly. Many men would aspire to own it, but most would fritter its wealth away because they are too idle to keep proper control. I cannot allow that to happen.'

'No, of course not.'

Anne understood that perfectly well. What was less clear was why she could not have a say in her choice of husband. She did not bother to pose a question that would only lead to a serious disagreement, but still wanted to scream that it was unfair. She did not care about wealth, privilege, or even Rosings. She would settle for a very great deal less, if only she could follow her heart. But then again, if she did not have wealth and privilege, what man would be interested in her?

'May I ask why you chose to replace Mrs. Jenkinson with Mr. Asquith, Mama? The decision raised more than one set of eyebrows. I overheard Mr. Collins advising you quite forcibly not to take the chance.'

'Mr. Collins sometimes assumes too much. Besides, he does not know Mr. Asquith's history.'

'Whatever do you mean?'

Mama's expression became distant. She was quiet for so long Anne thought she wouldn't give an answer. When she spoke again her tone was remote, her expression even more so.

'Mr. Asquith's mentor in Jamaica, Sir Marius Glover, was a very close friend of your papa's.'

'Oh, I did not realise.'

'Sir Marius and your father, Sir Lewis, were inseparable as young men. I knew them both very well.'

Anne had never heard her mother sound so wistful before; nor had she seen her look so pensive. She understood then that she probably had loved both men. How extraordinary. Mama clearly had buried secrets that accounted for her decision to employ Mr. Asquith. Anne sat forward expectantly, hoping her mother would say something more. It took a great deal of imagination to think of Mama as young and in love — not with one gentleman, but with two.

'When Mr. Asquith returned to England looking for a position as a teacher, Sir Marius suggested he tried Hunsford and sent a letter of recommendation, which Mr. Collins received. At the same time, Sir Marius wrote urging me to give the young man an opportunity.' Mama stared through the window, her back turned to Anne. 'Mrs. Jenkinson had just left us. I interviewed Mr. Asquith, liked what I saw of his manners and intellect, and thought he might imbue you with a little self-confidence.' Mama paused, screwing her features into a more recognisable expression of distaste. 'He seems to have managed the task better than I anticipated.'

'Mama, I do not mean to — '

'You will marry Colonel Fitzwilliam, Anne.' Mama whirled around, her earlier pathos replaced with a look of stark determination. 'Mr. Asquith is charming, and I can quite see why you are so taken with him, but he is not well born. Rosings cannot be entrusted to his care, and neither can you.' Mama's voice softened. 'Do not imagine me to be quite so heartless that I care nothing for your happiness, since nothing could be further from the truth. Even so, we must all make sacrifices in this life.' She paused. 'Even you.'

'I do not believe Colonel Fitzwilliam wishes to marry me, Mama. He has not shown the slightest partiality towards me.'

'He will, once he considers the advantages of the match. He will ensure that Rosings prospers. I can trust him absolutely in that respect.'

Anne said nothing, quelling a rare burst of temper she knew better than to reveal. She wondered if her mother could even begin to imagine how worthless it made her feel to know a gentlemen would only marry her for material benefits. Even then, it appeared Colonel Fitzwilliam was still hesitating.

'Mr. Asquith may remain with us,' Mama continued, presumably mistaking Anne's silence as acquiescence. 'Provided you promise me you will remember your duty and do as I ask.'

'Colonel Fitzwilliam does not love me, nor I him.'

Mama flapped a hand. 'Love has nothing to do with the matter.'

'Did you not love Papa?' Anne canted her head as she dared to ask the question. 'You always speak of him with great affection.'

'I married him because my father said he was the right man for me, much as I am telling you Fitzwilliam is right for you. My father knew best, and so do I.'

Which does not answer my question. 'I had always hoped to fall in love with the man I marry.'

'Don't be such a fool! That only happens in penny novels.'

'Mr. Darcy married for love.'

'Darcy is a great disappointment to me.' Mama pursed her lips. 'I thought he had more sense than to be swayed by a fine pair of eyes. I am happy my sister is not alive to see who has become mistress of Pemberley in her place.'

'I like Mrs. Darcy,' Anne said daringly. In danger of incurring her mother's ire, she persevered, mainly because Mama had never spoken to her so frankly before, and Anne thought it important to show she did have a mind of her own. 'I think she makes Mr. Darcy happy.'

Mama snorted. 'For now, perhaps, but it will not last, and he will then be at leisure to regret his foolishness. But enough of the Darcys. I need your word that you will accept Fitzwilliam. Only if I have your promise will I permit Mr. Asquith to remain for a moment longer.'

Anne paused, sorrow and resignation twisting her insides into a vicious knot because she knew she had no real choice in the matter. 'Yes, Mama,' she replied, suppressing a sigh which nevertheless managed to slip past her guard. 'I will behave as you expect me to.'

★　★　★

Joshua awoke to a sky heavy with dark clouds. However, it was not raining for now, which was all that mattered to him. He broke his fast early and was out on horseback long before the hour when he had agreed to meet Mrs. Sheffield and now walked his horse around the spinney that separated the two estates, anxious with anticipation. He felt like a callow youth about to confront an attractive lady for the first time rather than the seasoned campaigner he actually was.

He heard her approaching before he actually saw her, which gave him a moment to quell his ridiculous nerves. A pretty bay mare appeared on the path ahead of him and Mrs. Sheffield, perched elegantly on a sidesaddle, raised a hand in greeting. She wore a form-fitting pale blue velvet habit with matching hat that sported a whimsical plume. Significantly, she was alone, no groom in sight.

'Good morning, Mrs. Sheffield.' Joshua raised his hat.

'Good morning, Colonel. I trust you have not been waiting for long.'

'Not long at all.' He turned his horse in the opposite direction. 'If we go this way, we will reach the folly at the top of the hill. It is quite a climb, but the view makes the effort worthwhile.'

'It is not us who will be making the effort,' she replied, patting her mare's neck. 'But I have often wished to see that folly, and Molly is keen to stretch her legs.'

'Then we are agreed.'

They rode in silence as the horses commenced the upward incline. Joshua cast sideways glances at his companion, feeling ridiculously privileged to have her to himself. She looked fresh this morning, but there was evidence of strain around her eyes, as though she had not slept well.

'Darcy and I spent hours playing in these woods as boys,' he said. 'We set up camps, enlisted boys from the farms to our respective sides, and plotted to breach one another's headquarters.'

Mrs. Sheffield's smile lit up her eyes, banishing the sadness from them. 'You were a soldier in the making, even then?'

'Perhaps I was. Wearing a red coat held a certain appeal to a young man who did not understand the brutal realities of soldiering.'

'And yet, you rose to the rank of colonel. Seldom have I met a gentleman better suited to soldiering than you are.'

'How can you tell? You barely know me.'

'Oh, I can tell. I have had a lot of contact with military men over the years.'

Joshua laughed. 'You make yourself sound as old as the hills.'

She wrinkled her nose. 'I feel that way sometimes.'

'A positive old crone,' Joshua said, laughing at her.

'Thank you, but I was not fishing for a compliment when I made that remark.'

'Nonetheless, your presence here is like a breath of fresh air.'

Mrs. Sheffield shot him a sideways look. 'With such charming manners, I find it hard to believe you are still unmarried. I feel persuaded more than one young lady must have set her cap at you.'

'Since we appear to be speaking frankly, you might as well know I am a younger son.'

'Yes, I thought that must be the case. You are obliged to make your own way and marry for money.'

'If I marry at all.'

'You definitely should,' she replied, sending him a shrewd glance. 'You would do a disservice to my sex by remaining single.'

'Now, it is my turn to assure *you* I was not looking for compliments.'

'And mine to confess I already knew your circumstances. My sister, you understand. You are Lord Braithwaite's younger son, are you not?'

'Yes. But my father died some years ago. My brother now holds that title.'

She offered him a wry smile. 'You do not think highly of your brother?'

'Good heavens, your sister is well informed.'

Mrs. Sheffield's laughter filled the air. 'No, not my sister this time. You just gave yourself away. A look of extreme distaste crossed your face when you mentioned your brother.'

'I can see I shall have to guard my expressions more closely while in your company.'

'For my part, I hope you do not.'

Their conversation came to a halt when the path narrowed and they were obliged to ride in single file, with Joshua leading the way. He glanced back to ensure Mrs. Sheffield was keeping up with him, impressed with the easy way in which she handled her mare; her balance precise, her seat elegant, her hands light on the reins.

'I can see that you really do enjoy being on horseback,' he said when they were able to ride side by side again. He watched her as she steered her mare around a rut in the path, still wondering what to make of her previous comment and how to respond to it. 'You certainly ride well.'

'I enjoy being outdoors. While I have been here, it has been frustrating not to be able to ride without a groom. I don't know the lie of the land, you see, and it would be easy to get lost. My sister does not ride, and Lord Briar doesn't have the time to oblige me.'

'Ah, I see.' Joshua sent her a smile of mock reproach. 'And there was me, thinking it was my sparkling wit and engaging personality that persuaded you to accept my invitation.'

She hooted with laughter, and Joshua found her uninhibited personality refreshing. 'Colonel Fitzwilliam, I hope you do not expect me to respond to such an infamous remark.'

Joshua laughed as well. 'Forgive me, Mrs. Sheffield. I cannot imagine what came over me. However, I blame you.'

'Me?'

'Your outspokenness appears to have rubbed off on me.'

'Oh no, you must do better than that.'

'Then I shall reapply myself to the task.'

As they crested the hill, Mrs. Sheffield looked around and gasped. 'This is wonderful! Thank you so much for bringing me here. One can see for miles.'

'It's the wrong weather for it. Dark clouds are rolling in and we shall have the promised rain. On a clear day, it is so much more worth the effort of coming up here.' He threw his leg over the pummel of his saddle and jumped to the ground. He secured his horse's reins to prevent them being trodden on and turned him loose to crop at the thin grass. 'Shall we walk?'

Joshua reached up his hands, placed them on Mrs. Sheffield's waist, and lifted her down. He paused when her face was on a level with his. He was intoxicated by the sight of her lovely features, her skin slightly flushed from the exertion of the ride, her glowing eyes, and was slow to place her on her feet. Their gazes locked and a strange feeling gripped Joshua — a premonition, a sun responding to a gravitational pull — something. She felt it, too. He was sure of that when her eyes widened, and then darkened.

'There we are.'

His voice sounded thick and raw as he turned his attention to her mare. Satisfied the horses could not stray far, he offered Mrs. Sheffield his arm, and they slowly strolled along the ridge. She continued to admire the view, exclaiming every so often as Joshua pointed out landmarks to her. Joshua preferred to admire his companion, willing the rain to hold off and time to stand still.

'You can see the entire layout of the Pemberley house,' Joshua said, pointing in the appropriate direction.

'My goodness, it is extensive.'

'It certainly is.'

'I hear Lady Catherine was set upon combining Pemberley and her own estate in Kent.'

'Yes, but as soon as Darcy met his wife, there was not the slightest possibility of that ever happening.'

'That cannot have pleased Lady Catherine. She seems like a lady who is accustomed to having her own way.'

'She has sufficient wealth and consequence to ensure most people do as she wishes.'

'But not her nephew, it seems.'

'My aunt failed to take into account that Darcy inherited the same stubborn streak as Lady Catherine's from his mother, Lady Catherine's sister.'

'I was not referring specifically to Mr. Darcy.'

'Ah, I see.'

But Joshua did not see — not precisely. Whom had Lady Catherine told about her expectation of Joshua wedding Anne? It seemed unlikely she would speak about it, especially to strangers, until terms had been agreed. There again, perhaps she sensed Joshua's reluctance and was trying to make it happen by openly implying it was all but settled. Either way, it was clear Mrs. Sheffield knew, or suspected. So why was she here with him now?

'And what of your own plans? How long do you intend to remain in Derbyshire?'

She sent him a teasing smile. 'Are you tired of my society already, Colonel?'

'Quite the contrary, but I understood you inherited an estate from your husband.'

'Yes, in Buckinghamshire.' Her laughter abruptly faded. 'But I have no immediate plans to return there.'

91

'Your husband made his fortune in Jamaica, I collect.'

'Yes.'

'Did you enjoy living there?'

Mrs. Sheffield absently plucked a leaf from a bush as she considered the question. 'At first, but I soon became homesick.'

'I understand. I have spent some time on the island myself, and found it rather limiting after a while. If you enjoy riding, I can understand why living in Jamaica would have been frustrating.'

They had reached the end of the path and paused to admire a different prospect. 'You and Mr. Asquith met one another in Jamaica,' Joshua suggested as they turned to retrace their steps.

Her entire body tensed. 'Why ever would you think that?'

'Tell me to mind my own business if you like, but if we are to be friends I would prefer it if you did not prevaricate. I am a colonel, Mrs. Sheffield — a leader of men. It is my job to recognise, or at least suspect, when things are not all they appear to be.'

'You take a very great interest in my affairs, Colonel.'

He covered the hand that rested on his sleeve with one of his own, and was slow to remove it again. 'Yes,' he said. 'I do. You must forgive me, but I cannot seem to help myself. I know you are in trouble, have anxieties that keep you from your own property, and if I can be of service in any way, you have but to say the word.'

She swallowed several times, and her eyes looked moist. 'Thank you,' she said softly. 'I was not aware I was in such very great need of a confidante, until now.'

'You are assured of one in me, if you will honour me with your trust.'

They walked in contemplative silence for several minutes. Joshua was unsure whether he had overstepped the mark. No, that was not precisely true. He knew that he had. What was less sure was whether Mrs. Sheffield would turn away from him, or look to him for the help she clearly needed. Either way, there was nothing more he could say or do to persuade her. It was now up to her.

'Mr. Asquith and I are acquainted,' she said eventually. 'There was nothing improper about our relationship but for reasons I cannot share with you, we prefer others not to know it.'

'You can rely upon my discretion.'

'Yes, I know.' She stepped around a muddy patch. 'Because of our differences, I was keen not to take part in the play Mr. Asquith is producing. I understand he has made alternative arrangements to fill the vacant role.'

'You dislike one another so much that you cannot bear to be in the same room?' Joshua flexed a brow. 'Now I am really intrigued.'

'You read too much into that particular situation.'

'What business took your husband to Jamaica?'

'Oh, the usual. He and his younger brother were involved in the exportation of sugar.'

'He had his own plantation?'

'Yes. He was known to Sir Marius Glover, Mr. Asquith's mentor.'

'Your husband died in Jamaica?'

'Yes, a fever went around, and he unfortunately caught it.'

Again, Joshua was convinced she was holding something back. 'I am very sorry,' he said.

'And the correct response would be for me to say I am too, but if we are to be friends, I ought to be frank.' She flashed a brittle smile. 'My husband was a bully and a tyrant, and I would be a hypocrite if I pretended to be sorry he's dead.'

'It is refreshing to hear you admit it, and you can trust me with as many of your secrets as you are willing to share.' Joshua fixed her with an inquisitive look. 'I assume your family persuaded you to marry him, since it's clear you did not do so voluntarily.'

'Yes, he was a charming gentleman from a good, if impoverished family, and my father liked him. I had neither the will nor inclination to go against my father's wishes, and so we were married. With the benefit of my dowry, Albert and his brother became involved in Jamaica.'

'His brother is still alive?'

'Unfortunately, yes.'

'And living on your estate in Buckingham-shire?'

She shuddered. 'Precisely.'

'I see.'

And this time he did, to a degree. The brother probably had designs upon Mrs. Sheffield. However, she was no longer the subject of parental dictate and wished to have nothing to do with him. Be that as it may, the property obviously belonged to her, and she ought not to be afraid to occupy it. Joshua was filled with a violent need to be of service to Mrs. Sheffield, and wondered how to make the suggestion. Before he could think of a way, a fat raindrop bounced off the brim of his hat. He glanced up and noticed a black cloud directly overhead. He had been so entranced by Mrs. Sheffield's engaging company that he had not noticed the weather closing in. He stripped off his coat, held it over her head, and together they rushed for the shelter of the folly.

By the time they reached it, Joshua, now in waistcoat and shirtsleeves, was soaking wet. Mrs. Sheffield, with the protection of his coat, had fared better. Even so, the plume on her hat wilted across her face, bedraggled and probably ruined. She blew it out of her eyes, and then laughed.

'Thank you,' she said, moving from beneath the protection of his coat. 'That was kind of you, and now you are soaked through.'

'Better I should be, than you.'

'How very gallant.' She crossed her arms over her torso and hugged herself, laughing as she watched the rain pounding down. 'I love rain. We had a lot of it in Jamaica, but that was tropical rain, of course. Not the same thing at all.'

Joshua stood directly behind her, somehow managing not to touch her. God's teeth, but it was a hard temptation to resist! Never had he felt a greater urge to embrace a woman. Never had circumstances conspired to make it so easy, and yet impossible. He wanted her to trust him, not fear his intentions. He wanted that trust very badly indeed.

'Then I am glad to have summoned up a

rainstorm for your enjoyment,' he said. 'Unfortunately, it is unlikely to last for long. I can see clear skies directly behind the clouds.'

'Perhaps that is just as well. My sister will worry. Besides, my solicitor is due from London today. We have matters to discuss regarding Albert's estate.'

'Mrs. Sheffield.' Joshua removed his hat and ran a hand through his damp hair, unsure how to phrase what was on his mind. 'I know you have difficulties. I know they somehow have to do with Asquith, and your brother-in-law. We are virtual strangers, but I feel as though I have known you for a long time.'

'Yes,' she said softly. 'I can understand that because I feel it too.'

'Whatever troubles you, you have clearly not told your sister or her husband. Please treat me as your confidante. You ought not to feel so alone.'

'Thank you, Colonel Fitzwilliam, but I could not burden you. You have enough problems of your own to be going on with.'

'If you refer to my aunt, then let me put your mind at rest. I might not have Darcy's resources, but I share his stubbornness. No one will make me do that which I do not wish to do, regardless of the monetary rewards.'

'Fine words, sir, and finer principles are at

play here, but even younger sons must have something to live on.'

Strange, Joshua thought, but he recalled saying more or less the same words to Eliza Bennet as she was then, when they first met at Rosings more than a year previously. He placed a hand on the small of Mrs. Sheffield's back, sensing her body heat searing through his glove, and turned her towards the door.

'Come,' he said. 'The rain has eased. I will escort you home.'

The horses had had the good sense to seek cover when the rain came and their saddles were only a little damp. He easily lifted Mrs. Sheffield into hers and helped her to find her stirrup. Satisfied that she was comfortable, he swung himself onto the back of his own horse.

'I must see you again,' he said as they descended the hill and turned towards Briar Hall.

'I would like that, Colonel.'

When they reached her destination, he kissed the back of her hand as he bid her *adieu*.

'May I call on you tomorrow?' he asked.

'Certainly you may, although what my sister will make of my entertaining gentleman callers, I can't begin to imagine.'

'You are out of mourning for a man you

98

did not love. Presumably, your sister knows that and will rejoice in seeing you making new acquaintances?'

Her teasing smile illuminated her eyes, banishing their haunted expression. Joshua's reaction to it was profound, and he shifted his position in his saddle, anxious to conceal its physical manifestation.

'I believe you are right about that, Colonel, just as you appear to be right about so many things. You see a great deal. I shall have to remain alert when in your company if I wish to retain even a degree of mystique.'

Her gaze clashed with his, and Joshua was conscious of the deep longing that whipped through his bloodstream as he drank in the sight of this feisty, mysterious, and slightly vulnerable widow.

'For you, Mrs. Sheffield, I shall ensure my insight is selective.'

She laughed, waving over her shoulder as she rode through the gates to Briar Hall. 'Where would be the fun in that?' she asked.

Joshua bit back the flirtatious response that sprang to his lips, waited until she had disappeared from view, and then turned in the direction of Pemberley, wondering what the devil he was supposed to do about his situation now.

7

'You are sisters. The Misses Dolores, Dorethea, and Daphne Downton all have their individual interests set upon the same gentleman,' Mr. Asquith explained. 'Originally there were four of you, but I was unable to persuade Mrs. Sheffield to become Doris. No matter, three will work just as well, if not better.'

'Don't t-tell me,' Captain Turner said, laughing. 'The object of their affections is Mr. David Doolittle.'

Georgiana and Kitty linked arms and smiled at Anne. 'I feel sorry for the poor gentleman, being bombarded with our attentions,' Georgiana said.

'But at least he only has to endure three of us now,' Kitty pointed out.

'I shall gladly play the part of that gentleman,' Major Halstead said with enthusiasm. 'I think I can tolerate the attention.'

Everyone laughed.

'At first, there is lively competition between you,' Mr. Asquith continued. 'But each of you secretly believes she will triumph. When none of you makes progress, you become less civilized and start sabotaging one another's campaigns.'

'Goodness,' Anne said. 'It all sounds rather brutal.'

'That is the beauty of comedy, Miss de Bourgh. One takes an ordinary situation and makes it farcical. I mean, how far would you go, what stratagems would you employ, to secure the affections of a man you supposed yourself to be in love with?'

Anne's cheeks warmed. She wished Mr. Asquith's question could be personal rather than hypothetical. He was so elegantly relaxed amongst Mr. Darcy's guests, as though he had been born to a position of consequence himself. Anne would never tire of listening to his voice as he instructed the players in their individual roles. She watched his fingers curling around the edges of the book while he read out parts of the play. The thought of those same long fingers stroking her skin had kept her awake on countless occasions as deep feelings of intense longing gripped her body, sending tremors down the length of it, awakening parts of her she hadn't previously given any thought to.

He looked at her so intently as he waited for her answer, she wondered if he had guessed her secret. Oh dear, this was so confusing. She had little experience, and no one whom she could go to for advice. Unless . . . Lizzy Darcy had been so patient and understanding. Dare she ask her? Anne's blush deepened at the prospect of exposing herself to ridicule. If Mr. Asquith had found her out then this ought to be a tragedy, not a comedy, since Anne had much to fear from any future that did not measure up to her mother's expectations and little to laugh at.

'Would you really put itching powder in your sister's clothing, Miss de Bourgh?' Kitty asked, giggling as she skimmed through her lines.

'Or ruin the trim on her best ball gown when there was no time left to repair it?' Georgiana added. 'Oh dear. I am afraid we are not very nice sisters at all, Mr. Asquith.'

'Which of the sisters finally triumphs?' Jane Bingley asked from her chaperone's chair in the corner of the room.

'None of them,' Mr. Asquith replied, smiling. 'Major Halstead's character is already secretly married to a woman his father does not approve of. He has to pretend to court the Downton sisters, just to put his father off the scent.'

'I s-say, what a bounder,' Captain Turner said, grinning.

'Shall we run through the parts?' Mr. Asquith stood up and indicated the dais at one end of Pemberley's ballroom. 'The opening scene sees the three sisters sitting together when their brother, played by Captain Turner, brings his friend Major Halstead to the house for the first time. Are we all ready?'

They read for half an hour, with much laugher, and many errors being made. At first, Anne was nervous, and her voice could barely be heard. When it occurred to her no one was laughing at her, she gradually relaxed and actually enjoyed herself.

'Well done, all of you,' Mr. Asquith said when a maid came in with refreshments. 'I think I can safely say there is only room for improvement.'

Everyone laughed.

'I thought we made a passable first attempt,' Major Halstead said. 'Although I will be the first to admit we are a long way from making a living through treading the boards.'

'Just as w-well we d-don't need to,' Captain Turner added.

Georgiana settled herself behind the teapot and poured for everyone.

'We need to think about costumes and scenery,' Mr. Asquith said as he sat down and elegantly crossed his long legs at the ankle. 'Mrs. Darcy has kindly said it will be all right to stage our performance in the music room, although it is better if we rehearse in here where we won't be in anyone's way.'

'Since we shall have such a small audience,' Kitty said, 'the music room is a good idea.'

'Quite.' Mr. Asquith shared a smile between them all. 'Your own clothing will be perfectly all right, ladies, but we do need to think about painting some scenery. A lot of the action takes place in the garden, you will recall.'

'We could hang up old sheets and paint garden scenes on them,' Kitty said.

'Absolutely,' Georgiana agreed. 'I shall speak with Mrs. Reynolds and see if she can supply us with sheeting.'

The conversation was lively with suggestions — many of them fatuous, some actually helpful. Only Anne remained silent, mainly because she was unable to think of anything sensible to contribute.

Everyone drifted away once tea was finished, and Anne found herself alone with Mr. Asquith. It had happened on many occasions since his appointment as her tutor, even though she was supposed to be chaperoned at all times. She had never felt nervous before, but today the atmosphere was charged with a feeling Anne was unable to identify.

'Are you glad I persuaded you to take part, Miss de Bourgh?'

'I beg your pardon.'

'I merely thanked you for agreeing to participate. I know you did not want to, but you have saved the day.'

'I enjoyed this morning, but unfortunately I was not very good.'

'You were every bit as good as the others.'

'You deceived me, Mr. Asquith. You promised I would only have a small part.'

His mouth curved. 'Would you have agreed to it if you had known?'

'Probably not.'

'Then you must forgive me. I am employed to help you overcome your shyness. What better way?'

She shook a finger at him, astonished by her brazenness. To her precise knowledge, she had never shaken a finger at anyone before now. 'You are very devious.'

He chuckled. 'I live to serve, Miss de Bourgh.'

A heavy silence ensued. In her desire to break it and prolong her moment alone with Mr. Asquith, Anne asked the first question that popped into her head. 'What shall you do when your position at Rosings comes to an end?'

'Find another one, I suppose,' he said with

a shrug of his impossibly broad shoulders, seeming disconcertingly unconcerned about leaving Rosings, and her, at some future date.

The thought of another young lady being the recipient of his wisdom and charm filled Anne with a virulent jealousy. 'In a school perhaps?'

'Wherever there is a place for my talents, such as they are.' He cocked his head to one side and sent her a lopsided smile. 'Are you in such a very great hurry to get rid of me?'

'Oh no!' *How can he possibly think that?* 'I was just curious. You are so very good with people, I cannot imagine you having any difficulty finding another situation, and I wondered where your preference lay. Mama will give you a glowing character.'

'You are to marry Colonel Fitzwilliam, which is the reason for your question.'

His was not a question, Anne realised, but more a statement of fact. It annoyed her that everyone seemed to think the matter was settled when the colonel had not said a word to her, and she had not actually agreed to anything.

'Why does everyone seem to think that?' she asked crossly.

'Excuse me if I speak out of turn. Before we left Kent, Lady Catherine told me that was the purpose of this visit, and well, I just assumed — '

'The colonel has not spoken to me, and even if he does, I . . . '

Anne became too choked with emotion to continue speaking. To her great mortification, she felt tears trickling down her face. Mr. Asquith knelt beside her and took one of her hands in his. He had never touched her so intimately before, and the gesture took her completely by surprise. He drew patterns on her palm with his thumb and passed her his handkerchief with his other hand.

'There, now I have overset you. Accept my apology. I assumed too much.'

'You thought, like everyone else including Mama, that I have no mind of my own.' Anne blew her nose, very conscious of the fact Mr. Asquith still held her hand and that his handsome face was creased with genuine-seeming concern. 'You just assume I will do as my mother tells me to.'

'On the contrary, I know you have a very fine mind, are a deep thinker, and have more strength of character than most people give you credit for.'

'Thank you, at least for that.' She dried her eyes and squared her shoulders. Somehow, she also found the strength to withdraw her hand from his. 'There, I am better now, and we shall not refer to the matter again.'

'May I ask you a personal question?'

She looked at him askance. No one had ever asked her permission to question her before. 'You may certainly ask,' she replied cautiously.

'Do you wish for the colonel's address?'

'No,' Anne replied without hesitation. 'But he needs a rich wife, and I have a duty to marry someone who will take good care of Rosings.' She rolled her eyes: an expressive way to show her feelings that would earn her mother's disapproval. 'Mama never tires of reminding me of that fact. She did intend Mr. Darcy for me.' Mr. Asquith shook his head, looking appalled. 'I agree. We never would have suited. The colonel does not frighten me quite so much, but . . . oh, never mind.'

'Please, say what is on your mind. I fancy you don't often get the opportunity.'

She offered him a wry smile. 'That is certainly true.' She straightened her spine and found the courage to meet his gaze. 'I see a very different side to Mr. Darcy since he made such a happy marriage. He was always so severe before, but he clearly feels deeply for his wife, and his entire demeanour has changed as a consequence. Mr. and Mrs. Bingley are a less extreme example of marital felicity. I never knew Mrs. Bingley before her marriage, and Mr. Bingley has always been agreeable. Even so, it is obvious they are very content with one another.' She fixed Mr. Asquith with a candid gaze. 'Is it such a very bad thing to want that sort of joy for oneself?'

'To marry for love?' Anne nodded. 'Not in the least.'

'Not that I ever shall.' She spread her hands. 'Even if I was free to receive addresses from admirers, I would never know if they liked me for myself or merely hankered after Rosings. Or rather, I should know.' She averted her gaze. 'Who would look at me for any other reason?'

'Oh my dear girl!' he cried passionately. 'I feel so very sorry for you.'

Anne elevated her chin. 'I do not require your pity.'

'I was not pitying you. I was merely expressing my despair at your self-image.'

'Why?' His statement surprised her. 'You've known me long enough to appreciate it is true.'

'I disagree.' He sat beside her, and she felt the full weight of his dark gaze resting on her profile. 'You are intelligent, thoughtful, exceedingly well read, and show promise as an artist.' His expression lightened. 'You also have the makings of a fine actress.'

Anne laughed. 'Hardly, but thank you for

trying to make me feel better about myself.'

'Has it occurred to you that you are actually free to make up your own mind about your future, or at least have a say in it?'

'If I did, I would not only upset my mother but also risk being disinherited.'

He stood up and paced the width of the room, standing at its opposite side with his back turned towards her. 'You have no money of your own on which to live?'

'Well yes, my father left me provided for, but my mother has control of those funds. I am not sure how much is involved, but I think there is enough to live modestly.' She lifted her shoulders. 'I had not considered that before.'

'Then my advice, if you will accept it, is to think about yourself for a change. Think about your own hopes and aspirations, and don't rush into anything you find distasteful.'

'That is easy for you to say, Mr. Asquith, but without Rosings I become invisible. Even more invisible than I already am, and anyone I find interesting would no longer be interested in me.'

'I find you interesting.'

His back was still turned towards her, and he spoke so quietly Anne could not be sure she had heard him correctly. Her heart soared, but she told herself not to be foolish.

She had probably read more into his words than he had intended by them, simply because they were what she so desperately wanted to hear. The thought of disobeying her mother terrified her, and she simply could not contemplate such a daring action — unless her future was with Mr. Asquith. That would put a very different light on matters. She loved him with a deep passion that overrode all other considerations.

But it was impossible to believe he could love her in return.

He was a fortune hunter, albeit a charming and agreeable one. Unless he could convince her his feelings mirrored her own, then she would never take the extreme measure of defying her mama. Ergo, she would most likely accept Colonel Fitzwilliam and make the best of it.

'You are compassionate, thoughtful, and kind,' he said softly, turning to face her again. 'Do not let others dictate the way you live your life, Anne.'

She gasped when her name slipped past his dear lips. She wanted him to say it again, to take her hand again, and reiterate his advice. When he failed to speak, she felt compelled to fill the silence.

'Thank you,' she stuttered inadequately.

'Your mother would dismiss me on the spot

if she heard what I just said to you.'

'She will never hear it from me, but in return you must answer a question for me.'

'Gladly.'

'How well do you know Mrs. Sheffield?'

'What makes you think I know her at all?'

'You disappoint me, Mr. Asquith. I hoped you would be completely honest and not treat me like a fool.'

'I apologise,' he replied, sighing. 'I knew Mrs. Sheffield slightly when I was in Jamaica, but knew her husband rather better.'

'Thank you.' She dredged up a smile. 'There, that was not so very difficult, was it? And yet, last night you treated one another as strangers. Why would you do that?'

'I will tell you about it one day, I promise you. But in the meantime, I must ask you to keep what I have told you to yourself.'

'You have not told me anything.'

'I want to be your friend, Anne,' he said, his eyes burning with sincerity. 'Not because of what you are, but because of who you are. There is a huge difference. Always remember, my dear, in this world there is one man who does appreciate you for yourself, even if he is not in a position to do anything about it.'

'Mr. Asquith.' Anne clapped a hand over her mouth, totally surprised. 'Whatever can — '

The door opened, Georgiana burst through it with a question for Mr. Asquith, and the opportunity to pose her question was lost.

★ ★ ★

With the actors occupied in the ballroom, and the rest of their guests otherwise engaged, Will and Lizzy enjoyed a moment's respite in front of the fire in Lizzy's sitting room. His arm circled her shoulders, holding her close as he rested his chin on the top of her head.

'You look tired,' he said sympathetically.

'Not tired precisely, but your aunt makes me anxious. All the time, I sense her watching me and mentally criticising everything I do. Naturally, I don't achieve anything as well as your mama did, and she congratulates herself on always having known I would pollute Pemberley by becoming its mistress.'

'If she thinks that way, she knows better than to say so to me. Besides, she must sense she is very much in the minority. Everyone else here loves you.' Will removed his chin from the top of her head and fixed her with an intense gaze. 'Especially me.'

'Thank you.' Lizzy lifted one hand and ran a finger down the cleft in his chin. 'Even so, I shall be glad when she is gone.'

'Which won't be until she gets her way and matters are settled between Fitzwilliam and her daughter.'

'Then she will be with us for a long time.'

Will placed a protective hand over the slight swell in Lizzy's belly. 'Whatever do you mean?'

Lizzy laughed. 'Honestly, you men are supposed to be the superior sex but you seldom see what is beneath your noses.'

Will rested his forehead against hers, his eyes heavy-lidded and seductive. 'What is it that you think you saw?'

'I don't think. I am perfectly sure. Your cousin is enamoured of Mrs. Sheffield.'

Will appeared taken aback. 'Good God, is he really?'

'Few men would not be. She is very beautiful and also of independent means.'

'Even so, that doesn't mean Fitzwilliam would — '

'He spent half the evening watching her across the dining table, then a long time in private conversation with her while we had music.'

'Oh lord, you don't think he plans to defy Lady Catherine's wishes too?'

'Before he saw Mrs. Sheffield, I think he might have been persuaded to go along with your aunt's wishes, which would be a great pity for Anne. It must be hard to be in her position, never knowing if she is admired for herself.'

'Georgiana will be able to sympathise.'

'Georgiana is an heiress, but not Pemberley's heir.'

Again, Will's hand touched her belly. 'Certainly she is not.'

'I think Mr. Asquith has done his job a little too well, and your timid cousin is developing a mind of her own.'

'Oh lord!'

Lizzy poked her husband in the ribs. 'Don't try to pretend you are not enjoying the drama.'

'I shall be sorry to see Lady Catherine disappointed again. However, I also think Fitzwilliam ought to do what is right for him and Anne, regardless of the repercussions.' Will's lips twisted into the parody of a smile. 'It's just I would prefer if they did it elsewhere and left us in peace to anticipate the arrival of our first child.'

Lizzy flexed her brows. 'Would that life was that simple.'

'Where is Fitzwilliam now? Don't tell me he has been dragged into Asquith's play too.'

'I happened to see him go out on horseback quite early this morning.' Lizzy sent her husband an impish smile. 'I am willing to wager he left early to avoid Lady Catherine, and I happen to know Mrs. Sheffield is fond of riding.'

'You like Mrs. Sheffield?'

'Very much,' Lizzy replied without hesitation. 'If she and your cousin were to . . . but what am I doing? It is absolutely none of my business.'

'Romantic speculation is every lady's business,' Will replied, running his forefinger gently down the curve of her face.

'Only because we are not permitted to do anything important and have no better way to occupy our time.'

'Running this house does not occupy you?'

'Mrs. Reynolds pretends to need me, but she is only being kind. She and Simpson have the place running like clockwork. I hesitate to interfere.'

'Are you suggesting you would take no interest in our friends' romantic intentions if I asked for your help in running the estate?'

Lizzy waved a hand in vague agreement. 'I would not give such matters another thought.'

Will's deep, throaty chuckle echoed through the room. 'Then let me seize the moment while your mind is still veering in that direction and ask you about Turner. The last time he was here, Kitty was depressed because he had been summoned by his father, who intended to marry him off to some suitable woman. What happened?'

'I have absolutely no idea.'

'Lizzy!'

She treated him to an innocent look. 'But you have no interest in rumour and speculation.'

'On the contrary, I thrive on the latest *en dits*. Besides, I bear some responsibility for your sister's welfare while she is under this roof, and I would not see her anticipation unnecessarily excited if nothing is to come of it.'

'My father was fond of telling us that next to being married, all young ladies enjoy being disappointed in love.'

'Your father spoke in jest.'

'Very possibly.'

'So will you enlighten me, or leave me to guess?'

Lizzy laughed. 'In other words, you are as curious as I am, but can't bring yourself to admit it.' She lifted her head from its comfortable resting place on Will's shoulder and placed a delicate kiss on his lips. 'Very well, I will tell you what I know, which is precious little. I have not spoken to Captain Turner on the subject but Kitty tells me he will not be marrying the lady his father chose for him. Whether he balked at the idea, or the lady decided against the match, I cannot tell you since that is all Kitty knows herself.'

'Well, that is encouraging, I suppose. It is evident he enjoys Kitty's society, and she his. Let us hope for a happy outcome.'

'Yes, by all means, let's hope for that. I want everyone to be as happy as we are.'

'I hesitate to spoil any pleasure of yours, but that would be impossible. No man could be as content in his marriage as I am, Lizzy.' His fingers played with the escaped curls at her nape. 'I am sorry if that makes me sound selfish, but there's no help for it.'

'Then I am selfish too. I feel exactly the same way and pity the rest of my sex since none of them are destined to be as happy as I am.'

Booted footsteps rang out on the tiled floor of the vestibule. Lizzy glanced over her shoulder, through the open doorway, and saw a dishevelled Colonel Fitzwilliam standing there, watching them embrace with a pensive expression on his face.

'You look as though you were caught in the rain, Colonel,' she said, removing herself from Will's arms. 'Pray, come and warm yourself in front of the fire and tell us about your morning.'

'Idle curiosity?' Will whispered, raising an

ironic brow at her.

'I showed Mrs. Sheffield the folly,' he said, striding into the room and holding his hands out to the flames.

Lizzy shot her husband a triumphant smile. 'It is not the best day to appreciate the view.'

'That is what I told Mrs. Sheffield.'

'But the weather did not detract from your enjoyment?' Lizzy asked, smiling.

'The weather did not,' the colonel replied, seating himself opposite Lizzy and Will, 'but I am concerned about Mrs. Sheffield's welfare.'

'Why?' Will asked.

Succinctly, the colonel outlined what he had learned of Mrs. Sheffield's unhappy marriage and her disinclination to return to her estate because her husband's brother was in occupation of it.

'Something unpleasant happened in Jamaica,' the colonel said in summary, 'but Mrs. Sheffield either does not know the full particulars, or is unwilling to share them with a comparative stranger. Either way, I am willing to wager her husband did not die of a fever.'

'I got the impression she and Mr. Asquith are acquainted, even though they pretended otherwise,' Lizzy remarked.

'They do know one another, but that is all I could persuade Mrs. Sheffield to say.' The colonel frowned. 'The lady is out of her depth, in danger of being cheated, and I'm damned if I will stand back and allow that to happen. Oh, I beg your pardon. Please excuse my language, Mrs. Darcy.'

'That's perfectly all right, Colonel. I can see you are upset by the prospect, as I am. But what shall you do about it?'

Colonel Fitzwilliam ground his jaw. 'I have not yet decided. Mrs. Sheffield's solicitor calls to see her this afternoon. I myself am engaged to call upon her again tomorrow, when I shall endeavour to gain her confidence.'

'What of Lady Catherine, Fitzwilliam?' Will asked. 'If you have definitely decided against Anne then you ought to tell her so and get the business out of the way.'

'I shall not marry Anne, regardless of how things develop between Mrs. Sheffield and myself. I had my doubts before, for her sake as much as my own. Now I am perfectly sure. But you are right, I ought to tell our aunt of my decision sooner rather than later.'

'Please let me know when you intend to do so, Colonel, and I shall make sure I am elsewhere,' Lizzy said, making them laugh and lightening the sombre mood.

'Are you absolutely sure, Fitzwilliam?' Will asked. 'Think of the benefits.'

'Do you imagine I have not already done

so? Lady Catherine has been dropping endless hints about her wishes, ever since you and Mrs. Darcy married. I have had ample opportunity to reflect.' He shook his head. 'If Anne was still the same frail, docile creature we are accustomed to seeing, then I might well have gone ahead. But Asquith has had a beneficial effect upon her and her personality has blossomed. That changes everything.'

'That is certainly true,' Lizzy said. 'I do not know her nearly as well as you and Will do, but I can see remarkable changes in her as well.'

'Quite so. I don't believe marriage to me would please her very much, but she would go through with it for her mother's sake if I was willing. I refuse to put her in that position.'

'But Lady Catherine will choose her husband, however noble your intentions, Fitzwilliam. She could finish up with someone far less sympathetic to her feelings than you are.'

'Oh, I wouldn't be so sure about that,' Lizzy said.

'God help us if Anne defies her mother, too,' Will said, rolling his eyes.

'I don't relish the idea of your aunt not having her way, but I do feel very strongly that Anne is entitled to have some say in her future.'

Will laughed. 'Not all young ladies are as strong-minded as you are.'

'Then I feel very sorry for them.'

Their private conversation came to an end when Kitty and Georgiana joined them, laughing, faces flushed with excitement, full of the parts they would perform in Mr. Asquith's play.

8

The afternoon's torrential rain failed to dampen the spirits of Pemberley's residents. Joshua passed the closed door to the ballroom and heard raucous laughter coming from the actors rehearsing within.

'I insist upon knowing how the play ends,' he heard Lady Catherine, who had taken over chaperone duties, insist. 'How can I be sure it is suitable for Anne to be involved with otherwise?'

Joshua couldn't make out what Asquith said in response.

'That is all very well, Mr. Asquith, but I don't see why Mrs. Bingley should know, yet I cannot be trusted with that information.'

Joshua's aunt being otherwise engaged gave him a legitimate reason to delay telling her of his decision not to marry Anne. He strode away from the ballroom, thinking about Rosings. If he were to become master of such a rich estate, he would be in a position to help his ungrateful brother restore the Braithwaite estate to its former glory. He had to be insane not to grasp the opportunity and make the best of things. Then he thought of Mrs.

Sheffield and the instant attraction he had felt towards her. The emotions she had engendered in him made it impossible to put financial expediency ahead of desire. He could survive on his army pay if need be. Money was not everything. He had nothing against Anne de Bourgh, but she was not in love with him, and she deserved to find true happiness.

With his conscience salved, Joshua whiled away the afternoon with Darcy and Bingley in the billiards room, losing a modest sum to those gentlemen because he was unable to concentrate on the game. His thoughts were at Briar Hall instead. He wondered if Mrs. Sheffield's solicitor had arrived, and what possible business could have brought him all the way from London. It had to be more than a routine affair or he would have consigned it to writing. Mrs. Sheffield was concerned about the impending visit, much as she tried to pretend otherwise. Joshua ground his jaw. Unless his judgement had become severely impaired, she had never had greater need of a confidante or reliable friend.

Dinner was a cheerful affair, with the players full of laughter at their afternoon's efforts. Lady Catherine only made the occasional complaint about the folly of the production, wondering aloud why young people nowadays could not find a more seemly way to occupy their time.

'Anne is proving to have remarkable talent for acting,' she informed the rest of the diners. 'You ought to have seen her, Fitzwilliam.'

'I would have been glad to watch, Lady Catherine,' Joshua replied, 'but the door to the rehearsal room is barred to those not participating.'

'Acting is hardly a ladylike pursuit,' Lady Catherine continued. 'But since she is determined to try it, and my daughter and niece are performing here at Pemberley for an audience of family and close friends only, I can see no harm in it.'

'No harm whatsoever,' Mr. Asquith agreed.

'Are you enjoying yourself, Anne?' Joshua asked.

'Actually I am, but Mama has greatly exaggerated my talents.'

'I am not given to exaggeration, child. I merely speak as I find.'

'Yes, Mama, but I am not nearly so good as Georgiana and Kitty.'

Good heavens, Joshua thought. It was the first time he had ever heard Anne contradict her mother. Presumably Asquith had persuaded her to form opinions of her own, and given her the courage to voice them.

'At least you remember your lines.' Kitty wrinkled her nose. 'I have to be prompted all the time.'

'I would exchange a good memory for a louder voice,' Anne replied with feeling.

'Really, it does not in the least matter if your voices are too low, or if any of you forget your lines,' Mrs. Darcy said, smiling at all the players.

Kitty laughed. 'I shall remind you that you said that when I dry up.'

'Y-you will n-not forget your lines, M-miss Bennet,' Captain Turner assured her. 'I s-shall be glad to help you remember them and make sure y-you are w-word perfect.'

'Who wrote the play, Asquith?' Joshua asked. 'Perhaps there's a copy in Darcy's library and I can look it up.'

'Don't spoil the surprise, Colonel,' Mrs. Darcy said, smiling. 'Just like the rest of us, you must contain your curiosity until the players are ready to perform.'

'You ask a lot.'

After dinner, the card tables were placed. Joshua found himself partnering Anne thanks, no doubt, to Lady Catherine's influence. He anticipated a dreary time, with Anne barely saying a word, but her new sense of self-worth manifested itself, and she proved to be engaging company. Joshua forgave her for constantly stealing glances at Mr. Asquith who was seated at one of the other tables, partnering Georgiana.

'Well done,' Joshua said when the game came to an end, and he and Anne triumphed.

'We were lucky,' Anne replied.

'My advice, for what it's worth,' he said, helping her with her chair and speaking softly so only she could hear him, 'is that one ought to make one's own luck.'

Anne looked at him with confusion. 'Whatever do you mean?'

Joshua glanced at Asquith. 'I think you know.'

'Oh.' Colour invaded Anne's cheeks. 'Colonel, I do assure you . . . besides, Mama would never — '

'What are you speaking to Anne about?' Lady Catherine demanded from an adjoining table. 'I must know why you feel the need to whisper, Fitzwilliam.'

Young people who were attracted to one another tended to do a great deal of whispering. By drawing attention to it, Lady Catherine could be accused of hampering Joshua's campaign, had he decided to launch one.

'We were discussing our strategy at whist, ma'am.'

Joshua inclined his head to Anne, offered

her the ghost of a wink, and strolled away to join Darcy in front of the fire. By reminding him of her autocratic, interfering manner, Lady Catherine had just eradicated any lingering doubts Joshua might otherwise have entertained regarding his decision not to become the master of Rosings.

★ ★ ★

The following morning was blighted by overcast skies. There was no rain, but it wouldn't hold off for long. Joshua didn't care. He would ride to Briar Hall, even if his horse sank hock-deep in mud and he became soaked to the skin in the process. The players were again hard at work in the ballroom, and Lady Catherine had not yet shown herself. Joshua made his escape while he could.

Mrs. Sheffield and Lady Briar received him with great civility. Lady Sheffield's countenance showed signs of strain, and there were dark circles around her eyes. She clearly had not slept well for the second night in succession.

'Celia told me you planned to call this morning, Colonel, but I did not expect you to keep the engagement in such appalling weather.'

Wild horses could not have kept me away.

'I am a soldier, Lady Briar,' he replied. 'Weather conditions seldom deter me when I make up my mind on a course of action.'

'How is everyone at Pemberley, Colonel?' Mrs. Sheffield asked.

'In the best of health, I thank you. Speaking of which, I come with an invitation for you all to dine in six nights' time. The young people are combatting the inclement weather by putting on a play.' Joshua smiled. 'We are to be the audience, if you can bear it.'

'It would be our pleasure.' Lady Briar clapped her hands. 'I once enjoyed play-acting myself and possessed some aptitude as an actress, though I do say so myself.'

'Are you not taking part, Colonel?' Mrs. Sheffield asked. 'I can just see you as a dashing hero, riding to the rescue of the hapless heroine.'

'I hesitate to disappoint you, ma'am, but my services have not been offered, nor are they required. They can manage very well without me. I gather there are three heroines, and I lack the courage to take all three of them on at once.' Joshua shuddered, making the ladies smile. 'Give me an enemy regiment to face on the battlefield instead. That is a situation over which I might be able to exert some control.'

'Really, Colonel, do you expect us to

believe that?' Lady Briar asked.

'You ought to ma'am. The players are rehearsing in strict seclusion in the Pemberley ballroom. Even so, they have managed to turn the place on its head. No one except Mrs. Bingley knows how the play ends, and she refuses to give a single hint.'

'I should think not.' Mrs. Sheffield laughed, and some of the wariness left her eyes.

'Then you will come?'

'Certainly we shall. Please thank Mrs. Darcy and assure her we would not miss it.'

The conversation turned more general as tea was served. When Lady Briar finished hers, she excused herself on some pretext and, at last, Joshua found himself alone with Mrs. Sheffield. As soon as their gazes clashed, an air of expectancy sprang up between them, and she abandoned all pretence of normality. She looked so crestfallen that Joshua impulsively reached for her hand.

'I cannot bear to see you looking so unhappy,' he said passionately. 'Will you not tell me what has overset you? You can be assured of my secrecy.'

'What is the point?' She flapped the hand he wasn't holding. 'There is nothing you can do.'

'I may not be able to act, Mrs. Sheffield,

but I am very resourceful in all other respects. I have yet to encounter a situation that cannot be resolved with a little guile or, if necessary, brute force.'

She managed a wan smile. 'Always the soldier.'

'No, not in this situation.' His fingers closed more firmly around her palm, and she made no attempt to pull her hand free. 'I am simply a man who wishes to be of service to a lady who has attracted his interest.'

'You would do better to go back to Pemberley and pay court to your cousin. I am an entirely lost cause.'

'Hang my cousin!' Joshua fixed her with an intense, probing look. 'It is you whom I wish to serve. Whatever troubles you, you have not told your sister or Lord Briar about it, have you?'

'No.' She shook her head. 'They cannot help me, and I would not worsen my sister's nervous disposition by visiting my problems upon her.'

'Always putting others ahead of yourself.' Joshua exhaled sharply. 'Do you not trust me? Perhaps I am being presumptuous, but I thought we understood one another better than that.'

Mrs. Sheffield moistened her lips with the tip of her tongue, clearly trying to come to a decision. Joshua waited her out in silence.

'My husband's brother is claiming that my estate in Buckinghamshire is rightfully his,' she said with a heavy sigh. 'And, as things stand, I am unsure how to refute that claim.'

Joshua wasn't entirely surprised. Her unwillingness to return to Buckinghamshire because her brother-in-law was in residence there and her obvious dislike for the man had set him wondering.

'What does your solicitor suggest?'

Mrs. Sheffield's despairing look gave way to one of anger. 'That I should leave the negotiations to him because, as a feeble woman, I cannot be expected to understand them — or words to that effect.'

'There is absolutely nothing feeble about you.'

She offered him a humourless smile. 'I believe Mr. Higgins is now aware of that fact.'

'The man sounds incompetent. What made you choose him?'

'I did not. He was engaged by my husband when he purchased the estate and took care of Albert's interests in this country while we were in Jamaica.'

'That was to be my next question. If the estate was not previously in your husband's family, and was only purchased after your marriage, then presumably your dowry paid for it.'

'Well no.' She looked away from him and spoke evasively. 'We only acquired the house after we had been married several years. His work in Jamaica was sufficiently profitable to make the purchase possible.'

'And I imagine his brother was a-party to that work, so he now deserves to own the estate?'

'Yes, that is precisely what he thinks.'

This was clearly not straightforward, and Joshua's suspicions were on high alert. 'Did your husband leave a will?'

'Yes, I am his sole beneficiary. His brother is not mentioned.'

'Then he has no claim.'

'That is what I tried to tell Mr. Higgins but, of course, he disagrees.'

'Then you had better tell me everything, from the beginning.'

Mrs. Sheffield glanced out the window. The intermittent rain had been blown away by a strong wind that caused tree branches to bend against it, and sent a scattering of leaves bowling across the recently cut lawns. 'Can we walk outside and talk about this? I feel trapped in here, restless, and . . . oh, I don't know. I think better out of doors.'

'I understand completely. Go and fetch a

warm cloak. I shall wait for you in the vestibule.'

Five minutes later, they strolled along the gravel walkway that surrounded Briar Hall and headed for the reflecting pools. Even though it was such an overcast day, their images were still cast back at them in the water's surface, as was the edifice of the house itself. The Pemberley estate had similar pools, but on a grander scale.

'Are you warm enough?' Joshua asked.

She threw back her head and breathed deeply of the crisp autumnal air. 'Thank you, yes.'

Joshua said nothing more, leaving her to gather her thoughts.

'Albert and his brother had a signed partnership agreement regarding their work in Jamaica that I knew nothing about until yesterday afternoon,' Mrs. Sheffield said after a prolonged pause.

'That seems rather strange. Surely, your husband would have mentioned the arrangement to you, even in passing?'

'He didn't ordinarily tell me anything about his work, but I agree, he should have said something about such an important agreement.' She shrugged. 'Perhaps he didn't anticipate dying quite yet.'

'You think the agreement is bogus?'

She lifted her shoulders. 'I don't know what to think. Albert's signature looks genuine, but I am no expert on such matters.'

'Let us leave aside the validity of the agreement and consider your brother-in-law's claim. I imagine he says he was not paid monies owed to him and so plans to take the estate instead.'

'Something like that.' She screwed up her features into an expression of disdain. 'Out of Christian charity, he claims I can still live there if I so wish.'

'How very obliging of him.' Joshua was consumed by a murderous rage, well able to imagine what this vile-sounding individual had in mind once he had Mrs. Sheffield beneath the same roof as him. Outwardly, he remained perfectly calm. 'We will not allow that to happen. You will live there again, of course, but your husband's brother will have to find alternative accommodation.'

She gasped. 'You make it sound so straightforward.'

'Excuse me for asking such personal questions, but I was under the impression that your dowry was adequate enough to enable the purchase of an estate.'

'And so it should have been.' They turned at the end of the walk and took a different direction, further away from the house. 'What my father did not know until after we were married was that Albert had very large debts to discharge. Not of his own making. Albert was many things, most of them disagreeable, but one thing he was not was careless with money. Quite the opposite, in fact. Unlike his father, he never went near a gaming table, nor did he squander his blunt. When his father passed away Albert inherited his debts, which he felt honour bound to settle.'

Joshua grunted. 'I want very badly to dislike your late husband, Mrs. Sheffield, and you are making it difficult for me.'

'Oh, don't worry, he was not a kind person, and I can tell you plenty of things about him that would validate your dislike. However, I was attempting to be fair. He ought to have explained those debts to my father, before he gave Albert permission to address me. Papa would not have entertained his suit if he had known about them.'

'Which is precisely why he didn't tell him.' Joshua found a bench beneath an ancient oak that was in the lee of the wind and steered Mrs. Sheffield towards it. 'Your husband's father did not own an estate of his own.'

'He did at one time, but — '

'Let me guess. He gambled it away.'

'Precisely.'

'And so after Sheffield discharged his

father's debts, there was not much of your dowry left, and you were obliged to rent lodgings.'

'Yes. We were in London, but didn't show ourselves much in society. There was no money to spare for that. Besides, Albert would have considered it money wasted. He was not afraid of hard work and established himself as a commodities broker. He opened an office close to the docks and found markets for products that were brought in speculatively by independent vessels. You can have no idea how many such ships there are, and he did reasonably well at it.'

'I suppose that is where he got the idea for going to Jamaica?'

'Yes. His brother, Percival, worked with him when the fancy took him. He is cut from the same cloth as their father. Albert wasn't one to tolerate shirkers, but he had a blind spot when it came to Percival, I know not why. Basically, he did as little as possible and claimed a great deal of the profits. Albert once referred to an event in their childhood. I think Percival somehow saved Albert from a life-threatening situation. Albert felt obligated to Percival because of it and allowed him to do more or less as he pleased.'

Joshua disciplined himself to pay close attention to Mrs. Sheffield's account without becoming transfixed by the delicacy of her profile, or moved by the desolation in her luminous eyes. Brother Percival was trying to swindle her. He knew it as surely as he sat here doing his level best not to pull her into his arms and comfort her in the manner that sprang spontaneously to mind.

'It was Percival who first heard about the opportunity in Jamaica. He used to go to the dockside taverns, and drink with the sailors. Percival is a viper, but blessed with the appearance of an angel. He is universally popular with the ladies and manages to remain on good terms with most men he meets as well. One of his sea-faring acquaintances told him about a plantation in Jamaica that was in decline because the owner had died unexpectedly. His heirs had no interest in going to the island and required someone to purchase the plantation at a bargain price because they needed the money quickly. Albert wasn't prepared to take the risk, but Percival kept on and on at him. He said the market for sugar was thriving and only a simpleton could fail to make a success of it. Eventually, Albert agreed.'

'Without knowing anything about managing a plantation?' Joshua flexed a brow. 'Was that not risky?'

'I thought so and tried to persuade him not

to do it, but he would never listen to anything I said. I hated the idea of going to the Indies and asked him to leave me behind, but he would not hear of it. I was his property, you see, and he would never have left me to my own devices.'

'But your husband made the plantation profitable?'

'He must have done so because, a year after he acquired it we returned to England and he purchased Everton Park outright. I have not spent more than two months beneath the roof of the house we now own because we returned to Jamaica again almost immediately.'

'How large is your estate?'

'Nothing compared to Pemberley, or even to Briar Hall. It is a large manor house, with about fifty acres.'

Joshua could imagine the place. A modest establishment, but also very desirable, and fairly easily managed. The sort of establishment any man would be proud to call home. Joshua reined in his imagination, scowling when he thought of the scoundrel, Percival Sheffield. He was relying upon Celia's lack of knowledge of her late husband's affairs to pull off this deception, but he had not counted upon Joshua's involvement. He hardened his jaw, silently vowing it would never happen while he had breath in his body to prevent it.

'You doubted your husband's ability to turn the plantation around, and yet he must have done so because he purchased an estate from the proceeds after little more than a year.'

'Yes, and paid for it with his life.'

'What were the conditions like on the plantation?'

'Deplorable. Our slaves were a wretched band of creatures who had been so badly treated, and were so under-nourished, that they could barely work.' She shuddered. 'It was awful. I felt so very sorry for them and tried to persuade Albert to treat them better, give them more food, so they would be more productive. He would not listen to me. His way of getting more out of them was to have the overseer whip them into submission.'

'If Sheffield made money with such a poor workforce, only imagine how much more profitable a well-run plantation, with well-treated workers, would be.'

'Quite so. Sir Marius Glover, Mr. Asquith's mentor, is a case in point. He called to see us soon after we arrived and was closeted with Albert and Percival for a long time, offering them the benefit of his advice, which included better food and housing for the slaves.

Unfortunately, the Sheffield men thought they knew better.'

There were a dozen more questions Joshua wished to ask, but he suspected she would not know the answers to them. Asquith, on the other hand, almost certainly would, and Joshua planned to have a frank conversation with that gentleman upon his return to Pemberley. Of immediate concern was the agreement between the brothers. Mrs. Sheffield's solicitor seemed to think it was genuine, and had travelled all this way to talk to her about it.

'You say your husband's signature appeared genuine on this supposed partnership document between the brothers, so I presume you saw the whole thing?'

'Yes. It was witnessed by a solicitor in Kingston, Jamaica whom I had never heard of. Nor did I ever hear Albert mention his name. There was also a will drawn up by that gentleman, dated after the one in England naming me as Albert's sole heir.' She wrinkled her brow. 'It is very peculiar.'

'What were the precise provisions of the agreement?'

'Albert was the senior partner, and Percival worked for an agreed percentage. That was all straightforward enough and hardly needed to be stated in writing. They had always worked that way. The agreement also said that in the event of the demise of one brother, ownership of the plantation would revert to the other.'

Joshua sat a little straighter. 'I see. But in that case, why cannot Percival simply take control of the plantation?'

'Because the slaves revolted, for which I don't in the least blame them. Their conditions were nothing short of a disgrace, and when people run out of hope and have nothing to lose ... well, I tried to warn Albert that feelings were running high, given all the talk about abolition. Word had reached us of slaves on other plantations taking matters into their own hands, but it was all rumour and speculation, which Albert chose to dismiss without trying to get to the truth. Anyway, the plantation was razed to the ground; all the buildings and the crop. Albert died trying to save his property.'

'Ah, I thought there was no fever.'

'It is an explanation that satisfies most people and saves all the inevitable questions.'

Joshua lost the battle to remain passive and raised a hand to gently stroke her face. 'I, my dear, am not most people.'

'No,' she replied after a long pause. 'You are not, but I must know, why are you so anxious to help me?'

'Mrs. Sheffield ... Celia.' Joshua paused,

too acutely aware of her close proximity, of the intoxicating aroma of her floral perfume, of an overwhelming torrent of protective feelings, to act with discretion. 'I will resolve this problem for you, one way or another, on that you have my solemn word, and you owe me absolutely nothing.'

'That does not answer my question.'

'Is it so unnatural for a man of integrity to offer his services to a lady in distress?'

She offered him the ghost of a smile. 'You are attracted to me, Colonel Fitzwilliam?'

He chuckled. 'Am I so very transparent?'

'You make me feel safe. Safer than I have for a very long time. I am not sure if that is such a good thing.'

'You have nothing to fear from me,' he replied, gently stroking her cheek with a gloved finger. 'Just so long as you refrain from looking at me in the way you are at this precise moment. There is only so much temptation a man can be expected to withstand.'

'I cannot help the way I look.'

'And I cannot help the way I respond to that look.'

Her eyes burned with an unfathomable emotion, robbing Joshua of what little common sense he had managed to retain. With a smothered oath, he pulled her into his arms and covered her lips with his own, kissing her with determination and brutal passion. She responded with a sweet urgency that drugged his mind. Joshua deepened the kiss, disciplining himself to accept this would be the first and only time he allowed his feelings to get the better of him. Her arms had worked their way around his neck, and he could feel the softness of her breast pressing against his chest, even through the thick layers of their clothing. He cursed beneath his breath, not having expected her to respond with such abandonment.

Joshua broke the kiss and released her, breathing heavily. Her eyes were now muddy with passion, and she looked at him with a combination of surprise and total confidence in his abilities.

'I did warn you,' he said softly, taking her hand and pulling her to her feet. 'Come, I will take you back to the house. Have the goodness to give me the name of your solicitor, his direction and written authority to act on your behalf.'

'What do you intend to do?' she asked in a husky voice.

'I shall speak with Asquith first. See what light he can shed on matters.'

'He did not like my husband or brother-in-law.' They walked slowly towards the house.

'He disapproves of me, too.'

'Be that as it may.'

A short time later, Joshua was in possession of the information he had requested and had no further reason to delay his departure. Anyway, Lady Briar had re-joined them, and so the intimacy of the moment was lost.

'I shall call again tomorrow,' Joshua said, kissing the back of Celia's hand before taking formal leave of Lady Briar.

'I look forward to it,' Celia replied.

As Joshua rode away, mulling over all he had just learned, he doubted whether her anticipation could be greater than his own.

9

'A word if you please, Asquith.'

'How can I be of service to you, Colonel?' Asquith asked with an affable smile.

'Let's talk in here.'

Joshua led the way into the library and closed the door after them. He took a chair on one side of the fire and gestured Asquith towards its twin.

'I won't keep you long. You have rehearsals to occupy you and enthusiastic players to keep amused.'

Asquith draped himself elegantly in his chair, appearing to be perfectly at ease. 'The ladies are painting scenery this afternoon, and so I am entirely at your disposal.'

'What can you tell me about the plantation Sheffield purchased and the manner of his death?' When Asquith raised a brow, Joshua felt the need to explain himself. 'Sheffield's brother is attempting to swindle Mrs. Sheffield out of her property.'

'I see.'

'You don't appear surprised.'

Asquith twisted his lips into an expression of distaste. 'Nothing that blaggard does would surprise me.'

'Ah, so you dislike him. I don't know him myself, and only have Mrs. Sheffield's word that he does not hold a legitimate claim. But he has a cowardly way of staking that claim, hiding behind solicitors instead of coming straight out and discussing the situation with Mrs. Sheffield.'

Asquith looked genuinely startled. 'He has not communicated with Mrs. Sheffield himself?'

'His claim to the property came as a complete shock to her. When they arrived back from Jamaica he said he needed to live there until her husband's affairs were put in order. She assumed he would receive something from his brother's estate and had nowhere to live until he was in funds again. Anyway, Mrs. Sheffield chose to come here to her sister, rather than live beneath the same roof as him. Perhaps that was a mistake, since it gave the impression she was happy for Sheffield to take her property.'

'Or he has made the false claim to exact revenge, because Mrs. Sheffield decided not to dwell with him.'

Joshua's head shot up. 'You think he would stoop that low?'

'I think there is little he would not do to get his way.'

Joshua ground his jaw, stood up and braced both arms against the mantelpiece. 'Tell me more about Percival Sheffield.'

'Presumably you have Mrs. Sheffield's permission to ask such questions?'

Joshua shot Asquith a castigating glance. 'In writing,' he said curtly.

'Forgive me if I caused offence, but you have put me in an awkward situation. One cannot be too careful.'

'Is that why you pretended not to know Mrs. Sheffield when she dined here?'

'Ah yes, that was awkward.' He rubbed his chin. 'Perhaps I had better start at the beginning.'

Joshua resumed his chair and fixed Asquith with a steady gaze. 'That might be best.'

'My father worked as Sir Marius Glover's plantation manager, but died when I was very young. I don't remember much about him. My mother died when I was ten.' Asquith crossed one booted foot over his opposite knee and settled himself more comfortably in his chair. 'I assumed I would be sent back to England after her death, but Sir Marius wouldn't hear of it. His eldest son and I were of a similar age. Sir Marius kindly paid for me to be schooled in England alongside his son, and then supported me at university.'

Rather as old Mr. Darcy supported

Wickham, Joshua thought. 'Go on,' he said.

'Sir Marius spoke of me following in my father's footsteps and eventually managing his plantation, but by the time I finished university, talk of abolition was gaining momentum and everything in Jamaica became unsettled.' He waved an elegant hand. 'Don't misunderstand me, I shall be as happy as the next man to see an end to slavery, but at the current time the entire Indies are a maelstrom of uncertainty and unrest. No one knows quite what the future will hold, but things will never be quite the same again.'

Joshua inclined his head. 'I'm with you there.'

'Sir Marius's feelings closely mirrored my own. He understood I needed gainful employment and so had me school his younger children, and then escort his youngest son to England when it came time for him to complete his education here.'

'And you stayed on?'

'Yes, I felt it was time to support myself.'

Joshua nodded his approval. 'Most men in your position would have taken advantage of Sir Marius's good nature.'

Asquith waved the suggestion aside with a casual flip of his wrist. 'Sir Marius has eight children of his own. He does not need me adding to his burden.'

'You were still in Jamaica when Sheffield arrived?'

'Yes.' Asquith leaned an elbow on the arm of his chair and rubbed his chin in his cupped hand. 'The badly run plantation that Sheffield purchased against Sir Marius's advice was worked by half-starved slaves incapable of doing a full day's work through no fault of their own. When the owner of the plantation died, his sons couldn't wait to sell and leave the chaos that Jamaica had become. They were unable to believe their good fortune when Sheffield made them an offer for the place greatly in excess of its value.'

'I don't have the pleasure of understanding you.' Joshua shook his head. 'If the plantation was in such a sorry state, how did Sheffield make enough profit from it quickly enough to purchase the estate here in England that his brother is now laying claim to?'

Asquith flashed a humourless smile. 'What do you know of the Jamaican Maroons?'

'Not a great deal.' Joshua stretched his legs out in front of him, taking a moment to recall his history. 'Going back a hundred years, the Spanish colonists fled Jamaica and left a large number of African slaves behind. Rather than be re-enslaved by the British, they escaped into the mountainous regions of the island, joined forces with . . . er — '

'Very good, Colonel. They joined forces with the Tainos, intermarried with Amerindian natives and established independence in the backcountry, surviving by subsistence farming and by raiding plantations. Inevitably, there were wars because the Maroons were ruthless, becoming increasingly more powerful, and had to be stopped. Eventually, the British governor signed a treaty with the Maroons promising them two thousand five hundred acres of land in two locations, in exchange for living beneath their own chief and a British superintendent.'

Joshua nodded. 'I recall something about that.'

'In return, the Maroons agreed not to harbour runaway slaves but to help catch them. They were paid a bounty of two dollars for each returned slave, which was the start of a lot of tension between rival black communities.' Asquith ran a hand across the back of his neck. 'To summarise, another war recently ensued. Some Maroons remained neutral and were left alone, others were viciously hunted down and deported. Tensions were running high, and still are, hence the reason for a lot of British settlers selling up and leaving.'

'A lot of people in this country have been

made anxious by talk of abolition.'

'Mainly because they don't want to pay their slaves,' Asquith said with a cynical snort. 'Now that the place is in chaos, they are claiming they were in the right of it. Anyway, where was I?'

'Deportations.'

'Right, well, of those left behind, a large enclave of rogue Maroons occupied the hills close to Sheffield's plantation. They could see he had a decent crop, but no manpower to harvest it. They struck a deal with Percival. They would pick the crop and make sure it got refined and exported, without the necessity to pay the usual taxes. In return they wanted half the profits.'

'That is highly illegal.'

Asquith shrugged. 'And also highly profitable. It is not an uncommon practice, especially in these anarchic times when slaves are starting to organise themselves and make demands.'

'How do you know it was Percival's idea?'

'I overheard him talking to the Maroons and assuring them he would talk his brother round.'

Joshua would give a great deal to know what hold Percival had over his older sibling. It must have been something vital to persuade Albert, who everyone agreed had been a methodical and cautious man, to go along with such a risky scheme. 'What happened to the slaves who lived on the plantation?'

Asquith shot Joshua a look. 'What do you think?'

'Percival left them to fend for themselves?'

'Exactly, but in so doing, he miscalculated badly. To this day I don't know how they managed it, but they went off somewhere in the hills, were taken in, and recovered their strength. Then they were on the lookout for revenge, against the Maroons, but more especially against Sheffield, whom they blamed for making them homeless.'

'It was they who destroyed the plantation?'

'Yes, but here's a question for you, Colonel. Was Mrs. Sheffield's husband killed trying to save his property? Did his former slaves finish him off, or — ?'

'Or did Percival see an opportunity to take everything for himself?'

The two men locked gazes and neither spoke for several moments.

'Quite so,' Asquith said, breaking the brittle silence.

'You really think Percival Sheffield is capable of fratricide?'

'I assume you haven't met him?'

'No, I have not had that pleasure.'

153

'He is perfectly charming, but cunning as a fox, totally ruthless, and untroubled by his conscience. Percival has an added something about him that makes him dangerous. Put simply, he finds cruelty entertaining.'

Joshua's blood ran cold at the thought of this man having anything to do with Celia Sheffield. 'He claims he had a written agreement with his brother, leaving the English property to him.'

Asquith shook his head. 'I don't believe a word of it.'

'Nor do I.'

'There is nothing he would like more than to have Mrs. Sheffield beholden to him.' Joshua scowled at having his suspicions confirmed. 'I saw the way he used to look at her with such hunger in his eyes, but she never wanted anything to do with him, and it infuriated the man. He wasn't used to failing with the fairer sex.'

Joshua took a moment to reflect, feeling better informed but just as helpless as he had been at Briar Hall. 'I don't suppose you have any way of confirming what you have just told me?'

'Unfortunately not. It is all speculation and conjecture. Sir Marius's plantation was some distance away from Sheffield's. By the time news of the fire reached us, the damage had already been done. Even so, we thought it rather odd that while both brothers supposedly fought to save their home, Albert perished in the attempt, but Percival barely had a singed whisker.'

'Perhaps Mrs. Sheffield knows more. Presumably she was there.'

'No, she was visiting ladies on an adjoining plantation that afternoon. I have often wondered if Percival had some say in the timing of the attack and ensured Mrs. Sheffield's safety by arranging for it to take place when she was not at home.'

Joshua stood up and paced the length of the room, mulling this latest intelligence over. 'You still have not explained why you pretended not to know Mrs. Sheffield.'

'I regret that.' Asquith looked abashed. 'Seeing her here brought all those awful memories back. It was not a happy time, and many other people besides Sheffield died in that fire, a lot of them slaves who became trapped when the blaze spread far quicker than they had anticipated. I know the slaves were the ones who started it, but they had good reason to feel aggrieved, and — '

'Excuse me, but I overheard the two of you speaking privately in this very room. She thanked you for not giving her away. What did she mean by that?'

Asquith shifted awkwardly in his seat. 'I knew she did not much like her husband, and I couldn't blame her for that. But he *was* her husband, and she showed little remorse at his demise.'

Joshua furled his brow. 'She didn't pretend a grief she did not feel, and you blame her for that?'

'Well, yes. Several people were shocked by her attitude.' Joshua snorted. 'She also made little secret of the fact she hated Jamaica and couldn't wait to return to England. To her credit, she also had endless battles with her husband and his brother about the appalling manner in which they treated their slaves, but the Sheffield brothers adamantly refused to do the right thing by them. So all Mrs. Sheffield could do was spend time with the women and children, doing what she could for their illnesses and sneaking food to them when she was able.'

'And you hold that against her?' Joshua asked, feeling his temper rising.

'No, I applauded her efforts, but . . . excuse me, I did wonder if she encouraged her slaves to rise up against her husband and the Maroons who had moved in. They would do absolutely anything she asked of them, you see.'

'Careful!'

'I was wrong, I know that now, but you must see how it looked. She got what she wanted, which was release from an unhappy marriage, return to England, and financial independence. She wasn't to know that Percival would try to claim her property.'

'I am very glad you did not spread false rumours about Mrs. Sheffield's character,' Joshua said, narrowing his eyes at his cousin's tutor.

'I would never do that.'

'Well, that's something, I suppose.' Joshua paused. 'I assume Mrs. Sheffield is aware of what you thought about her.'

'Things were said in the heat of the moment that I now regret,' Asquith replied evasively.

'Apologise when next you see the lady, throw your support behind me in my efforts to restore her property to her, and we will say no more about the matter.'

'That is very generous of you.' It was Asquith's turn to pause. 'Will you permit me to ask you a personal question, sir?'

Joshua sighed, suspecting he knew what was coming. 'Ask away.'

'Lady Catherine told me why she wished to come to Pemberley, and why you are here also.' He cleared his throat. 'Excuse me, but you obviously have a personal interest in Mrs. Sheffield. Where does that leave Miss de Bourgh?'

'Anne and I would not suit,' he replied shortly.

Asquith elevated both brows. 'You would pass up the opportunity to be master of Rosings?'

Joshua shrugged. 'Apparently so.'

'Have you told Lady Catherine of your decision?'

'Not yet, and nor shall I for a few days more.' Joshua slapped the younger man on the shoulders. 'That ought to give you time.'

'Me?' Asquith laughed. 'If Lady Catherine even suspected — '

'I have watched you and Anne together. You have done a great deal to bring her out of herself. I hardly recognise her anymore.'

'It is what I am paid to do.'

'Anne is no longer quite so afraid of Lady Catherine. If there is something she wants enough, she might even defy her mother in order to get it.'

Asquith shook his head. 'Lady Catherine would disinherit her.'

'I doubt it. Lady Catherine likes you.' Joshua paused. 'There is something in her expression when she looks at you, especially when you mention Sir Marius.'

'They knew one another when they were younger.'

'I suspect my aunt liked him, which accounts for her taking you on as Anne's tutor. The question is, do you return Anne's feelings?' Joshua waved a hand. 'I don't expect you to answer that. It's none of my business. But I would prefer it if you did not excite her expectations if you don't plan to act on your feelings.'

Asquith expelled a long breath. 'She will never believe I have anything other than the acquisition of Rosings in mind.'

'Well then, you have some work ahead of you.'

The two men shook hands and went their separate ways. Joshua was unsure what he had just set in motion, and where the repercussions might lead. All he knew was that everyone, no matter what their circumstances, deserved a chance of happiness. If he could achieve that for his cousin by encouraging Asquith to think the unthinkable, then the devil take the consequences.

10

Painting huge areas of sheeting to resemble a garden was exhausting yet exhilarating work. Within half an hour, Anne had almost as much paint on her as she had applied to the sheet, but she was enjoying herself too much to mind. She couldn't remember the last time she had actually got dirty, or if she ever had.

When Papa had died and Mama showed no inclination to remarry, she made it clear the de Bourghs did not discriminate against female succession and that Anne was her sole heir. What she failed to mention was that Anne's life would never be her own from that point onwards, and that she would be cosseted and protected to a ridiculous extreme. She had nothing to compare her upbringing to, until she came to Pemberley and spent time with Georgiana and Kitty. Now she was starting to realise what she had missed all these years.

'You have paint on the end of your nose, Anne,' Georgiana said, laughing.

'We all have paint on our exposed parts,' Kitty pointed out. 'It is fortunate these pinafores cover our gowns or they would be ruined.'

Georgiana stood back to examine the rose garden she had just painted. 'It looks more like a rambling jungle,' she said, screwing up her nose in disgust.

'Oh no, Georgie, it's very realistic.' Kitty examined Georgiana's efforts with a critical eye. 'Mr. Asquith explained that when the sheets are lining the walls, they will look very different. Something about perspective, I think he said.'

Georgiana grimaced. 'Dim lighting would better serve.'

'Or else we will put on such a dazzling display of acting no one will notice the scenery,' Kitty suggested, not sounding convinced. 'Anyway, when we put the scenery up in the music room, I think Mr. Asquith said something about having potted palms put in front of it.'

'Very wise.' Georgiana flashed a rueful smile. 'How are your trees coming along, Anne?'

'About as well as your roses.' Anne stood up and stretched. 'Where is Mr. Asquith, by the way? I thought he would be here to advise us.'

Anne noticed Georgiana and Kitty share an amused glance. 'I think he was detained by

Colonel Fitzwilliam,' Kitty said. 'Don't worry, Anne. I'm sure he will not neglect you for long.'

Anne felt heat invade her face. 'I simply wanted to ask him something about the trees.'

'Of course you did.'

'It's all right,' Georgiana said. 'We are only teasing you, even if we can't help wondering what the two of you find to talk about when you are closeted together for so many hours at a time.'

'Literature,' Anne replied, causing both girls to burst out laughing. 'It's true,' Anne protested. 'We both share a love of the written word, but I have had no one with which to discuss what I read before now. If Mama knew how much time I secretly spend with my nose in a book, she would scold me for straining my eyes, but really, I cannot think of a better way to pass the long hours in each day. Escaping into a literary world is . . . well, my guilty secret.'

'That is so sad,' Georgiana said. 'I am very glad you now have someone to share your . . . er, passion with, and we promise not to tease you about it anymore.'

'Thank you.' Anne actually giggled. Mama did not approve of young ladies who giggled, but then there were a lot of things Mama did not approve of.

'You are entirely welcome.' Georgiana smiled before turning her attention to Kitty. 'Talking of passions, has Captain Turner said anything more about his duty visit to his father?'

'No, surprisingly little.' Kitty pouted. 'All he said was that the meeting with his father had not gone well, and he would not be marrying the lady his father wanted him to.'

'That is a good thing, surely?' Anne couldn't understand why Kitty seemed so glum. 'It is obviously you he wants for his wife.'

'If he does, he has not said a word, or done anything to suggest a preference.'

This time, it was Georgiana and Anne who shared a laugh at Kitty's expense.

'You goose,' Georgiana said affectionately. 'The captain adores you. Whenever you are in the same room together, his gaze seldom leaves you.'

'You exaggerate.'

'Indeed, she does not,' Anne said. 'Even I have noticed. Do not be downhearted. The captain is shy, and this is only your second meeting.'

'He has clearly had a falling out with his father,' Georgiana added. 'Even though he has independent means and can please himself, I am sure he would wish to be on

163

good terms with his family before admitting to his feelings.'

'Don't think I don't know your game.' Kitty shook a paint-stained finger beneath Georgiana's nose. 'You are deliberately turning the conversation towards mine and Anne's aspirations in the hope we will not cross-question you about yours.'

Anne raised a speculative brow. 'Is that what she is doing?'

'Undoubtedly.' Kitty grinned at Anne. 'As though we didn't both know she is madly in love with Major Halstead.'

'You are wrong about that.' Georgiana sighed. 'I like him and enjoy his society, but love . . . well, I'm not so sure. Besides, I don't think my brother would allow me to become betrothed yet, even if the major declared himself.'

'What do you want, if not Major Halstead?' Anne asked.

'I want what my brother and Lizzy have,' she replied without hesitation. 'I envy them so much. You know, sometimes I can be in the same room as them, but they are so completely involved with one another they don't seem to realise I am there. Nothing has yet persuaded me I could feel that way about the major.'

'Yes,' Anne said. 'I have noticed that about

them. Even with a houseful of guests, they still seem to be totally absorbed with each other.'

'Lizzy didn't feel that way at first,' Kitty said. 'So perhaps your feelings for the major will change.'

The door opened to admit Mr. Asquith, bringing their conversation to an end. Anne was pleased to have been included in it and to offer advice, such as it was. She had never had the pleasure of another female to swap confidences with before.

'How are you progressing, ladies?' Mr. Asquith asked.

It was Georgiana who answered him. 'Not terribly well, Mr. Asquith, as you can see. Sketching is one thing, but painting on this scale is entirely another. I had not realised it would be quite so challenging.'

'Could we not just close the drapes in the music room and make do with them as a backdrop?' Kitty asked.

Mr. Asquith took a close look at their handiwork and nodded his approval. 'From a distance, this will look very well indeed,' he said. 'Who is responsible for painting the sun dial?'

'That was me,' Anne admitted reluctantly. 'I know it is too large. I got a little carried away. Unlike with sketching, it is impossible to start afresh if things go awry.'

Mr. Asquith turned towards her and offered her a dazzling smile. 'I think it a very realistic touch, skilfully executed and not at all out of proportion.'

Anne blossomed beneath such fulsome praise. 'I am not sure about that. Besides, it was Kitty's idea.'

'Well, I have had quite enough for one afternoon,' Georgiana said, putting aside her brush and unfastening her pinafore. 'I had no idea painting scenery could be quite so exhausting.'

'No, nor I,' Kitty agreed, also abandoning her painting equipment. 'Please excuse us, Mr. Asquith. I for one intend to idle the rest of the afternoon away. Oh, and study my lines, of course,' she added, giggling.

'As do I,' Georgiana added.

Mr. Asquith opened the door for the girls. Anne blushed when Kitty looked back over her shoulder and winked at her. It was clear they were not really tired. Anne had wondered about that. She was supposedly the weakest of the three, and yet still felt full of energy. This was their clumsy attempt to leave Anne alone with Mr. Asquith. The silence hung heavily between them once the girls' chattering voices had faded.

'Are you tired as well, Miss de Bourgh?'

Mr. Asquith asked. 'I have been working you all very hard.'

'Not in the least.'

'What is it?' he asked softly, moving to stand closer to her. 'You look very pensive.'

'Oh, take no notice of me. I was just thinking how much I have enjoyed my time here with Georgiana and Kitty. I have never had friends my own age before, you see. But I also can't shake the feeling we are marking time, waiting for something significant to happen.'

'You refer to Colonel Fitzwilliam?'

'Yes.' Anne twisted her hands together, wondering what could have possessed her to instigate this line of conversation. She had become accustomed, over the years, to keeping her thoughts and opinions to herself for fear of earning her mother's disapproval. With Mr. Asquith, she seemed to say whatever came into her head, despite the fact he probably thought her immature and undeserving of her privileged position. 'Mama warned me to expect an offer of marriage from the colonel while we were here, and yet he has made no effort to speak to me alone.' She wrinkled her brow. 'Does he find me so unattractive he cannot make himself do it, even though he would have Rosings to make up for his disappointment?'

Mr. Asquith looked agitated, or perhaps embarrassed, by her candour.

'Take no notice of me,' she said, turning away from him. 'I am not feeling myself today.'

'You are anxious to receive the colonel's address?'

'You know I am not, but if he does not propose Mama will probably say the fault is mine for not encouraging him.'

'The blame is definitely not yours.'

Anne shuddered. 'I feel so much stronger nowadays, but the prospect of arguing with Mama saps my energy and resolve.' She managed a droll smile. 'I have always found it easier to do whatever she asks of me. Rosings is a much pleasanter place when Mama is in good humour.'

Mr. Asquith glanced out of the window. Anne followed the direction of his gaze, and saw the earlier rain had given way to patchy blue skies.

'We have been cooped up in here for two whole days,' he said. 'Shall we take a walk together in the grounds?'

The suggestion was as surprising as it was welcome. 'By all means. Give me a moment to fetch my bonnet and pelisse. Providing I can avoid Mama and her intrusive questions, I shall meet you in the vestibule in ten minutes.'

'Lady Catherine is in the conservatory writing a letter. You ought to be able to slip past her if you are quick.'

Anne managed to reach her chamber, don her outdoor clothing, and run back down again without encountering her mother or her maid. She wondered why she felt the need for secrecy. There was nothing out of the ordinary about her walking with Mr. Asquith. They did it all the time at Rosings, even if they did take a servant with them. There was really no necessity for that, but Mama would insist, or worse, inflict her company upon them and then dominate the conversation.

'You were very quick,' Mr. Asquith said when she returned to the hall.

'Mama has eyes and ears everywhere,' she said in a conspiratorial whisper that made her handsome tutor smile.

He led her to a side door, presumably so they wouldn't be seen leaving together. The wind was brisk, and yet invigorating. The air smelled fresh and clean. Damp leaves, whipped up by the wind, whirled around their feet and clung like natural decoration to the hem of Anne's gown.

'I love this time of year in England,' he said. 'It was one of the things I missed most while in Jamaica.'

'And yet you were born in Jamaica. I should have thought you would have found our autumn and winter far too cold.'

'I did when I first came over here to school. I actually thought I might freeze to death, but I soon learned to prefer it to the heat and humidity of the tropics.'

'I have never set foot outside of England, so I am not qualified to give an opinion. However, I am sure I would not enjoy being too hot.'

They turned a corner that brought them close to the famous Pemberley maze.

'Have you ever tried this?' he asked.

'Goodness no. I would get lost for a month.'

'Nonsense.' He offered his arm, and she placed her hand on it. 'Come along, Miss de Bourgh. Let us be brave. We shall either triumph or be lost together for all time.'

Anne would greatly prefer the latter. 'Very well, Mr. Asquith.' Anne squared her shoulders. 'Lead on.'

Smiling, she followed beside Mr. Asquith as he plunged into the confusing construction of beech hedges.

'The trick is always to turn in the same direction and never deviate. What shall it be, Miss de Bourgh, left or right?'

'Oh right, by all means.'

He briefly covered the fingers that rested on his arm with his opposite hand. 'I shall never knowingly do wrong by you,' he said with a gaze of dark intensity.

Anne turned away, wondering what he had meant by that oblique statement. Mama would consider it highly inappropriate for her to be alone in the maze with Mr. Asquith, but simply didn't care. She felt light of heart, daring, defiant, and intended to enjoy every second of her momentary rebellion.

'Are you sure about this, Mr. Asquith?' she asked when they had taken several turns that took them deeper into the maze with no clear end in sight. The hedges were far too tall even for Mr. Asquith to see over them. 'I am sure we just passed down this walkway in the opposite direction.'

'Have faith.' He dropped his voice to a soft purr. 'Have I ever guided you wrong?'

'Well no, but perhaps not all mazes are designed the same way. It is a little daunting.'

'We could leave markers as we go, to ensure we find our way out. A ribbon from your hair, my handkerchief, things like that, but it would be cheating.'

'Yes, I suppose it would be.' It would also make Anne feel a lot safer, but her mood was capricious and danger suddenly seemed far more attractive than safety.

'If all else fails, we will simply wait to be found.'

'But no one knows where we are, so how would they know where to look?'

'Ah, so they do not.' He sent her a charming smile, the one that always seemed to melt her insides and send agreeable sensations rioting through her body. 'In which case, we must hope I know what I am doing. Now, which way, I wonder.'

They had reached a crossroads. The path they were on continued straight ahead, but there were also turnings to the left and right.

'Right,' Anne replied, without hesitation. 'This junction is supposed to confuse us, and trick us into not turning.'

'Exactly so.'

The right hand turning took them to a large clearing in the centre of the maze, and Anne was delighted with their success. It boasted a magnificent statue of a winged horse that was as tall as the hedges. There was a small fountain and a bench seat perfectly situated so that visitors could enjoy the prospect of the statue.

'Oh, it is beautiful!' Anne stared at the statue, awestruck. 'I should love to draw it.'

'Do you not recognise it?'

'Should I?' Anne tilted her head, examining the statue from all angles. 'Pegaz?'

'Yes, from the ancient Persian legend we read together.'

'Did you know it was here, Mr. Asquith?'

'No, but it occurred to me that Mr. Darcy would put something special in the centre of his maze to reward those brave enough to make their way through all the wrong turns.'

A bit like her life, Anne thought, briefly closing her eyes and pretending she was here with Mr. Asquith because he intended to go down on bended knee and request her hand in marriage. That would make the agonies of her lonely childhood, and the confusion of impending adulthood, more than worthwhile. She shook her head to dislodge the thought, telling herself not to be so foolish. Even if he did pretend affection for her, that is all it would be. Pretence. It wasn't her he wanted, but Rosings. That was all everyone saw when they looked at her. She shivered at the thought, and her pleasure in the moment was spoiled.

'Are you cold?' he asked.

'Not really.'

'Then what is it?'

He took her hand in his, and she felt compelled to meet his gaze. What she saw there unbalanced her. There was sympathy and understanding in his eyes, and compassion too. It was as though he grasped the reasons for her turmoil and cared, really cared, about her as a person. It did no harm to pretend.

'I am afraid,' she said simply. 'Afraid of what will happen if Colonel Fitzwilliam addresses me, but even more afraid that he will not.' She swallowed down her apprehension. 'But whatever happens, I will have to part with you,' she said, turning her head away. 'Mama never intended for you to remain with me for long, but in the short time we have been together you have opened my eyes to the world beyond Rosings, given me the courage to think and to hold opinions of my own I am no longer afraid to express and . . . well, I have said too much.'

'My dear girl!' he cried passionately. 'You need never concern yourself about my leaving you.'

She blinked, unsure she had heard him right. 'You have to earn a living, Mr. Asquith. We both know that.'

'Miss de Bourgh . . . Anne.' He reached out an arm and pulled her against him. Anne was breathless with delight when her name slipped past his lips again so naturally, and she willingly allowed herself to be embraced by him. 'Don't make the mistake of underestimating me. At first I looked upon you as a challenge. A lonely young lady afraid to open her mouth for fear of earning ridicule. I saw your potential, but you have surpassed my most optimistic expectations. You are like a flower that has blossomed beneath my nurturing. I take all the credit for that, you know,' he continued, his capable hands sliding to her back and holding her more firmly against him, 'and I never walk away from what I create.'

Anne felt dazed, disorientated, euphoric, and barely able to believe this was happening. Not altogether sure what *was* happening. She had absolutely no idea what he meant by her being his creation, nor did she much care. All she wanted was to enjoy being held by him, to feel the warmth and strength from his body seeping into her own. This was where she was supposed to be. He made her feel safe and protected, as though a great weight had been lifted from her shoulders. She screwed her eyes tightly closed, willing him to kiss her.

To her intense disappointment, he did not.

'Come,' he said with a heavy sigh, his voice gravelly and rough. Her eyes flew open, and she sent him an enquiring look, wondering what she had done to cause such an abrupt change in him. 'We have stayed out for too long. We ought to get back to the house before we are missed.'

Joshua found Mr. and Mrs. Darcy together in the drawing room. He paused in the doorway to observe them, heads close together, laughing at something one of them had just said. Darcy reached out a hand and gently touched his wife's face, his eyes soft, adoring. She leaned her cheek into his palm and sent him an enticing smile that prompted Darcy to groan, lower his head, and cover her lips with his own.

The intimacy of the snatched moment reinforced Joshua's long-held opinion that Darcy had found his soul mate, a woman who would be the making of his intelligent yet rigidly correct cousin. With her irreverent attitude and lively wit, Eliza's character was diametrically opposed to Darcy's and could only have a beneficial effect upon his mercurial temper. Joshua was glad. Darcy took life far too seriously and deserved to put his own happiness ahead of duty.

Joshua hesitated on the threshold, feeling like the intruder that he was, wondering if he ought to leave them alone. Unfortunately, his business was too urgent to brook delay. He needed the benefit of his cousin's advice and was unlikely to find a better opportunity for a quiet word.

He cleared his throat and walked into the room.

'Colonel Fitzwilliam.' Mrs. Darcy offered him a warm smile. 'You look as though you have lost a guinea and found a farthing. Pray sit down and tell us what bothers you.'

'It is not quite as serious as that,' he replied, smiling as he sat across from them.

'You have made yourself scarce all day, Fitzwilliam,' Darcy said, a cynical twist to his lips. 'If I didn't know better, I would say you were avoiding our aunt.'

Joshua grunted. 'The very idea.'

'I believe the colonel has been to pay a call on our neighbours,' Mrs. Darcy said, her eyes sparkling with lively interest.

'Indeed I have, and I was rather taken aback by what I learned from Mrs. Sheffield. The fact of the matter is that I'm unsure what to do about it and need of your advice, Darcy.'

Mrs. Darcy stood. 'Then I will leave you gentlemen to talk.'

'No, don't go.' Joshua grimaced. 'If you can spare the time, I would appreciate a lady's point of view.'

'I have all the time in the world for you, Colonel.' She resumed her seat. 'Besides, you have made me curious.'

Succinctly, Joshua outlined all Mrs. Sheffield had told him and all he had subsequently learned from Asquith.

'It sounds to me as though Percival Sheffield is definitely trying to bamboozle your Mrs. Sheffield out of her inheritance,' Darcy said, after a moment's contemplation.

'There is no doubt in my mind,' Joshua agreed. 'The question is how do I prove it?'

'If Asquith is to be believed — '

'You doubt his word?' Mrs. Darcy asked, looking rather shocked.

'It's not that I doubt him precisely. It is more that he seems a little too good to be true.'

'He is in the same position as Wickham was as a young man,' Darcy said. 'The favoured son of an employee who has enjoyed his master's largesse. Unlike Wickham, Asquith appears to have made the most of that opportunity.'

'He certainly knows how to behave in society,' Mrs. Darcy added. 'His manners are faultless.'

'True enough, but he had the temerity to suggest Mrs. Sheffield might know more about her husband's death than she said, or that she might even have arranged it.'

Darcy chuckled, something Joshua had seldom heard him do before his marriage. 'You are not looking at the broader picture, Fitzwilliam. Think like the soldier you are.

Would you not suspect her too, if you had all the facts at your disposal?'

Joshua stood up. 'I came to you for sound advice,' he said hotly. 'But if all you can do is cast aspersions on an innocent lady's character, then I have obviously wasted my time.'

'Sit down, Fitzwilliam.' Joshua scowled at his cousin and was slow to react. 'I am merely playing devil's advocate — '

'He does that a lot,' Mrs. Darcy said with a wicked smile that lightened the tension.

'I still think Asquith is not all he appears to be.' Joshua crossed his arms in a defensive pose. 'However, that is nothing to me. What is important is finding a way to disprove Sheffield's claim.'

'Will you allow me to think about it?' Darcy asked.

'By all means.'

'It will be difficult to do anything with Sheffield in Buckinghamshire and his solicitor in London,' Mrs. Darcy remarked. 'They are the main characters in this real life drama playing out alongside Mr. Asquith's fictional one, and we will never get at the truth at arm's length.'

'True,' Darcy replied. 'But even to oblige my cousin and forward his matrimonial ambitions, we are not going to London.'

'Who said anything about matrimony?' Joshua asked.

Both Darcys sent him wry smiles, but before either of them could speak, Lady Catherine joined them, bringing the conversation to a premature end.

'Oh, there you are Fitzwilliam. I thought you must be with Anne,' she said accusingly. 'I cannot find her anywhere.'

'Is she not in the ballroom, practising her lines?' Joshua asked politely.

'No one is in the ballroom. I just checked.' Lady Catherine settled herself in the chair closest to the fire. 'Anne is not in her room either, but her maid says her pelisse is gone.'

'Then presumably she is walking in the grounds,' Darcy said calmly.

Lady Catherine seemed scandalised by such a reasonable suggestion. 'In this weather?'

'It isn't cold,' Mrs. Darcy pointed out. 'In fact, it is now a rather bracing autumn day. The girls have been indoors for two entire days. I expect they felt the need for fresh air and exercise. I know I do.'

'We are not all fortunate enough to share your robust health, Mrs. Darcy.'

'Anne seems much stronger these days,' Darcy remarked.

'She thinks she is, but I know better.

Besides, it is bad enough, all this play acting.'
Lady Catherine's expression radiated disapproval. 'I am still unsure why I permitted it. It will sap her strength.'

'She appears to be enjoying herself enormously,' Darcy remarked.

'Bah, life is not all about pleasure.'

'I shall ring for tea,' Mrs. Darcy said diplomatically.

Before she could do so, Simpson entered the room and waited for Darcy to acknowledge his presence. 'What is it, Simpson?'

'Mr. Collins is here, sir.'

'Mr. Collins?' Lady Catherine looked astonished. 'My Mr. Collins? What on earth could possibly bring him all this way?'

'You had best show him in, Simpson,' Darcy said with a glance at his wife. 'And then, we shall find out.'

'Have some tea sent up please, Simpson,' Mrs. Darcy said.

'At once, ma'am.'

The butler left the room, returning almost immediately. 'Mr. Collins, sir,' he said, standing back and allowing the clergyman into the room.

Mr. Collins was much as Joshua remembered him — red of face, thin-lipped, full of self-importance. He bowed low to Lady Catherine, and then to Darcy and Joshua.

'Cousin Elizabeth,' he said to Mrs. Darcy. 'I trust you will excuse my unexpected arrival. I can assure you nothing but the most urgent business would have brought me here uninvited. Indeed, I must apologise for my dishevelled appearance since I have been on the road these past three days.'

'What can possibly be so urgent that you could not commit it to an express letter, Mr. Collins?' Lady Catherine asked.

'Well, ma'am, it is . . . er, very delicate. Perhaps your ladyship would be kind enough to grant me an audience in private.'

Heavens, Joshua thought, trying hard to maintain his countenance. The damned man makes Lady Catherine sound like the pope.

'Nonsense, man,' Lady Catherine replied briskly. 'Whatever you have to say can be said in front of my relations.' Her gaze lingered on Mrs. Darcy, as though she still couldn't decide if she qualified as a relation and was considering asking her to leave her own drawing room. Common sense prevailed, and she remained silent on the point.

'Please take a seat, Mr. Collins, and recover your breath.'

Mrs. Darcy looked as though she too found the situation amusing. Joshua had heard rumours that Collins once aspired to marry Eliza Bennet. The rejection of his suit wounded his pride and he transferred his imaginary affections to Eliza's friend, Charlotte Lucas, with astonishing speed. This time his proposal met with success. Lady Catherine, it transpired, had deemed it time for Hunsford's clergyman to find himself a wife. Mr. Collins would die rather than return home to Kent and disappoint his patroness, so everyone was satisfied with the arrangement.

'Tea will be here directly,' Mrs. Darcy said when her uninvited guest stopped talking for long enough for her to get a word in. 'When you are refreshed there will be ample opportunity for you to explain your reasons for coming to Pemberley.'

'Thank you, Cousin Elizabeth. I confess that refreshment would be welcome. I cannot seem to dislodge the dust of the road from my throat.'

'How did you leave Charlotte?' Mrs. Darcy asked.

'In the best of health, I thank you. She is much occupied with our daughter, of course, but sends you her most affectionate best wishes. Naturally, she is also taken up with the affairs of the parish, as becomes the wife of a clergyman, and I . . . '

Joshua only half-listened to Mr. Collins's monologue about life in Hunsford. Collins

183

was perfectly capable of conducting a conversation entirely on his own and Joshua saw no reason to listen to it. However, he had no intention of removing himself from the drawing room since he too was curious as to the reason for Collins's arrival at Pemberley.

Only when tea was finished and Collins had talked non-stop throughout it, his obsequiousness already starting to grate on Joshua's nerves, did Darcy remind him he had urgent news for Lady Catherine.

'Thank you for reminding me, Mr. Darcy.' He shook his head. 'As though I could forget about this unfortunate business.'

'What unfortunate business, Mr. Collins. Pray out with it,' Lady Catherine said irascibly.

Looking exceptionally sombre, Collins cleared his throat, grasped his lapels, and finally had the goodness to explain himself. 'Your ladyship will recall I was not impressed with Mr. Asquith and advised your ladyship against exposing Miss de Bourgh to his company. Such a delicate young lady should be protected at all costs.'

More to the point, Joshua thought, Collins disliked another man having Lady Catherine's ear. He probably felt as though his influence at Rosings had diminished with the arrival of such a well-educated, charismatic young man as Asquith. Even so, Joshua's interest was piqued, especially given his own reservations about the gentleman's character.

'This is about Asquith?' Darcy asked.

'Indeed it is, Mr. Darcy. I take no pleasure in being proven right in my advice to you, Lady Catherine. But you see a lady called at the vicarage, having been directed there in search of Mr. Asquith.'

'A lady?' Lady Catherine frowned. 'What lady?'

'A Miss Miranda Glover, my lady.'

Lady Catherine appeared startled, and rather discomposed. 'One of Sir Marius's daughters?'

'Apparently so.'

Lady Catherine frowned. 'What on earth brings her to England?'

'Was she travelling alone?' Mrs. Darcy asked at the same time.

Collins paused, presumably getting to the point at last. Even by his long-winded ways, Joshua thought he had dragged this matter out to its lengthiest extreme because he enjoyed being the harbinger of bad tidings.

'She came in search of Mr. Asquith.' Collins clearly tried for a disapproving look but instead appeared smug and self-satisfied. 'She said they were engaged to be married, but Mr. Asquith ran away to England and deserted her.'

11

Lizzy felt as shocked as everyone else appeared to be at this startling revelation. No one spoke, or knew quite what to do, until Lady Catherine broke the silence.

'I don't believe a word of it,' she said forcibly. 'There must be some other explanation. I am never wrong about people. Besides, I trust Sir Marius's judgement implicitly. He recommended Mr. Asquith to me and would not have done so if he had jilted one of his daughters.'

'Perhaps he sent the recommendation before he became aware of the broken engagement?' Colonel Fitzwilliam suggested. 'Asquith has not been in England long enough for another letter from Sir Marius to reach you, ma'am. Letters from such far-flung places as Jamaica can take months to arrive.'

'That is possible,' Lady Catherine conceded grudgingly.

'You didn't answer Mrs. Darcy's question, Collins,' Will said. 'Was the lady travelling alone?'

'She travelled to England with her father.'

Lady Catherine gasped, and her face lost all colour. Lizzy became quite concerned about her. Will filled a glass with water and handed it to his aunt, who looked as though she was about to swoon. How curious. Lady Catherine was the last person on this earth whom Lizzy considered capable of swooning. She would look upon it as a weakness, a character flaw, and Lady Catherine did not hold with weaknesses or flaws. Lizzy was now truly intrigued. Could it be Lady Catherine had some sort of dark secret in her past that was to do with Sir Marius? That would explain the peculiar situation with Mr. Asquith being engaged to tutor Anne, and Lady Catherine's disinclination to think badly of him.

'Sir Marius is in England?' Lady Catherine asked faintly.

'Apparently, he had business in England and his daughter, suffering as she was, persuaded him to bring her along for a change of scenery and society,' Mr. Collins replied.

'Sir Marius never comes to England.' Lady Catherine appeared to recover a little of her customary fortitude. She straightened her spine as she asserted the fact, as if by so doing she would make it a reality. 'Did you actually see him, Mr. Collins?'

'No, my lady. Miss Glover was accompanied by her maid. Sir Marius had business in Dover, and she travelled on to Hunsford in the hope of seeing Mr. Asquith. I am unsure if Sir Marius knew she planned to do so. In fact, I am persuaded he could not have done. He would not wish his daughter to face the awkwardness of seeing Mr. Asquith alone.'

'That all sounds rather questionable,' Will said, sharing a glance with Lizzy, who was thinking exactly the same thing.

'And easily resolved. Ring the bell, Darcy, and summon Asquith,' Lady Catherine said. 'If there is a grain of truth in Miss Glover's claim, or the slightest stain attaching to Asquith's character, then of course he must not be allowed anywhere near Anne ever again.'

Lizzy glanced at Mr. Collins, noticed his smug expression still firmly in place, and disliked him more than ever as a consequence. No matter what Colonel Fitzwilliam thought, Lizzy was convinced Mr. Asquith was not a cad or a fortune hunter.

'We ought to leave you to conduct this interview alone,' Lizzy said, standing. 'I would not have Mr. Asquith feel this is some sort of inquisition.'

'Nonsense.' Lady Catherine sniffed. 'You now all know the particulars, and I see no occasion to think of his finer feelings, especially if he is culpable.'

'Very well.'

Lizzy felt uncomfortable. She was usually a good judge of character and had taken to Mr. Asquith upon first acquaintance. Then again, she had taken to Wickham, and look how that had turned out. Lizzy wanted to leave the room, but had a feeling Mr. Asquith might be in need of a supporter. Mr. Collins and the colonel were both disposed to think badly of him, albeit for differing reasons. Lady Catherine liked Mr. Asquith but regretted employing him because Anne was so taken with him that she had developed a rebellious streak. Only Lizzy and Will were truly neutral, prepared to give the young man the benefit of the doubt.

Simpson answered the bell and despatched a footman in search of Mr. Asquith. An uneasy silence descended upon the drawing room as its occupants waited for him to respond to the summons.

'I simply refuse to believe Mr. Asquith capable of such base behaviour,' Lady Catherine said after several minutes.

'I agree with you, ma'am,' Lizzy said. 'He seems far too honourable.'

'Forgive me, Cousin Elizabeth, but as a well brought up lady you cannot be expected to know how certain men behave when given sufficient licence.'

Of all the pompous, self-opinionated . . . Will squeezed her hand, as though understanding the nature of the thoughts running through her head. 'And you must forgive me, Mr. Collins, if I assure you that I understand far better than you could possibly imagine.'

Mr. Collins looked as though he wished to argue the point. One glance at Will and he wisely held his tongue.

'You wished to see me, Lady Catherine,' Mr. Asquith said as he strode into the room. 'Oh, excuse me, I did not realise you were not alone. Mr. Collins. It is a pleasure to see you here.'

Mr. Collins mumbled what, for him, was a very short, and exceedingly ungracious response. Mr. Asquith's congenial expression faltered.

'Has something happened?' he asked.

'Mr. Asquith,' Lady Catherine said with asperity. 'Mr. Collins felt it necessary to come to Pemberley in person because he has received a visit from a most unexpected quarter.'

'Someone known to me, I assume, accounting for your wish to speak with me.'

'Quite so.' Lady Catherine paused. 'Miss Miranda Glover.'

Lizzy watched Mr. Asquith carefully when this disclosure was made and noticed the profound effect the mention of that lady's name had upon him. His eyes widened, his jaw slackened, and his manner became rather agitated.

'Miranda is in England?'

'Apparently so.' Lady Catherine fixed her daughter's tutor with a steely gaze. 'You know the lady.'

'She is one of Sir Marius's daughters. I know all of his children. I taught many of them, especially the younger girls, including Miranda, since they did not go away to school.'

'Mr. Asquith, you know me well enough to appreciate I prefer plain speaking and so I shall come straight to the point.' But Lady Catherine paused, as though unwilling to do so. 'Miss Glover left her father in Dover and travelled to Hunsford in search of you. She told Mr. Collins you and she were engaged to be married and that you deserted her.' Lady Catherine's lips tightened. 'There, what do you have to say to that?'

Mr. Asquith didn't immediately respond. Instead, he paced the length of the room, hands clasped behind his back, muttering something unintelligible. For the first time, Lizzy doubted him. If it was untrue, why did he not immediately refute Miss Glover's claim?

'You must accept my word, Lady Catherine,' he eventually said, turning to face his employer with an expression of complete sincerity, 'that Miranda and I were never engaged.'

'Then why would she suggest otherwise, and come all the way to England in search of you?'

'That I cannot tell you, nor am I prepared to discuss the matter further. If you require proof that I speak the truth, then I must refer you to Sir Marius. Only he can explain why his daughter has acted in the way that she has.'

He is protecting the lady's reputation, Lizzy thought, feeling vindicated for having placed her faith in him.

Lady Catherine made an unladylike scoffing sound. 'I am asking you.'

'I hesitate to appear disobliging, but I cannot prove what I know to be the truth, and will not reveal the circumstances that led to Miranda's claim. If being a man of honour is sufficient grounds for you to dismiss me from my post, then there is nothing I can do to prevent you.'

'Lady Catherine,' Mr. Collins said, when his benefactress did not immediately do precisely that. 'I beg you to consider Miss de Bourgh's situation. You cannot take the risk — '

'Be quiet, Mr. Collins. If I require your opinion I will ask for it.'

Lizzy could understand Lady Catherine's dilemma and felt a certain sympathy for her. Ordinarily she would not give Mr. Asquith the benefit of the doubt and risk the corruption of her daughter's morals. Anne was beyond the age where continued education was strictly necessary, but Lizzy knew that was not why Mr. Asquith had been employed. Lady Catherine wasn't prepared to act without definitive proof of his duplicity, but it was obvious she took exception to his refusal to explain himself.

'If I dismiss you, I shall not give you a character, and you will find it impossible to gain suitable employment without one.'

'I understand that, but unfortunately I am still unable to oblige you, ma'am.'

'If Sir Marius is in Dover, a letter will quickly find its way to him,' Lizzy said.

'But what of the mean time?' Mr. Collins asked. 'Miss de Bourgh's education.'

'I will permit you to continue mentoring Anne,' Lady Catherine said after a moment's contemplation. 'For now. But I am most displeased by this development, and intend to get to the bottom of things. If you are not being honest with me, Mr. Asquith, you will soon be found out and it will be the worse for you.'

'I understand.'

With a bow for Lady Catherine, and another for Lizzy, he left the room, closing the door quietly behind him.

★　★　★

Anne was tired after her active day, but lay on her bed unable to sleep. She picked up a novel Mr. Asquith had recommended, anxious to finish it so she could discuss it with him. Their tastes in literature were so similar, just as they were in many other respects. Mama would not approve of the book, but Anne found it enlightening and informative. Did Mr. Asquith ask her to read it for any particular reason, other than that he thought she might enjoy it? The heroine was in a remarkably similar situation to Anne's, burdened by a rich inheritance. Unlike Anne, she was beautiful, and sure of herself, determined to marry for love rather than allow her Papa to choose the right man for her.

Anne marked her place, unable to absorb very much of what she read in her current confused state of mind. Her head was still full of her walk in the garden with Mr. Asquith, the things he had said and done, his use of her name, and his abrupt change of mood just when things were getting interesting. She had felt as though she turned a corner in her mind at that moment. She was no longer a sickly child, but a grown woman with opinions of her own, and thoughts she was entitled to keep to herself.

Anne heard light footsteps approaching her room. She recognised her mother's rapid tread, hid the book beneath her pillow, and closed her eyes. Mama burst into the room without knocking.

'Anne, are you awake?'

'Yes, Mama.' She leaned up on one elbow and rubbed non-existent sleep from her eyes. 'What is it? You look distressed. Has something happened?'

'Where have you been? I have been looking for you all over.'

'I was painting scenery with Georgiana and Kitty, and then I took the air with Mr. Asquith.'

Mama looked scandalised. 'Alone?'

'Yes, the others wanted to rest.'

'Anne, it is not seemly for you to be with Mr. Asquith unchaperoned, not under any circumstances.'

'I fail to see why not. He is a perfect gentleman. Besides, no one saw us.'

'He is the son of a plantation manager and you are an innocent heiress who might be seen by some as ripe for the plucking.'

'Mama!'

'Don't pretend not to understand me. More importantly, never lose sight of that fact.'

'As if I could,' Anne replied, almost to herself.

'Did you say something?'

'No, nothing.'

Mama seated herself in the window embrasure. 'What of Fitzwilliam? Has he spoken with you yet?'

'No, he has not.'

'Probably because you are never to be found. Instead of spending your time play-acting and taking illicit walks, you ought to make yourself available. The man cannot address you if he can't find you.'

The colonel had had ample opportunities to express himself but Anne knew it would do her no good to say so. 'You are blaming me because he has no interest in me?'

'Don't be so impertinent.' Mama looked down her nose in the disapproving manner she had perfected to terrorise her servants. 'If this new-found manner of speaking back to me is the result of Mr. Asquith's influence then I made a grave error in engaging him.'

'I disagree.' Anne surprised herself at finding the courage to refute her mother's assertion. It was so unjust that she couldn't allow it to pass unchallenged.

'You look pale and fagged out,' Mama said, examining Anne's face closely and not appearing to like what she saw. 'You think you are capable of doing the same things as Georgiana and Miss Bennet, but that is patently not the case.'

'Again I must disagree with you, Mama. I am having a perfectly splendid time, and don't feel the least bit short of breath. I no longer cough hardly at all, either. I believe that with maturity I have outgrown my illnesses.'

'Nonsense, one does not outgrow such weaknesses. They remain with one for life. You do not have a strong constitution, Anne, and cannot manage the same things as other young ladies. The sooner you accept that, the happier your life will be.'

Anne knew it was an argument she would never win, and so didn't risk angering her mother by attempting to persuade her otherwise.

'Go down half an hour early this evening and situate yourself in the conservatory. I shall tell Colonel Fitzwilliam you will be there and he can speak with you without interruption.' Mama exhaled. 'If he cannot contrive a simple conversation alone with you, then I shall just have to arrange it for him. I have had quite enough of this shilly-shallying. Besides, if things are settled between you and the colonel, then the other matter does not signify.'

Sadness gripped Anne's heart. She should not have allowed herself to take hope from Colonel Fitzwilliam's indifference, only to have those hopes dashed. 'What if the colonel does not wish to speak with me?'

'Don't be ridiculous. Of course, he wishes to. He is very fond of you.'

'And more so of Rosings.'

Mama tutted. 'Stop acting as if you were the only child who ever had to make a sacrifice for the sake of her family's honour. You have been behaving most peculiarly since we arrived here and I feel as though I no longer know you. That being the case, I must have your assurance that you will oblige me in this matter.'

Anne swallowed down a burst of anger, wanting to tell her mother she was no longer a child, and resented being told what to do, and whom to marry. No one had ever asked her opinion before, certainly not her mother, who would not have listened even if Anne had found the courage to challenge one of her decisions. But now, suddenly, Anne had grown tired of being invisible. Her anger gave way to incredulity when she realised that with maturity she had also developed a rebellious streak. Whether she would find the courage to put it to use remained to be seen.

Her mother tapped her fingers impatiently on the window ledge as she waited for Anne to give her the assurance she sought. Anne was conflicted, unsure if she could casually commit herself to a lifetime beside a man whom she respected but did not love. Then the implication behind her mother's words struck home, and Anne's curiosity was piqued.

'Did you make sacrifices, Mama?'

'Never mind that.' Anne could tell from her mother's set expression that no further revelations would be forthcoming. How vexatious. She knew precious little about her mother's life when she had been Anne's age. Could it be that she had been disappointed in love? 'Of course Colonel Fitzwilliam will be tempted by Rosings. It would be unrealistic to think otherwise. We cannot change what we were born to be, Anne, much as we might sometimes wish that we could.'

'Did you ever wish that, Mama?'

'We are not discussing me. I made the best of my life, and you must do the same. You will be perfectly comfortable as Mrs. Fitzwilliam. In fact you will continue to live in the only home you have ever known, and nothing will be very different.'

Anne opened her mouth to protest, and then closed it again. She had learned enough from books to know things would be very different indeed. That was partly what worried her.

'What other matter, Mama?'

Mama was gazing out of the window. Her head snapped around at the sound of Anne's voice. 'I beg your pardon.'

'You said that if things were settled between myself and the colonel then the other matter would not signify.'

'Mr. Collins is here.'

'Oh.' That was all Anne needed. Mr. Collins seemed to think that being Hunsford's clergyman gave him the right to interfere in her affairs. 'Was he expected?'

'He came with alarming news.'

Anne gaped at her mother when she related the reason for Mr. Collins's visit.

'It cannot be,' she said faintly. 'The Mr. Asquith I know would never act so dishonourably.'

'Perhaps not, but if you fix your future with

the colonel then I will have no further need of his services and it will not matter anyway.'

'Yes, I understand that much.' *Oh, I understand better than you could possibly imagine.* 'But you must give him a character, otherwise he will starve.'

Mama adopted a haughty, stubborn expression. 'I must do no such thing.'

'Mama, be reasonable. What explanation did Mr. Asquith give for this lady's claim?'

'He said it was untrue, but he could not explain why.'

'Well, there you are then.' Anne struggled to hide her relief. 'He would not tell an outright lie.'

Mama huffed. 'Which just goes to show how little you understand of the world. A young man in need of employment will do or say many things in order not to lose his position.'

'Not Mr. Asquith,' Anne replied stubbornly.

'Mr. Asquith, Mr. Asquith.' Mama threw her hands in the air. 'I must have been out of my senses when I engaged him. You seem to think of no one else. You certainly think nothing at all of the sacrifices I have made to get you to this point. I did not expect any thanks, but I do expect your obedience.' Mama stood up and brushed down her skirts.

'I shall ring for your maid. Wear your best gown and be in the conservatory to receive the colonel's address within the hour.'

And with that, Mama swept regally from the room.

Anne watched the door close behind her, feeling close to despair. There could be no turning back now. The colonel would not ignore such a direct order from her mother, and Anne would have no choice but to accept him. Unlike the heroine in the novel still buried beneath her pillow, she did not have the strength of will to stand up to her mama and reach out to grasp happiness. Besides, even if Mr. Asquith offered for her, she would not accept him for the simple reason that he couldn't possibly return her feelings. One-sided love could never prosper.

She sat perfectly still as her maid helped her out of her afternoon gown. Poor Mr. Asquith. Whatever the circumstances behind this woman's claim, she was absolutely sure he could not have jilted her. Anne might accept he was lost to her, but her soft heart melted at the thought of him being unable to find alternative employment because there was a question mark against his character. She loved him with a passion that surprised her, and there was one thing she could do for him to prove it, even though he would never know it. She would marry the colonel, do whatever her mother asked of her, but only if her Mama promised to give Mr. Asquith a glowing reference.

* * *

'What did you make of all that?' Will asked Lizzy as they made their way up to their chambers to change for dinner.

'I believe Mr. Asquith,' Lizzy replied without hesitation. 'He made no promise to the young lady, but is too gentlemanly to explain what really happened.'

'I agree. If a letter had to be sent to Jamaica to apply for the truth, I might think differently. But Asquith knows Sir Marius is in this country, and that verification of Asquith's innocence can be obtained in a matter of days. I can see no profit in being untruthful under such circumstances.'

'I admire the way he stood up to Lady Catherine with such polite determination. It shows an honourable disposition that does him credit.'

'Do I need to worry about him?' Will asked with a mock scowl as he opened the door to Lizzy's chamber and stood back so she could precede him through it.

'Well,' Lizzy replied playfully, plucking her

lower lip with her forefinger as she pretended to consider the question. 'He *is* remarkably good looking.'

'Wench!' Will lifted her from the floor and closed his arms tightly around her waist. 'Have you no shame?'

Lizzy laughed. 'Apparently not, but just because I can appreciate Mr. Asquith's handsome face, it does not mean I fail to appreciate yours also.'

Will kissed the end of her nose and sat her on the edge of her bed. 'Said not a moment too soon.'

'Ah, but I am safe from your punishments in my current condition so I can say whatever I please.'

Will harrumphed. 'You say precisely what you please anyway.'

'Which is one of the traits you most admire about me.'

'I wish I could deny it, but you know me too well.' Will sat beside her and took her hand, running his fingers gently down the length of hers. 'Why do parties at Pemberley never proceed smoothly?'

Lizzy rested her head against the breadth of his shoulder, wondering if she would ever get tired of using it as a pillow. 'Where would be the amusement in that?'

'We never did get around to offering

Fitzwilliam advice about his situation with Mrs. Sheffield.'

'I have some thoughts on that.'

Will rolled his eyes. 'Somehow that doesn't surprise me.' He fell back onto her bed and pulled her with him. 'And I suppose I had better hear what you have in mind, much as I would prefer to occupy our time with more pleasurable pursuits.'

Lizzy lightly punched his chest. 'There is no reason why we should not do both.'

'Other than you need to rest, none whatsoever.'

'I knew you would be like this,' Lizzy complained. 'Overprotective and domineering.'

Will's throaty, suggestive chuckle sent shivers of anticipation tingling down her spine. 'You like me best when I am at my most domineering. You have said so more than once.'

'Hmm, it depends upon the circumstances.'

'Name your circumstances, Lizzy, my love.' His expression turned passionately, ardently sincere. No longer teasing her, his dark eyes smouldered with intense emotion, stealing her breath away as his face hovered mere inches from hers and his lips brushed gently against her own. 'You must know I would give you the moon itself, if it was mine to give. Everything I have is yours. Everything I am is because of you.'

'Oh, Will, I love you so very much, especially when you turn poetic.' She leaned in, taking her turn to steal a kiss. 'But as far as your cousin is concerned, I think we should invite the odious-sounding Sheffield to Lambton, or rather Mrs. Sheffield should.'

'Go on,' Will said, stroking her hair.

'She ought to write to him, say she has had a chance to reflect since her solicitor's visit, and that they should discuss the matter face to face. She will not invite him to Briar Hall, of course. I am sure she can think of a good reason not to.'

Will chuckled. 'I am equally sure Fitzwilliam wouldn't sleep a wink if she did. So why have him come to Derbyshire?'

'Because he doesn't know Mrs. Sheffield has allies here. He must be aware that she seldom shares her affairs with Lord Briar for fear of oversetting her sister. That being the case, he will assume she is ready to capitulate.'

'But she has no intention of giving up what is rightfully hers.'

'Nor would I ask her to, but if Sheffield puts up at the inn in Lambton I dare say he will while away his spare time in the taproom.' Lizzy sent her husband a mischievous smile. 'There is no telling whom he might encounter in that establishment. Perhaps even a military man who does not at all relish the idea of being leg-shackled to an heiress.'

Will scowled. 'I see what you are thinking, and it is very clever. Fitzwilliam befriends Sheffield and complains about being obliged to marry his cousin when he is in love with another lady.'

'Well, that part is certainly true.'

Will flexed a brow. 'You think Fitzwilliam is as far gone as that.'

Lizzy shook her head in faux despair. 'You men are blind when it comes to such matters. I have seldom seen any man more lovestruck.'

'Oh dear. Poor Lady Catherine.'

'Hang Lady Catherine,' Lizzy replied impatiently. 'Now, where was I? Oh yes, I understand Sheffield is popular with the ladies and very sure of himself in that arena. He is also unquestionably greedy. If he thinks there might be an opportunity to meet this elusive heiress and make himself agreeable to her, he will be obligated to the colonel. Naturally, the colonel will ask his new friend what business brings him to the district. They will start talking about Jamaica and it will all come out. Fitzwilliam can then say his plan won't work because in order to pursue Anne, Sheffield will have to give up his claim to Mrs. Sheffield's estate. If they have this conversation when Sheffield has consumed enough brandy to loosen his tongue, I dare say he will admit he has no legitimate claim to the estate anyway. Men like him can never resist bragging, especially when they are in their cups. Needless to say, Colonel Fitzwilliam will have someone else situated in the taproom, close enough to overhear the conversation and bear witness to it if necessary.'

'It's ingenious, Lizzy, but for one snag.'

'Oh, did I overlook something?'

'Something rather important as it happens. This could endanger Anne.'

'Not if we don't allow Sheffield to set foot on Pemberley, or Anne to leave it.'

'Even so.' Will shuddered. 'I dread to think what Lady Catherine would have to say if she got wind of the scheme.'

'You underestimate your cousin's new-found determination. Anne has no wish to marry Fitzwilliam. Her affections are engaged elsewhere.'

Will sighed. 'Perhaps, but Anne marrying Asquith was always going to be out of the question, even before these accusations against his character came to light.'

'Maybe so, but she lives in dread of the colonel paying her his addresses. If he is otherwise engaged in pursuit of Mrs. Sheffield, and if he manages to restore her estate to her, I feel persuaded it isn't Anne who will benefit from his attentions.'

'Leaving Anne free to persuade her mother to let her follow her heart.'

'Precisely.'

'She will never succeed in that ambition,' Will said.

'Oh, I am not so very sure about that. Lady Catherine has a weak spot when it comes to anything to do with Sir Marius.' Lizzy wrinkled a brow. 'I would give much to understand why. Anyway, it must be so, otherwise she would never have given Asquith the benefit of the doubt and permitted him to remain in his post.'

'Yes, that was rather peculiar.' Will lapsed into thought, idly twisting one of Lizzy's many escaped curls around his forefinger as he did so. 'I will put the proposal to Fitzwilliam later, and let him decide. If we are to do this, time is of the essence. Lady Catherine won't stay here much longer, nor can Fitzwilliam avoid addressing Anne indefinitely.'

'Or not doing so and have Lady Catherine

leave Pemberley in a high dudgeon.'

'Quite so. But apart from all that, I have one condition of my own.'

'What is it?'

'That Anne must be made aware of the plan, and decide for herself if it goes ahead or not.'

Lizzy grinned. 'In that case, it is as good as agreed. Miss de Bourgh is hungry for adventure and even if there is an outside chance of her procuring Mr. Asquith as a result she will grasp it with both hands. You just see if I am not right.'

'Talking of occupying one's hands, Mrs. Darcy.'

Lizzy treated her husband to a flirtatious smile. 'Yes, what did you have in mind?'

Will spent the next half hour allowing his actions to answer that question for him.

12

Joshua was dressing for dinner when Darcy knocked at his door.

'Mrs. Darcy is nothing if not inventive when it comes to righting wrongs,' he said by way of greeting.

'Really?' Joshua dismissed Cox and gave his cousin his full attention. 'You refer, I presume, to Mrs. Sheffield's problems.'

'Yes, she has made a proposal that is a little irresponsible. My initial reaction was to dismiss it out of hand. Then I decided you ought to hear it first.'

Joshua listened with growing astonishment as Darcy related his wife's suggestion.

'I see what you mean about inventiveness,' Joshua said when Darcy ran out of words.

'But the dangers. It could easily fail. We don't know enough about the man's character to be sure he would give himself away. And then, of course, there is a risk to Anne, to say nothing of Lady Catherine's reaction, were she to find out that we had involved her.'

'Only Mrs. Sheffield will know if her brother-in-law is likely to fall for the ruse,'

Joshua replied thoughtfully. 'I must consult her as a matter of urgency.'

Darcy flashed a half-smile. 'Naturally you must.'

'As to Anne, I have just received a not-so-subtle message from our aunt to say she will be in the conservatory a half-hour before dinner.'

'So you will speak with her?'

'Yes, but not on the subject Lady Catherine expects me to.' Joshua flexed his jaw. 'I know there are many risks and uncertainties connecting to Mrs. Darcy's plan, but I have been racking my brains all the afternoon and can't think of an alternative that is half as likely to work. But whether Anne will agree — '

'Lizzy thinks she will jump at the opportunity, and I tend to agree with my wife. Asquith has encouraged Anne to think for herself and express her opinions freely.'

'Anne has no wish to marry me and I don't see why she should be forced into a union when we both know it would be for all the wrong reasons. It is time we discussed the matter between ourselves and decided on a plan.'

'I know you are keen to help Mrs. Sheffield,' Darcy said, his expression sombre. 'But if Anne even hesitates to go along with the scheme, I need your assurance that you will not put undue pressure on her.'

Joshua scowled. 'What sort of cad do you take me for?'

'Sorry, Fitzwilliam.' Darcy slapped his shoulder. 'I intended no insult.'

Joshua straightened his cuffs, optimism filtering through his earlier feelings of ineffectiveness. 'You must excuse me. I have an engagement with our cousin which I am suddenly anxious to keep.'

Darcy chuckled. 'Then don't let me detain you.'

Anne was already in the conservatory when Joshua arrived. He watched her from the open doorway, before she realised he was there. She stared out of the window without appearing to take in the view, her expression remote as she repeatedly pleated the fabric of her skirt between her fingers. She looked nervous and upset, as though her life was about to come to an end. Anne's spirit had been suppressed for too long, and she needed to live a little before settling into marriage.

At least Joshua came with a scheme that, if she was willing, would help to restore the balance. His plan would require absolute secrecy, and would give her a taste of adventure. Of course, it would also set her mind at rest about being obliged to marry Joshua.

'Anne, I hope I have not kept you waiting.'

She started at the sound of his voice. 'No, not at all.' She spoke distractedly and didn't turn to look at him.

'May I sit?' he asked.

'Please do.'

'I think you know why I am here.'

She lowered her eyes. 'Yes, of course.'

'Anne, look at me.' Slowly she lifted her eyes and turned her head in his direction. She looked pale and afraid. 'There, that was not so very difficult, was it?'

'You must forgive me, Colonel. I am a little nervous.'

'And distressed, because you don't wish to receive my address but your mother has insisted.'

'Oh no . . . well, yes.' She bit her lip, her anxiety giving way to animation Joshua had never seen light up his cousin's narrow face before. 'I am sorry, Colonel, I didn't mean to make light of this situation. I realise it is as awkward for you as it is for me.' She sighed. 'It all seems so very . . . well, cold and formal, I suppose.'

'Supposing we decided not to marry?'

She gasped, and this time Joshua didn't need to request her full attention. He most assuredly had it. 'How can that be? My mother, she — '

'I hold you in great respect, Anne, and I am considerably attached to Rosings. But I don't think those are strong enough foundations upon which to build a successful marriage, do you?'

'I feel exactly the same way about you, Colonel,' she replied breathlessly. 'But it does no good. Mama is quite determined, you see.'

'I am not afraid of Lady Catherine.'

Anne wrinkled her nose. 'Unfortunately I am, although not as much as I used to be.' She fixed Joshua with a curious gaze. 'Since we appear to be speaking plainly, how can you afford to pass up on Rosings?'

'I have fixed my interest elsewhere, as I think you have.' She lowered her eyes again but remained silent. Joshua wondered if she found his admission insulting but, as she had just pointed out, this was definitely a time for plain speaking. 'Nothing has been agreed between myself and the lady in question, and probably never will be, but I cannot bring myself to marry for money when my heart is not in it. That would not be honourable, or fair to you.'

'You certainly do believe in plain speaking, Colonel,' she replied with a nervous little laugh.

'Whereas you find the prospect of marrying the man your mother tells you to appealing?'

She shook her head. 'What would you have me say, Colonel?'

'Plain speaking, remember.'

'Yes, all right. I enjoy your company, but I do not think we would suit, either.'

'I can see we understand one another perfectly.' Anne's uncontrived smile seemed too wide for her face. 'But Mama will be beside herself if you don't do as she asks, and will probably blame me for not encouraging you.'

'I will not allow any blame to be directed upon you.' Joshua matched her smile. 'But I do have a suggestion to put to you.'

'By all means.'

'Firstly, we ought not to tell her quite yet that we have decided against matrimony.'

'She will want to know what passed between us.'

'Tell her we have agreed to go for a drive in the morning and get to know one another better.'

'We have known one another for years.'

'Not in the manner your mother has in mind. Any young lady on the brink of matrimony is entitled to be courted.'

'But you don't intend to court me, Colonel.' She lifted her shoulders. 'And so why — '

'Instead of courtship I require your help.'

She elevated her brows. 'My help? How can I possibly be of help to you?'

'The lady I have fixed my interest on has a problem but, with your permission, I think we might have devised a way to resolve it for her.'

'Mrs. Sheffield?' It was Joshua's turn to flex both brows, causing Anne to laugh. 'Colonel, I saw the way you looked at her when she dined here the other night and I was seated beside you. Your manners were perfectly correct, and I cannot claim you neglected me. However, I saw how frequently you glanced across the table at Mrs. Sheffield, and didn't seem to be able to look away again. You were completely fascinated by her.'

And I thought she was not worldly wise. 'Oh dear.'

'Don't worry, everyone else was far too busy trying to be witty and amusing to take much interest in you.' Joshua was too astonished by her powers of observation to respond. He had definitely underestimated his quiet cousin's hidden depths. 'I tend to be overlooked in company, you see, and so I occupy my time by watching the reactions of others.'

'Since you have guessed my secret, I shall explain Mrs. Sheffield's problem to you, together with Mrs. Darcy's proposed resolution of it. First, I will require your word that even if you do not agree to help, you will not reveal any of this to anyone else; especially not to your mother.'

'You have my word,' Anne replied, clearly intrigued.

Joshua spoke for ten minutes. Anne listened without once interrupting, a series of unreadable expressions passing across her face.

'Certainly you may use my name, Colonel,' she said without hesitation when he came to the end of his narration. 'If it helps you to achieve your heart's desire, it will be my pleasure to have assisted you in some small way.'

'Thank you, but as to achieving my heart's desire as you put it, I have no way of knowing if that will be possible, even if we are successful, which is far from certain. Mrs. Sheffield is a beautiful woman and can do far better than me.'

'You underestimate your attraction, Colonel. Besides, has it occurred to you that her feelings might mirror your own?'

Joshua couldn't conceal his surprise. 'Whatever makes you say that?'

'Oh, nothing in particular.' She sent him a teasing smile. 'It is just that I noticed she was observing you across the table, just as often as you were looking at her, and I am sure it wasn't the cut of your coat that engaged her attention.'

'Good God!'

Anne laughed at his discomfiture, and Joshua eventually joined in. He had certainly not started this interview with any thought of being the one to feel embarrassed.

'As to your own situation, if we go ahead with this plan, there is no danger to you, Anne,' he said, regaining his composure, 'provided you remain here at Pemberley. Sheffield won't be able to get anywhere near you, but he will learn all about you from anyone he talks to in Lambton. You know very well that everyone in the village knows everything that happens at Pemberley. That ought to be enough to convince him I speak the truth, especially if I have my man spread rumours about our impending nuptials.'

'Mr. Sheffield sounds most disagreeable.'

'Not precisely the word I would choose, but I shall not offend your sensibilities by using more appropriate ones.'

'Oh, I do wish you would. No one ever says anything inappropriate within my hearing. It is most vexatious.'

Joshua threw back his head and laughed, making no attempt to hide his relief at her ready capitulation and lively curiosity. 'Ask Asquith. I have already led you quite far enough astray.'

'I have asked him, repeatedly.' Anne tossed her head. 'But he has a way of distracting me with some interesting fact or other, and manages not to answer me without giving offence.'

Mrs. Darcy had been right about her, Joshua thought. She had matured and was hungry for adventure and rebellion. But he needed to be absolutely sure she understood.

'Do you wish to consider the matter? You can give me your answer in the morning.'

'Not at all. I am quite determined you should bring the odious Mr. Sheffield down to size. However, I should like to explain our plan to Mr. Asquith. I know you swore me to secrecy, but he knows Sheffield and might be able to suggest other ways to lure him in.'

'I have already discussed Mrs. Sheffield's problems with him, but he has problems of his own now.'

'Mr. Collins's accusations, you mean?' Joshua nodded. 'Well, I am sure there is nothing to them, but it is typical of Mr. Collins to come charging up to Derbyshire like an avenging . . . I hesitate to say angel, because a less likely looking angel I have yet to encounter.' Anne pulled a disgruntled face.

'He so likes to interfere, and never did approve of Mr. Asquith. I believe he is jealous because Mr. Asquith has displaced him at Rosings. I like Mrs. Collins very much and cannot imagine what made her marry Mr. Collins.'

Joshua was vastly entertained by this new, talkative side of Anne's character and would happily have listened to her prattling on. However, time was not on their side.

'By all means acquaint Mr. Asquith of our plan. And tomorrow you and I, in the spirit of a couple on the verge of engagement, will drive out together. Your mother will encourage the outing. She need not know that we are heading for Briar Hall to explain the plan to Mrs. Sheffield.'

Anne smiled. 'I cannot remember a time when I enjoyed myself more, or felt more useful. I am sorry for Mama, of course. She genuinely does have my best interests at heart and thinks she knows what is best for me and for Rosings, too, of course. Still, since you do not wish to marry me, there is nothing she can do about it.'

'Anne, you must not think — '

'Shush, I am just teasing you.'

His cousin Anne, having the confidence to tease? Who would have thought it?

'We do not have much time to make our

arrangements. In less than a week's time you perform your play, and by then I am sure your mother will expect us to do more than spend our afternoons out driving.'

'Yes, I am sure she will.' Anne furrowed her brow. 'Providing she doesn't get suspicious, she will be happy to remain at Pemberley for at least another week. She will be very angry and disappointed, but there is no help for that.'

'It is I who will do the disappointing. No blame will attach to you.'

'Is a week long enough for Mr. Sheffield to come up here and for this matter to be settled?'

'Oh yes. He is in London at present, according to Mrs. Sheffield's solicitor, and not in Buckinghamshire. If he doesn't mind the discomfort of long days on the road, which I am sure he will not if he thinks there is profit in it for him, he can be here within three days.'

'Well, in that case, I shall enjoy seeing him get his just deserts.'

'And you will have the satisfaction of knowing you helped to bring that about.' Joshua took her small hand, kissed the back of it, and pulled her to her feet. 'I am so glad we understand one another. Now come, we ought to join the others.'

A hum of polite conversation filled the drawing room. It seemed to Joshua as though it stalled when he and Anne entered the room. All heads certainly turned their way, some displaying more interest than others. Lady Catherine descended upon them, and Joshua diplomatically left mother and daughter alone. The Darcys were in conversation with Jane Bingley but joined Joshua a short time later.

'You and Anne look very pleased with yourselves, Colonel,' Mrs. Darcy said. 'Are we to wish you joy?'

'No, ma'am, but I certainly owe you my thanks.'

'She agreed then,' Darcy surmised.

'With alacrity. She is so pleased not to be forced into marriage with me that she will do just about anything.'

'Fitzwilliam!'

'Sorry, Darcy. You looked so severe for a moment that I couldn't resist shamming it.'

'Anne is more than ready for a little adventure,' Darcy said, taking Joshua's joke in good part.

'I hope you have given her leave to inform Mr. Asquith of your plans,' Mrs. Darcy said. 'He looks ready to cut his own throat at present. After he has cut yours, of course.'

'Yes, he will soon learn the truth, but Lady

Catherine must never know. Anne is telling her now that we have agreed to take some time to get to know one another. I shall drive her over to Briar Hall in the morning and meet with Mrs. Sheffield.'

'Will you just look at Mr. Collins strutting about my drawing room like a peacock in full plume.' Mrs. Darcy looked disgusted. 'He has taken great pleasure in casting doubt over Mr. Asquith's character, which is not very Christian of him. I believe he has grown even more pompous since we last met, and I did not think that was possible.' She sighed. 'Poor Charlotte.'

'Come, my dear, I believe Simpson is about to announce dinner,' Darcy said. 'Where shall you seat Mr. Collins?'

'As far away from me as possible.'

'Have him take Lady Catherine in,' Joshua suggested. 'He will butter her up for the entire meal, which will work wonders for her pride.'

'Oh, I think you and Anne already managed that when you walked into this room wearing identical smiles,' Mrs. Darcy replied, wandering off to organise her guests.

13

'Am I to wish you joy, Miss de Bourgh?'

Mr. Asquith posed the question early the following morning, at a time when he and Anne had fallen into the habit of spending an hour discussing literature before rehearsals commenced. He looked so crestfallen that Anne's soft heart went out to him. He had been unnaturally quiet and withdrawn the previous evening, she had noticed. Mr. Collins, on the other hand, had been his usually verbose self, dominating the conversation until Mr. Darcy had expressed his disapproval, cutting him with a look. Anne wanted to ask Mr. Collins when he planned to leave, but now that he was here, he appeared to be in no hurry to quit Pemberley. God forbid that he expected to return to Hunsford in their carriage.

'Are you asking me if I have accepted Colonel Fitzwilliam's proposal?'

He fixed her with an intent gaze. 'Have you?'

Anne took pity on him and laughing, shook her head. She knew his only concern was for his lucrative position, even if a tiny part of her wanted to believe he was disappointed for more personal reasons.

'The colonel and I have decided against marriage.'

'He does not wish to marry you?' Mr. Asquith's jaw dropped open.

She bit her lip to prevent herself from laughing at his expression — a mixture of surprise, disbelief, and dare she hope, a little relief too? 'Has it occurred to you, Mr. Asquith, that it might be me who does not wish to marry him?'

'I know you were not keen on the match, but I thought . . . well I — ' He stood up and ran a hand through his hair. 'Forgive me. I did not think you would go against your mother's wishes.'

'Sometimes I surprise myself,' she replied playfully.

'You were closeted together for so long, and Lady Catherine has been in a very light-hearted mood ever since. I just assumed everything had been settled between you.'

His words ground to a momentary halt. 'It is not my business, but if you wish to tell me what happened I would be happy to listen. If he did actually reject you and not the other way around, I would call him out for his incivility, were it my place to do so.'

'That would be very rash, Mr. Asquith. He

is, after all, a trained soldier.'

'You think me incapable of protecting your honour?' he asked passionately. 'I can assure you that Colonel Fitzwilliam does not frighten me.'

'I do not in the least doubt you.' Anne's heart swelled at his obvious determination to protect her. It was a new and very agreeable feeling. 'However, such drastic action will not be necessary.'

'I have never seen you like this before. So self-assured, so carefree. I understand you are relieved, but Lady Catherine . . . why is she so buoyed if the match is not to go ahead?'

'The colonel and I have reached a rather unique understanding, and he has given me his permission to confide in you,' she told Mr. Asquith.

He settled himself more comfortably in his chair and crossed one leg elegantly over its twin. He was like a large cat, she thought, probably not aware that he appeared sleek, sophisticated, glorious in his male splendour, and ever so slightly dangerous. 'Now I am really intrigued.'

'It has to do with Mrs. Sheffield.'

Mr. Asquith frowned. 'He spoke to you about his feelings for another lady?'

'Oh yes, we had a very free and frank discussion. It was highly illuminating.'

His frown intensified. 'I think you had best tell me everything.'

Anne did so, watching Mr. Asquith's face for any sign he might disapprove or decide to warn Lady Catherine. When she ran out of words, she looked at him expectantly.

'I am very glad you will not have to marry a man whom you do not love.'

'Oh, I will have to do that, Mr. Asquith. I have merely been granted a stay of execution.'

'I cannot believe he is prepared to put you in the path of danger, however indirectly.'

'He asked my permission and I agreed. I feel very sorry for Mrs. Sheffield and intend to help her if I can. I hope you are not going to say you know what is better for me and inform my mother.' Anne narrowed her eyes at him. 'I thought you were my friend and that I could trust you.'

'As you can.' His voice softened, and the deep vertical lines around his nose dissipated as the grip of winter left his eyes. 'My concern is entirely for your welfare.'

'And your position,' she said before she could stop herself.

He shrugged his broad shoulders. 'My position is at best tenable.'

'I spoke with Mama about you last night. Remember, she thinks I am to accept Colonel Fitzwilliam and that she will no longer need your services. I made her promise to give you a glowing character.'

Mr. Asquith sent her a devastating smile. 'In the middle of all the things that are happening in your life, you spared a moment to think of me?'

'Certainly I did. I would not see you turned away with no means of making a living. Anyway, I happened to hear Mama asking Mr. Collins if he knew where Sir Marius is lodging. Naturally, Mr. Collins did know, being so eager to engineer your downfall. Apparently, he asked Miss Miranda's coachman for that information and ensured the young lady was put safely on the road back to Dover. Not that the coachman needed his interference but Mr. Collins does so like to make himself useful. Anyway, I believe Mama intends to apply to Sir Marius and the truth will come out, proving your innocence and enabling her to give you a character with a clear conscience.'

'You are remarkable,' he said softly. 'I have offered you no explanation for Miranda's extraordinary claim and yet you have complete faith in my innocence.'

'That is because I believe you incapable of jilting a lady,' Anne replied, firm conviction in her tone. 'I am guided by my instincts in this matter.' She paused, somehow finding the courage to meet his gaze. She seemed to have a plethora of courage these days, and wondered where it had been hiding itself all these years. 'I have spent enough time in your company these past months to know that you have the highest standards of conduct.'

'I rejoice in your faith in me. Few other people in this establishment feel the same way. They all have their doubts, thinking there must be some truth in Miranda's claim, even if they don't actually come out and say so. The shadow of false accusation will dog me for a long time to come.'

'Only if people do not know you for whom you really are.'

Anne felt a deep oneness with her handsome tutor that broke through the boundaries of rank separating them. Mr. Asquith held her gaze for a prolonged moment, an elusive warmth in his dark eyes that caused her body to react with a series of deliciously disturbing tremors. She enjoyed them for a fleeting moment before shaking her head to clear it. She was being fanciful again, reading more into their relationship than existed, and it really would not do.

'Colonel Fitzwilliam is driving me over to Briar Hall before today's rehearsals, so that we can explain the plan to Mrs. Sheffield. If she is in agreement then we will require your help to bring it about.'

'I am entirely at your disposal.'

'After today Colonel Fitzwilliam will wish to call upon Mrs. Sheffield daily. Obviously, he can't be seen to be doing that and courting me. Even Mama might notice something amiss. And so, we thought he could drive me to the end of the lane, you could meet me there and we could . . . well, read or something, until the colonel returns to collect me.'

Mr. Asquith laughed. 'The colonel is a good strategist.'

'How could he be a colonel otherwise?'

'Many far less capable men rise to that rank. However, as to his plan, I think I could tolerate your company.'

'Excellent.' Anne canted her head 'Do you think Mrs. Sheffield will get her property back?'

'If you are asking me whether I think Sheffield is making a false claim, then the answer is yes. As to his admitting it . . . well, that is something else. The man is wily. I once thought Mrs. Sheffield might know something about the destruction of the plantation — '

'Oh no, I hope you did not tell the colonel that.'

Mr. Asquith shrugged, his expression rather sheepish. 'I admitted I was wrong.'

She stifled a smile. 'Your problem is that you judge others by your own high standards. You are not guilty of lacking integrity, but possess too much of it. You are a man of principal and honour, and your standards are if anything too rigid.'

'My goodness. What happened to the shy young lady who didn't have two words to say for herself?'

'She grew up.'

'I noticed,' Mr. Asquith replied softly.

The room fell so quiet, it felt to Anne as though the air had been sucked out of it. This time her breathing difficulties had nothing to do with her supposedly weak chest and everything to do with the disturbingly poised specimen of male beauty sharing the room with her. There was a tangible excitement between them now, brought about by them being partners in deception. If Mr. Asquith's part in it was discovered, he really would lose his position. Anne should have thought about that, instead of insisting upon involving him because . . . well, because she was selfish and wanted an excuse to spend more time alone with him.

He fascinated and compelled her in a manner she had never imagined possible. Her every conscious thought was of him. His was the last face she imaged before closing her eyes at night, and the first that sprang to mind when she opened them again in the morning. She was being unreasonable expecting him to compromise his standards, knowing he had little choice but to do as she asked. He was an honourable man, and she had asked him to behave in a manner that wouldn't sit comfortably with his conscience. She opened her mouth to say as much, but no words emerged.

'I know what you are thinking,' he said, reaching out to touch her cheek gently. 'But you must not concern yourself on my account. I am perfectly willing to be of service to you.'

★　★　★

'Do you think anyone suspects?' Joshua asked the following morning as he drove Darcy's curricle, with Anne seated beside him, down Pemberley's long driveway.

'Mama was put out that we had not made an immediate commitment, but I knew that would be the case. After complaining at length about needless delays — '

'Why is she in such a tearing hurry to have the matter settled, I wonder.'

'That I could not say, but she does seem extraordinarily anxious to marry me off.'

'Lady Catherine does enjoy having everything in her life in proper order.'

'And everyone in it doing what she wants,' Anne added with a wry smile. 'Anyway, she didn't ask any awkward questions that required an outright lie. I mean, it is not as though you have actually asked me to marry you, and so I could not have rejected your suit.'

Joshua laughed at her irrefutable logic. 'What of Asquith?'

'I spoke with him this morning and he is perfectly willing to play his part.'

'Are you still absolutely sure about all this, Anne. I shall not hold it against you if you have had a change of heart.'

'I wouldn't think of withdrawing my help.' Reassuring determination underscored her words. 'I cannot remember a time when I enjoyed myself more.' She put up her parasol when the sun broke through the light cloud cover. 'Quite apart from anything else, we cannot allow Mrs. Sheffield's property to be taken from her without at least trying to prevent it.'

'Then nothing remains except for me to offer you my heartfelt thanks'

'Oh, there is no need. If you think about it,

we are being of service to one another in our different ways.'

Once again, Joshua could find no fault with her logic and they made the rest of the journey in companionable silence.

Upon arrival at Briar Hall, they learned that Lady Briar was not at home and they were received by Mrs. Sheffield alone. She appeared confused by Anne's presence but hid it well. Without the need to make polite conversation with Lady Briar, Joshua wasted no time in apprising Mrs. Sheffield of the reason for his visit, which he did the moment refreshments had been served and the footman who delivered them had withdrawn.

'Well.' Mrs. Sheffield said, looking exceedingly shocked after hearing him out in silence. 'I am unsure what to say.'

'Do you think it will work?'

'Possibly, but I would not think of asking Miss de Bourgh to risk her reputation, and — '

'Oh, don't spare a thought for me,' Anne replied, flapping a hand. 'I shall remain at Pemberley, and your odious brother-in-law will not get within a mile of me.'

'Yes, but what if word reaches Lady Catherine?'

'I cannot see how it would.'

'Servants talk.'

'Yes, that's true,' Joshua replied. 'But I will charge my man with ensuring nothing untoward is mentioned within the hearing of Lady Catherine's retainers.'

'Is that possible?' Mrs. Sheffield asked in a dubious tone.

'No offence, Anne, but if half of what my man tells me is true, no one below stairs at Pemberley thinks much of your mother's maid, or yours. Or your coachmen either for that matter. Apparently they had inflated opinions of their own worth.'

Anne nodded. 'I am not surprised to hear it.'

'Prejudices below stairs can be brutal.' Joshua grinned. 'No, it is safe to assume Lady Catherine will hear nothing of our plans from the servants' hall.'

Mrs. Sheffield stood up, obliging Joshua to do the same thing. She paced the length of the room, her gown swishing about her ankles as she thought the matter through. 'I am perfectly sure Percival would come rushing up here, given the slightest encouragement.'

'Yes,' Joshua replied, scowling. Just the thought of another man desiring Celia Sheffield sent him into a murderous rage. 'I dare say. The question is, would he be sufficiently tempted by the prospect of a vulnerable heiress to become indiscreet about his claims on your property?'

'With respect to Miss de Bourgh, unquestionably. It's just the sort of challenge he would enjoy. As to revealing the true nature of his claim on my estate . . . well, that is another matter entirely. I cannot say for sure.'

'Greed has a way of loosening tongues,' Joshua replied. 'And I can be very persuasive when I wish to be.'

Their gazes clashed, and Mrs. Sheffield's lips quirked. 'I am perfectly sure you can be.'

'Well, there you are then. Would he expect to be welcomed here to Briar Hall?'

'Oh no. Lord Briar detested my husband, and made no secret of the fact that he disliked Percival even more. My sister feels the same way, and Lord Briar would never let him sleep beneath his roof for fear of oversetting my sister, and me.'

'I am very glad to hear it. My main concern is that if you summon him here with the intention of speaking with him, that meeting must take place somewhere.'

'I am sure he will be permitted to call here, if I advise Lord Briar in advance. That way he can ensure my sister is out of the way, and that I have a servant with me all the time. He will want to know why I have invited him, of course.' She pondered upon that for a moment. 'Hmm, I will have to indulge in a small untruth, I suppose, since I do not wish him to know of your involvement, Colonel, and especially not of yours, Miss de Bourgh. No matter, I am sure I shall think of a plausible reason to have invited him that will satisfy Lord Briar.'

'Then, if we are agreed, perhaps you ought to write your letter now,' Joshua suggested. 'I will ensure it is sent immediately by express. If you were to say that your plans are not settled and you intend to leave Derbyshire very soon, it will hasten his arrival.'

'Before I commit pen to paper,' Mrs. Sheffield replied, resuming her seat and fixing Anne with an inquisitive glance, 'I would very much like to know how you came to be drawn into this, Miss de Bourgh.'

Joshua felt almost surplus to requirement as the two ladies fell into a conversation that excluded him. One of those ladies he was expected to marry, and the other he would very much like to wed, but would never propose to. They were so very different in appearance, experience and every other possible way. And yet they chatted together now as though they had known one another for years. Anne was quite open about her disinclination to marry Joshua and explained how relieved she had felt when she discovered he was of a similar mind.

'I wish I had possessed the strength to defy my parents when they insisted I marry Albert,' Mrs. Sheffield said wistfully.

'I can accept no credit for strength of character,' Anne replied. 'If the colonel had proposed marriage, I would have accepted him, simply because . . . well, I swear if I hear one more time I have a duty, I shall scream. However, I am very glad he did not . . . propose, that is. We now understand each other perfectly and are the very best of friends.'

'You are proving your friendship by offering to help me.' She shot a glance Joshua's way. 'Now if I could only decide what motivates the colonel.'

Joshua raised a brow and sent her a teasing smile. Mrs. Sheffield cocked a brow in return, almost as though she was issuing some sort of challenge, and returned her attention to Anne. Leaning forward, she patted her hand. 'I want you to know that however matters turn out, you will always have my eternal gratitude. I cannot remember the last time anyone helped me without wanting something in return.'

'That is something else we have in common then.'

'I hope that I too can be your friend,' Mrs. Sheffield said.

Anne smiled. 'I would like that very much.'

'Your letter, Mrs. Sheffield,' Joshua said softly.

'Yes, of course. Pray, excuse me. It will take but a moment.'

'I suggest you say you have reserved a room for him at the inn in Lambton for three days' time and that he should let you know by return if he intends to make use of it. That way we shall know his intentions and it will give us time to prepare.'

'A good suggestion.'

She disappeared and, good as her word, returned a short time later with a letter in her hand.

'Here is what I have written. Tell me if you approve, Colonel.'

Dear Percival, I was disturbed and overset to receive a visit from Albert's solicitor earlier this week. I had no idea there was a partnership agreement between you and Albert, or a will in existence that gifted our estate to you. As you can imagine, this news came as a great shock and has caused me considerable worry. I cannot believe Albert meant to leave me destitute and can only hope a resolution can be reached that will satisfy us both. We ought to speak face to face, to avoid further misunderstanding.

240

Involving solicitors always complicates things.

I leave Derbyshire in a week's time for a prolonged stay with relations in Scotland. Could I prevail upon you to travel north at the earliest opportunity? I have reserved a room for you at the inn in Lambton for three nights' time. Please advise me by return if you plan to make use of it.
Yours etc.

'Perfect,' Joshua said, sending her an approving smile. 'He will find the prospect of meeting with you too tempting to resist.' In Sheffield's place, Joshua certainly would have. 'You have made it sound as though you are on the point of capitulation, which is exactly the right way to tempt him. He is anxious to get his hands on your property and cannot do so until the matter of ownership is established beyond question. Seal the letter, if you please, and I will arrange to have it sent.'

'This is all very well,' Mrs. Sheffield replied, affixing her seal and handing the letter to Joshua, 'but what am I to say to him when we actually meet?'

'If you will allow it, I shall call on you tomorrow afternoon, when I am supposed to be driving Anne, and we will be at leisure to discuss the matter then.'

'I look forward to it. But what of you, Miss de Bourgh? How will you occupy your time?'

Anne blushed. 'Don't worry about me. The colonel and I have arranged matters.'

'Ah, I see.' Instead of ringing the bell, Mrs. Sheffield conducted them to the door herself. 'I am very greatly indebted to you both,' she said as they took their leave.

14

Three days later, Lizzy and Will snatched a few minutes alone in the small salon. Lizzy was reclined with her head rested in her husband's lap and his hands stroked her hair.

'What's troubling you, Will?' Lizzy asked. 'You keep scowling and so I know there must be something.'

'Other than allowing my cousin Anne to take part in a dangerous deception?'

'You are not allowing her to do anything. Anne is perfectly capable of making up her own mind.'

'I would never have given permission for Georgiana to become involved in anything so rash. I now have grave reservations about Anne doing so.'

'Anne will be safe and well protected here at Pemberley. Stop brooding.' Lizzy smiled up at her husband. 'Anne is being rewarded by spending an hour or more every afternoon when she is supposed to be driving with the colonel, in Mr. Asquith's company.'

'Which gives me something else to be concerned about.'

Lizzy laughed. 'I am convinced Mr.

Asquith is a man of the highest integrity.'

'I agree, but Lady Catherine would not approve.'

Lizzy rolled her eyes. 'When does she ever approve of people enjoying themselves?'

Will shrugged. 'True, but talking of my aunt, I am worried about her.'

Lizzy lifted her head and looked intently at her husband. 'Why?'

'I have never seen her beset by a fit of the blue devils before. Ever since Collins arrived — '

'That would be enough to cast anyone into despair.'

'My aunt is one of the few people who likes and approves of the man.'

Lizzy snorted. 'She only likes him because he hangs on her every word, treating them more reverently than the gospel he reads from his pulpit on a Sunday.'

'Even so, ever since he arrived with tales of Asquith's nefarious wrong-doings, we have hardly seen my aunt, except at meal times.' Will shook his head. 'I am worried she might be unwell, seriously unwell, which would account for her desire to see Anne married.'

Lizzy sat up and gave Will her complete attention. Lady Catherine could be overbearing, but she was still Will's aunt and he was fond of her in his way. 'I cannot see anything different about her. She looks as strong to me as she did when we met in Kent. She is a little less forthright than I have grown to expect, but then she is not in her own home and knows you will never permit her to usurp my position here.'

'Even so, something is not right about her.'

'If you want my opinion, I think it has to do with Sir Marius.' Lizzy flashed a playful smile. 'She knew him years ago, which would account for her willingness to employ Mr. Asquith.'

'How do you know this?'

'Anne told me. It came out in a conversation with her mother. I also happen to know that Lady Catherine has written to him — I saw her letter on the table in the hall waiting to be posted. Presumably she wants to know the truth about Mr. Collins's allegations, and I think she is nervous about the prospect of meeting Sir Marius again.'

'Good God!' Will looked shocked rigid. 'Could that be all it is?'

'Why not? She pretends to have no time for romantic love, but perhaps that is because she was once disappointed.'

'But all these years later. To still feel — '

'If we were separated for twenty years, would that change your feelings for me?'

Will's eyes glowed as he gently covered her lips with his own. 'What a question. You know very well, I would never allow that situation to occur. If we were parted for any reason I would come after you, throw you over my shoulder and carry you back to Pemberley if necessary.' His lips worked their way down her neck, nipping and kissing until she was in a fervour of need. 'Nothing and no one will ever keep me away from you, Lizzy.'

'Perhaps Lady Catherine felt the same way about Sir Marius,' she said, reluctantly shuffling so there was a little distance between their bodies and Will was obliged to stop nibbling her neck. 'Everyone deserves to be happy, even your curmudgeonly aunt.'

'You have a romantic soul, Mrs. Darcy.'

'Whose fault is that, Mr. Darcy?'

'Anyway,' Will continued. 'Lady Catherine isn't likely to see Sir Marius again. All she has done is write to him, and for all we know, she could have been doing that for years.'

'But equally, she very well might not have done, either. You know how disciplined she is.'

Will shook his head. 'I find it difficult to imagine my aunt suffering from love-sickness.'

'Whereas I think it the most natural thing in the world.'

A burst of laughter and chattering voices warned Lizzy her precious time alone with

Will was about to come to an end.

'It sounds as though the morning's rehearsal is over,' Will said.

'So it does.' Lizzy sighed. 'Poor Jane. Since Lady Catherine has stopped offering her services as chaperone, my sister has to sit in on all the rehearsals. It hardly seems fair.'

'What isn't fair?'

'We were sympathising that you must supervise the actors, Jane, because you're the only one entrusted with the play's ending.'

Jane smiled good-naturedly as she took a seat. 'I don't mind in the least. Mr. Asquith is wonderful at getting the girls to perform. It actually might turn out quite well.'

'If enthusiasm equates to success,' Will said, 'then they are sure to please.'

'Not that their enthusiasm could have anything to do with the involvement of a certain major, captain and tutor,' Lizzy remarked playfully.

'Lizzy, how could you suggest such a thing?' Jane asked, laughing.

'I cannot begin to imagine. Anyway, Jane, I am glad you feel useful. Personally, I still can't get used to the fact that we now qualify as chaperones.'

Jane glanced down at her expanding waistline and smiled. 'How quickly times change.'

They were joined by the girls, who were chattering about the play.

'I hear rehearsals progress well,' Lizzy said, smiling.

'I remembered all my lines today,' Kitty said. 'Who would have thought it?'

'Not you, obviously,' Lizzy replied. 'This time yesterday you despaired of ever knowing them all.'

'I expect I shall forget them again when the time comes to perform.'

'Nonsense,' Anne said. 'You are a natural.'

Will shook his head, but smiled as he stood up and left the ladies to their chatter, presumably going off in search of male company.

'Mr. Collins tried to intrude on our rehearsals again,' Kitty said, wrinkling her nose. 'He seemed to think he could order Mr. Asquith about, but did not succeed.'

'Mr. Asquith was very polite, but firm,' Anne added, her eyes glowing. 'Mr. Collins soon realised he had met his match, and took himself off somewhere else.'

'He has been pacing about in the garden for the last hour,' Lizzy said. 'Even the gardeners try to keep their distance from him.'

'Oh dear,' Jane said. 'I feel rather sorry for him.'

'Dear Jane!' Lizzy sighed. 'No one invited him here. I should have thought he would be needed back in Hunsford, but he shows no inclination to leave.'

'He is very thick-skinned when it suits him to be,' Anne said.

'Kitty and I are finishing up the scenery this afternoon,' Georgiana said, 'while Anne goes driving with Colonel Fitzwilliam.'

Anne caught Lizzy's eye, blushed, and said nothing.

'Come along, girls.' Lizzy stood up. 'It is almost time for luncheon.'

Jane and Lizzy ushered the girls ahead of them and made their way to the dining room. Will's mood had rubbed off on her and Lizzy now felt unsettled. Tomorrow would see the arrival of Sheffield and her plan to catch him out would be put into action by the colonel. Lizzy was gripped with a sudden desire to call it all off, sensing they had overlooked something important that could have catastrophic consequences for them all.

And if that happened, the blame would be entirely hers.

* * *

Celia Sheffield was waiting for Joshua in the woods adjoining Briar Hall, a location they

249

used as a meeting place for the third consecutive day. It was a convenient distance for Celia to walk and the chances of their being seen together were slim. Joshua halted the curricle, secured the reins, and jumped down from the box seat, raising his hat by way of greeting. He took Celia's hand, kissed the back of it, and tucked it into the crook of his arm.

'I hope you haven't been waiting for long,' he said, smiling down at the top of her straw bonnet.

'I arrived early because I was anxious to see you.'

'I would be delighted, if I could bring myself to believe it was my company you desired.'

She looked up at him, and blinked in evident surprise. 'Why ever would it not be?'

'I know how anxious you must be feeling. Sheffield will arrive in Lambton this afternoon, and tomorrow you will have to face him. It would be peculiar if you didn't want to talk about it to the only person who knows the truth.'

'You are quite wrong, Colonel.'

'I thought we had agreed upon Joshua.'

Her distracted smile was almost Joshua's undoing. 'So we had.'

'I shall visit Lambton Inn this evening and

make Sheffield's acquaintance.'

She shuddered. 'How nice for you.'

'I want to get his measure as soon as possible.'

'He is sure to be found in the taproom, but has a strong head for liquor, so it won't be easy to get him intoxicated.'

Joshua patted the hand trapped on his arm and sent her a reassuring smile. 'Just worry about what you will say to him when he calls on you tomorrow morning.'

'We have discussed that endlessly.'

'Even so, oblige me. I need to be sure you have not forgotten anything.'

'Very well. I shall pretend not to understand the new will, and ask to see it. He's sure to have a copy with him. He will assume I am incapable of grasping the particulars and explain them to me, odious man! I shall act confused, tell him I'm unsure about the document's authenticity — '

'Be careful not to anger him.'

'I shall say I don't blame him for believing it is legally enforceable, at which point he will probably suggest we occupy the estate together.'

'Come,' he said when she shuddered. He led her to a stone bench and seated himself on it. After a moment's hesitation, he pulled her onto his lap and enfolded her in his arms, waiting for a protest that didn't materialise. 'You are cold?'

'No.' She rested her head on his shoulder and sighed. 'I just want tomorrow to be over with. I am being weak and foolish. I know there is nothing he can do to harm me in Briar Hall, or coerce me to return to Buckinghamshire with him, but still . . . '

During his previous meetings with Celia, Joshua had called upon all his military discipline not to overstep the mark. He sat her on his knee now purely to infuse some of his strength into her, and to protect her skirts from the muddy ground. Obviously, those were his only reasons. But seeing a fat tear trickling down her cheek, noticing just how badly she was trembling, cut through his crumbling resolve. His arms tightened around her, and he placed a finger beneath her chin, tilting it upwards until she could no longer hide beneath the brim of her bonnet. She looked so pale, so vulnerable, so scared, that his heart melted, and the desire to comfort her overrode common sense.

With a smothered oath, he lowered his head and captured her lips in a slow, incendiary kiss that promised so much more than he could allow himself to deliver. It would expose a great deal more about his feelings for her than was wise, but she responded with enthusiasm, which was almost Joshua's undoing. His tongue tickled the corner of her mouth as his lips played against hers and he tried to remind himself of all the reasons why this was such a bad idea.

Powerless to help himself when gripped by the fierce, burning desire that had grown stronger with every meeting between them, Joshua deepened the kiss, pulling Celia firmly against him as it turned unashamedly carnal. Their breathing quickly grew ragged as Joshua's control slipped. The reward he had been dreaming of claiming since first meeting Mrs. Sheffield was within a hair's breadth of becoming a reality, and yet he could not allow that to happen. Not now, certainly not here in the open air.

Not ever.

When Celia groaned around their fused lips and settled herself more firmly against his burgeoning desire, the extent of which she could not fail to notice, it actually brought Joshua to his senses. He broke the kiss and released his hold on her.

'I am sorry,' he said, not meeting her gaze. 'I should not have done that.'

'I disagree.' It was the last thing he had expected her to say. 'There is no need to look so shocked,' she said capriciously.

'You wanted me to kiss you.'

'I hope you are not this slow when you are in command of your men, Colonel, or the enemy would run rings around you.'

'I want you very much,' he said softly. 'I didn't think you could possibly doubt it, but I will not take advantage of your reliance upon me, and there's an end to the matter.'

'I am not being fair to you, am I?'

'We need to get through the next few days, deal with Sheffield, and then we will be at leisure to discuss anything you wish.'

'It is not what I wish that concerns me. I know my own mind.'

Joshua wanted to ask her what she meant by that comment, but restrained himself. Once she had her property restored to her and was no longer obligated to Joshua, her feelings would change. He had nothing to offer her other than his undying love and a colonel's pay. Marrying for money, which he had always known was his only recourse, hadn't seemed so bad because he had never anticipated falling quite so violently in love. Now that it had happened, it seemed ungentlemanly to use her fortune to support them both. Especially since the fortune in question had been amassed through the exploitation of slaves.

Joshua expelled a prolonged sigh. Having a

conscience could sometimes be damnably inconvenient.

⋆   ⋆   ⋆

Anne sat beside Mr. Asquith on a bench in a pretty part of the Pemberley Park, a good distance away from the house. She had a poetry book open on her lap but wasn't reading aloud from it as she had done the two previous days. Instead, she looked up from it and smiled.

'What do you find so amusing, Anne?' Mr. Asquith asked.

'Mr. Collins.'

'Collins?'

'He came here to cause you harm, and took considerable pleasure from doing so, yet calls himself a man of God. How can he justify such behaviour?'

'Many worse crimes have been committed in the name of God.'

'Hmm, but Mr. Collins is my personal cross to bear.'

'And yet he has managed to make you laugh.'

'I am laughing at him, not with him, there is a difference.'

'Certainly there is.'

'I overheard him telling Mama this

morning that I ought not to be allowed to drive out with Colonel Fitzwilliam alone, and that he would be happy to bear us company, just to ensure the proprieties were observed.' Her smile widened. 'Only imagine if he could see the two of us now. He would probably have apoplexy.'

'And would also have a legitimate reason to disapprove of me.'

'But we are not doing anything wrong.'

'We are alone.'

'Yes, but quite innocently.' Anne bit her lip. She had rather hoped that Mr. Asquith — Pierce, as he had invited her to address him in private — would use the opportunity to . . . well, to do something to show his true feelings for her. Perhaps he had. By behaving in a gentlemanly fashion, he had made it clear that he did not return her rather transparent regard.

'I trust Lady Catherine told him to mind his own business.'

'Oh, but I am his business, or so he thinks.' Anne continued to smile, until Pierce reluctantly did the same thing. 'The problem is that no one at Pemberley wants anything to do with him.'

'He would be best advised to take himself back to Hunsford, where he has a legitimate excuse to interfere in his parishioners' lives.'

'He will not leave here until he is sure Mama intends to dismiss you.' Anne's smile widened. 'I don't think Mr. Collins likes you very much, Pierce.'

'The feeling is entirely mutual.' He fixed her with a penetrating gaze. 'You should smile more often, by the way. It suits you.'

Perversely, his words caused Anne's smile to fade abruptly. 'A few more days and I will have little to smile about. When Mama learns Colonel Fitzwilliam and I have decided not to marry, she will be furious.' She felt tears welling but impatiently brushed them aside. 'She will take you away from me as a punishment, because she knows I enjoy your society.'

'Hush now. Don't get upset on my account.' He gently brushed an escaped tear from her cheek. 'I am a survivor.'

'That is not what I meant.'

'I know you did not.' Pierce stood and half turned away from her, probably embarrassed by her immaturity. 'Let us worry about the here and now and leave the future to take care of itself.'

In other words, he is anxious to leave me, Anne thought desolately. 'What shall you do?' she asked.

'Find another position,' he said, not looking at her. 'What else can I do?'

15

'You had best be off to Lambton, Cox,'
Joshua told his valet later that afternoon.
'Even if Sheffield hired a saddle horse from
Newcastle instead of springing for a private
carriage to complete his journey, he ought to
have arrived in the village by now.'

'Right you are, sir. I shall see you there
later.'

'Keep your wits about you. Sheffield is
nobody's fool.'

Joshua stared out the window for a long
time after Cox had left, wondering if there
was the remotest possibility of this plan
actually working. They intended to play on a
greedy man's rapacious nature, along with his
arrogant assumption that no female on the
planet could help but fall for his looks and
charm.

Joshua forced himself to give Cox an hour's
head start, filling the interminable wait by
pacing the length of his chamber, deep in
thought about his meeting with Celia earlier.
Even if he did manage to get the better of
Sheffield, he had come to the agonising yet
incontrovertible decision that he would

definitely not ask her to marry him. The only way he could show how much he loved her was by restoring her property to her and setting her free of all commitment to him.

He tightly compressed his lips as he withstood the debilitating pain brought on by his decision. Her desire to be kissed by him implied she enjoyed his society. She definitely hadn't kissed him solely out of a sense of gratitude, but that was neither here nor there. Celia deserved time and solitude in which to consider her future, without Joshua around to muddy her thinking. He would leave here as soon as this matter was resolved and, of course, after he had weathered the storm that would rage after he told Lady Catherine he would not be marrying Anne.

With a heavy heart, Joshua slid his arms into his greatcoat and left the house by the side door that led to the mews, anxious not to draw attention to himself.

He left his mount in the care of the head groom at Lambton Inn and pushed open the door to the taproom. It was crowded with thirsty men eager to wash away the dust from a day's work with a tankard of ale or two. The noise of a dozen different conversations filled the air, as did smoke from a fire fuelled by peat that was obviously still damp. The odour of unwashed bodies and spilt ale barely registered with Joshua as he scanned the crowd, looking for Cox. He panicked when it occurred to him that a man of Sheffield's ilk may prefer not to share the taproom with farm labourers, market traders, and assorted locals. If he had chosen to hire a private room instead, Joshua's plan would not even get off the ground. He released a long breath when he observed Cox at a corner table with a man who could only be Sheffield.

Joshua caught the landlord's attention and ordered a tankard of ale. Then he stood to one side of the room for a moment, watching Sheffield, sizing him up. Even to someone as predisposed as Joshua was to dislike him, he had to concede the man was blessed with good looks. Long fair hair fell across a face with features that attractively complimented one another — no crooked nose or jutting jaw to spoil the picture. He was dressed elegantly in the latest style, his boots still showing signs of dust from the road. He banged his empty tankard on the table to attract the attention of the barmaid and was served quickly. Millie had received instructions from Cox, and a healthy tip, to ensure the ale flowed. She flashed a flirtatious smile as she placed a full tankard in front of Sheffield and then bustled away to serve others.

'Hey, Fitzwilliam. I did not know you

planned to come into Lambton this evening.' Cox waved to Joshua. 'I thought you preferred to drown your sorrows with Darcy's expensive brandy.'

'Needed to get away from Pemberley,' Joshua replied, pulling out a chair next to Cox and throwing himself into it.

'This is the friend I was telling you about,' Cox said to Sheffield. 'Sheffield, meet Fitzwilliam, the luckiest man on earth with a face like a badger's arse to prove it.' Cox laughed at his own joke and slapped Joshua's shoulder. 'Sheffield here has just arrived from London.'

Joshua grunted and kept his attention focused on his ale.

'Sorry about my friend's lack of manners,' Cox said. 'You'd think that marrying one of the richest heiresses in the country would be cause for celebration.' Cox chuckled. 'As you can see, Fitzwilliam is in raptures at the prospect.'

Joshua shot his valet an evil look that caused Cox to laugh harder.

'I've only been here for an hour,' Sheffield said, 'but all I hear mention of is the great Pemberlcy. Is that where you're staying?'

Cox nodded. 'Darcy is Fitzwilliam's cousin. I'm here for moral support.'

Joshua snorted. 'Nothing moral about you.'

'I aim to please.'

'I hear there's a Miss Darcy. Is she your intended, Fitzwilliam?'

'Miss Anne de Bourgh is the lady in question,' Cox replied, because Joshua was concentrating on brooding. 'She is ten times more consequential than Miss Darcy.'

Cox took a sip of his ale, warming to his theme. 'Imagine an estate at least as grand as Pemberley, run by a widow, who has just one child set to inherit the lot.' He paused for effect. 'A daughter.'

'Is that what you're in such a funk about, Fitzwilliam?' Sheffield asked, looking incredulous. 'What great good fortune. Every man in the land would give his right arm to be in your boots.'

'Any man with half a brain would agree with you, Sheffield, except, it seems, for the would-be bridegroom.'

'And why is that?' Sheffield's tankard was empty again. Glancing up, Joshua noticed that his eyes were glazing over. Good. Millie had obviously remembered Cox's instructions and put a tot of rum into each of Sheffield's tankards. He would never notice the addition against the strong spicy taste of the famous local ale. 'I say, this ale is just the thing. Damned odd aftertaste, but it grows on a man.' He banged his tankard down, and once again, Millie replenished it in double-quick time, saving a saucy wink for Cox as she turned away.

'My lunatic of a friend has taken a fancy to another lady,' Cox said, rolling his eyes. 'Claims to be in love, whatever that's supposed to mean.'

'What is this heiress like?' Sheffield asked, his expression calculating.

Joshua continued glaring morosely at the table and Cox provided the answer. 'Small, quiet as a church mouse, biddable, not bad looking but shy and unworldly. Spent most of her childhood fighting illness so she ain't seen much of life beyond Kent.'

Sheffield, now definitely the worse for drink, leaned back in his chair and stared at the soot-blackened beams above his head. 'Let me see if I understand you a'right. You have the chance to become master of a vast estate, Fitzwilliam, with just a sickly wife and her compliant mother in your way.' A bark of a laugh escaped Joshua at the thought of Lady Catherine ever being compliant, but he quickly turned it into a cough. 'Are you out of your senses, man? You can buy a dozen other women once you've married into that sort of money.'

'That's what I keep trying to tell him, but it don't do me no good.' Cox pulled a disgruntled face. 'He's got it bad for this lady of his.'

'Must be quite a stunner,' Sheffield remarked.

'She would never agree to be my mistress,' Joshua said, addressing the comment to his ale. 'Anyway, she deserves better than that.'

'We always want what we can't have.' Sheffield took another long swig of his rum-laced ale and smacked his lips together in appreciation. 'I'll tell you what. I will do you a good turn and change places with you.' He chuckled to show he was joking, but Joshua could tell the idea had taken root. 'Far be it from me to stand in the way of true love. Besides, it sounds like your Miss de Bourgh is ripe for the plucking.'

'Reads lots of romantic fiction, so she does,' Cox replied, 'and expects to be swept off her feet with grand, romantic gestures. A good-looking man like you could probably melt her precious little heart in no time flat, but it wouldn't be any use. Her mama has quite made up her mind that only Fitzwilliam will do.'

Sheffield burped. 'Changing the minds of mamas is something I excel at, along with avoiding irate husbands, of course.' He chuckled. 'Whoops, bit indiscreet there.'

'You haven't told us what brings you to this

part of the world,' Cox said.

'Ah, I've come to see my late brother's wife. He made a fortune in Jamaica, brought an estate here, and left it to me. Problem is, his lovely wife didn't know it and ain't too happy about the way things have turned out. I reckon she'll soon see sense though 'cause she sent for me.' Sheffield's lecherous grin caused Joshua to clench his fists impotently beneath the table. 'I think her and me could make ourselves very cosy back in Buckinghamshire.'

'Dare say you could,' Cox replied. 'Shame about that. Perhaps you could have done Don Juan here a favour and taken Miss de Bourgh off his hands, but it won't serve, not if you already have a love nest set up elsewhere. What you do after you tie the knot is another matter, but Lady Catherine would check up on you if you turned her daughter's head and the slightest whiff of scandal would give her the excuse to cut off all relations.'

'What are you talking about, Cox?' Joshua asked, slamming down his tankard. 'I might not want to marry Anne, but you can't just try and palm her off onto a stranger.'

'Just trying to be of service.'

'Hmm.' Joshua staggered to his feet, giving every impression of being in his cups when in fact he was icily sober. 'We had best get back

265

to Pemberley. It's almost dinner time.'

'So it is.' Cox stood up and shook Sheffield's hand. Joshua couldn't bring himself to do the same. 'Nice meeting you, Sheffield, and good luck with your business. We might meet again if you're here for a while. Fitzwilliam seems to find his way in here most nights to drown his sorrows, and someone has to make sure he gets back to Pemberley in one piece.'

Joshua and Cox walked away, leaving Sheffield in a pensive frame of mind.

'Well done, Cox,' Joshua said when they reached the mews and reclaimed their horses. 'You sowed the seed perfectly.'

'What will happen now?'

'Sheffield will ask more questions about Pemberley and Lady Catherine. Everyone here will tell him the same thing. That Rosings is as grand as Pemberley and he will discover that everything we told him is true. You know how every tiny detail connected to the Darcy family is the equivalent of folklore around these parts. He had his eye on Millie, and she will certainly set him straight.'

They mounted up and trotted down the village street, side by side.

'All we can hope for now,' Joshua added, 'is that Mrs. Sheffield plays her part right.'

The next morning Joshua waited impatiently for Celia to join him in their usual place. When their appointed time came and went, and there was no sign of her, he became anxious that something had gone wrong. He was at the point of making his way to Briar Hall, no longer caring if he exposed himself to Sheffield, when she ran breathlessly into the clearing. She was bareheaded, her face flushed and her eyes huge and luminous. Joshua could see she was distressed, and his resolve not to touch her in an inappropriate manner did not survive the first minute. He opened his arms and she flung herself into them.

'Sorry, he was late arriving.'

'That is probably my fault. We managed to get him intoxicated.'

'Ah, that explains it.'

'Was it so very bad?' he asked, brushing his lips across the top of her head when he felt her entire body tremble.

'I hate being in the same room with that man,' she cried passionately. 'There is just something predatory about him that makes me shudder. He reminds me of a wild animal on the prowl.'

'A very apt description.'

Joshua forced himself to release his hold on her. 'Tell me what he said, and how you responded. I need to know it all.'

'I asked to see the will, and he had the original in his coat pocket. I got the impression he always carries it with him.'

'Which is exceedingly foolish of him, but typical of his arrogance.'

'He was at his most charming and persuasive, suggesting there was no reason why we shouldn't share the property.' Celia tossed her head and sniffed. 'He made it clear, without actually saying so, that was not all he expected to share.'

Joshua was filled with a murderous rage, but quelled it with difficulty. As a soldier, he knew rational decisions could not be made when one allowed passion to overcome reason. 'I hope you told him you planned to have the will authenticated.'

'Certainly I did, and he wasn't at all pleased to hear it. He said it could take months, all but implying he didn't have months to wait.'

'You think he has pressing debts?'

She wrinkled her nose. 'He usually does. He enjoys playing cards but doesn't always win. Anyway, he was not impressed by my procrastination, and went to a lot of trouble to try and talk me around. I told him I had no desire to share my house with him, and insisted he leave.'

'You did well.' He broke his resolve for a second time by reaching out and gently touching her face. 'But now it is over. You can leave the rest to me and need never see him again.'

'What happened at the inn last night?'

They walked together, her hand on his arm, as he told her.

'Cox and I will return this evening, and I have every expectation of getting him to admit the will is a forgery. He is desperate for easy money, will have asked about Anne and found out what I told him, or rather what Cox told him about her situation, is true.' Joshua allowed himself a prolonged glance at her lovely profile, dying a little inside when he recalled his decision not to press her into matrimony. To walk away and leave her to live her life on her own terms would be like tearing his own heart out with a blunt spoon. But he would do it because it was the right, the honourable, thing to do. He should never have allowed himself to get carried away by thoughts of what could never be. 'I have met men like him before. He will not be able to resist.'

She sighed. 'You make it all sound so straightforward.'

'There isn't any reason why it should not be.'

'And will you let me know as soon as you possibly can. I shall be in a fervour of expectation.'

'I promise to send word immediately.'

'Will you not come yourself?'

Joshua avoided making an answer, unwilling to commit himself to a promise he could not afford to keep. His resolve was not that strong. He escorted her back to the house, but declined her invitation to go inside. He had every wish to prolong his time with Celia, but what would be the point? His mind was made up. He raised her hand to his lips, kissed the back of it, and bid her *adieu*. He sensed her confused gaze boring into his back as he strode away to the position where he had left his horse but didn't look back. He couldn't allow her to see his expression, which he suspected was as bleak and desolate as his empty heart.

Joshua had just spent the last moments he would allow himself to be alone with the only woman he would ever love.

★　★　★

Joshua and Cox arrived earlier at the Lambton Inn that evening, and Sheffield wasn't yet in the taproom. Millie sent Cox a cheerful wink, implying Sheffield had asked all the questions they had anticipated and received the right answers. Confident Sheffield would appear, they took their tankards to a table by the window and waited. They heard booted feet clumping down the wooden stairs a short time later. Joshua pretended not to see Sheffield and continued to stare into his ale.

'Let him come to us,' he told Cox.

Sure enough, he did precisely that. Raising a hand in greeting, he pulled out a chair at their table.

'Evening,' Sheffield said, looking and sounding a little less chipper than he had the previous day. 'Mind if I join you?'

Joshua merely shrugged. Cox was more forthcoming. 'By all means,' he said. 'How did your business go today?'

Sheffield grunted. 'Damned woman thinks she can lead me a merry dance. Why the devil can't women just do as they're told and leave the thinking to us men?'

'See,' Cox said. 'I told you Sheffield and Miss de Bourgh would be a perfect match. She would never dare to answer back.'

'Miss de Bourgh, Miss de Bourgh,' Joshua growled, scowling. 'I come here to get away from the sound of her name.'

'Is she really that biddable?' Sheffield asked.

'Oh aye. Brought up to be seen and not heard,' Cox replied. 'You would think, what with her being such a grand heiress, she would be high and mighty, but she hardly opens her mouth.'

'She sounds too good to be true.' Sheffield shook his head. 'You're a few farthings short of a guinea, Fitzwilliam, and don't know when you're well off.'

'His latest plan, if you can believe it, is to propose to his lady love and ask her to live on a colonel's pay.' Cox grimaced. 'She would be a damned fool to even consider it. She can do much better than that, but Fitzwilliam won't listen to a word I tell him.'

'Money ain't everything,' Joshua replied.

Cox rolled his eyes, but made no comment.

'It is when you don't have any,' Sheffield said with feeling.

'Darcy will give me a helping hand,' Joshua mumbled.

'Are you really serious about passing the heiress up?' Sheffield asked, tucking into his second tankard of ale in ten minutes.

Joshua shrugged.

'You can take it from me that he is,' Cox said. 'I know him when he makes up his mind about something. Wild horses couldn't change it.'

'Then I don't suppose you could arrange for me to accidentally meet the lady. I might be able to help you out by turning her head.'

'Hardly.'

'It is possible, I suppose,' Cox said in a pensive tone. 'Nothing to stop you inviting Sheffield to Pemberley for dinner, Fitzwilliam. I'm sure Mrs. Darcy won't mind.'

'It will never work,' Joshua said. 'Miss de Bourgh won't go against her mother's wishes.'

'Care to take a wager on that?' Sheffield asked smugly. 'I have a way with the ladies. Besides, if I do manage to pull it off, I'd make it worth your while, Fitzwilliam. Give you enough for you to keep your lady in style.'

'It don't sound as though you have much of a way with the lady you came up here to deal with.' Sheffield scowled at Joshua but said nothing. 'Talking of which, you can't even think about pursuing Miss de Bourgh if you're in dispute over this other property. Lady Catherine would cut her daughter off without a penny if she thought you were a-party to any questionable transactions, especially if there's a lady involved.'

Sheffield was quiet for a long time. Joshua's nerves were on edge, but he forced himself to remain quiet and let the man sup his ale while he thought things through. Cox opened his mouth to break the silence but Joshua kicked his shin and he quickly closed it again.

'Perdition, Mrs. Sheffield has left me with no choice.' Sheffield's expression filled with rage. 'I don't have time on my side, or I would — '

'But if you have genuine claim to the property, why would you give that up on the off chance that you might be able to woo Miss de Bourgh? I assume you have debts, who doesn't? But I dare say your creditors would be prepared to wait if they knew you have expectations.' Cox scratched his chin. 'This sudden desire to pursue a lady you've never met sounds a bit tenuous to me.'

'Stupidest idea I ever heard,' Joshua grumbled.

'Damned strong this ale.' Millie's rum measures were obviously generous this evening and Sheffield was already slurring his words. 'Truth to tell, I don't actually have a legitimate claim to the estate.' Joshua tensed. There, he'd said it, just like that. Cox had heard him. So too had Millie, who loitered directly behind their table. 'My brother intended to change his will, but didn't get around to it before he died. Didn't seem right that the cold bitch he was married to should get it all when I had toiled hard to get us to the point we were at. I'll admit I cut a few

274

corners, but taking chances is what I do best. My brother was cut from a different cloth and never would have had the nerve. Come to that, he never would have had anything if it weren't for me driving him on when all he could do was bleat about what might go wrong.' Sheffield leaned back in his chair and scratched his thigh. 'Anyway, Albert ain't no great loss, truth to tell. He died trying to save some damned useless slaves.' He rolled his eyes in disgust. 'What a fool!'

'If he was such a lost cause, how did he become a plantation owner?' Joshua asked.

'That was merely an accident of birth. He got all the help to get started simply because he was our father's favourite.' Sheffield focused a glower on his tankard, which was again almost empty. 'He was also better at routine than me, I'll give him that. Order, method, and prudence were his bywords. Me? I like to get something started, which I did by pointing out the opportunities in Jamaica to Albert, so the man owed me. No question about it.' He ground his jaw. 'And I aim to collect, one way or another. But I don't have time to wait for his widow to contest the will. There's an outside chance she might discover it's bogus.'

Sheffield was deranged, which made him dangerous and unpredictable. A cold chill worked its way through Joshua's body. He relaxed when he reminded himself that they had caught him out. He had condemned himself with his own words, and there was no further damage he could do to Celia or her property.

'Sounds as though you deserve something,' Cox agreed.

And he's about to get it, Joshua thought with satisfaction.

'Damned right I do,' Sheffield slurred.

'How did you come by a will?' Cox asked.

'I had someone in Jamaica forge it for me, along with a partnership agreement. It looks genuine and I figured she would believe it was. It fooled my brother's own solicitor, but the damned woman just won't lie down and accept it.' Sheffield jutted his chin. 'I really didn't think she would make so much fuss, and truth be told, I'm too hard pressed to wait on the off chance that she might feed me a few crumbs.' He sat forward and leaned both forearms on the table, suddenly appearing disconcertingly alert and sober. 'So, when can I meet the lovely Miss de Bourgh?'

'That won't be possible,' Joshua said, standing and pulling himself up to his full height.

'Hey, just a minute.' Sheffield's momentary

confusion gave way to anger. 'What is all this. You said — '

Cox stood also. 'No, I believe the suggestion came from you.'

'Did you just hear this man admit to trying to gull Mrs. Sheffield?' Joshua asked.

'Yes, sir,' Cox replied without hesitation. 'I heard him clear as day.'

'So did I,' Millie said cheerfully from behind them.

'Why should you care?'

'The game's up, Sheffield.' Joshua's harsh tone rang with the authority that usually saw the men beneath his command scurrying to carry out his orders. 'And here's what will happen. Firstly, you will write a letter confirming you are making no further claim upon Mrs. Sheffield's estate.'

'The devil I will!'

'When you have done that you will leave Derbyshire immediately. You will go nowhere near Mrs. Sheffield or her property ever again. If you do, I'll have you taken in charge to account for the crime you just admitted to in front of witnesses.'

'Mrs. Sheffield.' A slow grin of comprehension spread across Sheffield's face. 'She's the woman you've fallen for, ain't she? That's why you're trying to gull me. Well, you're wasting your time. She's as cold as ice. My brother told me as much. She's just used you to get the better of me, but you'll get nothing from her in return.'

The urge to strike the man grew more compelling by the minute. 'Unlike you, I do not help a lady in the expectation of receiving anything in return.'

Sheffield stood on unsteady legs and glowered at Joshua. 'This ain't over,' he said belligerently.

Before Joshua realised what he intended to do, Sheffield roared and aimed a roundhouse punch to his gut. Joshua turned sideways and deflected the worst of it, but it still hurt like the devil. Ignoring the pain, he drew back his arm and finally had the satisfaction of planting his clenched fist squarely in the centre of Sheffield's face. He thought of Celia and the pain this man had caused her, the future he ached to have with her but could not, and put all the force of his disappointment behind the punch.

Sheffield was knocked off his feet and landed on a stool that splintered beneath his weight. He cried out as blood spurted and bones cracked. Joshua had broken his nose.

Sheffield's features would never be quite as regular again.

A rough cheer went up from the watching crowd. Anyone connected with Pemberley was a firm favourite in this inn. Sheffield was an outsider. By throwing the first punch, the locals would know he had crossed Joshua and he would get no sympathy from them.

Joshua leaned over the prostrate man, felt inside his coat, and extracted the original copy of the will.

'Hey, that's mine.'

'I don't think so.' Joshua turned to a couple of the inn's servants. 'Help him pack and get him back on the road tonight,' he said, slipping them each a few coins. 'Cox, stay behind, make sure he writes that letter, and then ensure he leaves.'

16

'You are all to be congratulated.' Mr. Asquith's smile embraced all the actors. 'Everything is in readiness for tonight's performance. I suggest taking the remainder of the day to rest and prepare ourselves.'

A general murmur of accent greeted this suggestion.

'I shall never be able to settle to anything,' Georgiana said. 'I know it is only our family and neighbours we shall be performing for, and they are bound to be kind, but still . . . '

'Perhaps a brisk walk before luncheon will calm us all down,' Major Halstead suggested. 'It is a fine day, and a shame to remain indoors.'

'Very well.' Georgiana shared a brief glance with Kitty. 'Will you join us, Anne?'

'Thank you, but no.'

When applied to, Mrs. Bingley also declined. Anne couldn't blame her. Lizzy's good-natured sister had sat through endless rehearsals in her capacity as chaperone and probably desired some time for herself.

'Take a servant with you instead, Kitty,' she said.

The walking party went off to fetch outdoor clothing, leaving Anne alone with Mr. Asquith and Mrs. Bingley. Unsure what to do with herself, the decision was made for her when Mr. Asquith passed her a book, holding her gaze significantly as he did so.

'I believe you expressed an interest in this novel, Miss de Bourgh.'

Anne blinked. She did not recall discussing this particular tome with Pierce. She opened her mouth to express her surprise, looked down, and abruptly closed it again in an effort to stifle a gasp. There was a piece of paper jutting from between the pages.

'If you will excuse me, ladies,' he said, turning to leave the room.

'Certainly, Mr. Asquith,' Mrs. Bingley replied. 'I'm sure you would welcome a respite yourself.'

'I do have plans for the rest of the morning,' he said as he opened the door for them both.

Anne didn't think she would ever tire of his smile. Her heart lurched when she recalled that she would very soon have to. She sighed, absently waving to Mrs. Bingley when she excused herself from Anne and disappeared in the direction of her chamber.

Anne noticed Colonel Fitzwilliam lingering in the open doorway to the billiards room and gave him a little wave, to which he responded before returning to his game. His efforts to expose Mrs. Sheffield's brother-in-law for the fiend he was had been successful. Anne was very glad for the colonel's sake, but she also knew that after tonight's play they would have to inform Mama they had decided against marrying. Anne's stomach roiled in harmony with her already thumping heart as she anticipated that interview. Mama would be furious to have her hopes disappointed for a second time and Mr. Asquith would bear the brunt of her displeasure. Anne knew it, and so did Mr. Asquith. Pierce, she mentally amended.

Alone, Anne extracted the piece of paper from between the pages of the book and slowly unfolded it. It was covered by a few brief lines of Mr. Asquith — Pierce's — elegant hand.

> *Anne, please meet me beside Pegaz in half an hour. We have urgent matters to discuss and require absolute privacy in which to do so. PA*

Anne hugged the note to her breast — the first personal missive she had received from Pierce, and very possibly the last. Fearful of creasing it, because she knew she would never throw it away, Anne smoothed out the paper as she ascended the stairs. Naturally, she would keep the engagement. She couldn't refuse him anything. Besides, her curiosity was piqued. What could he possibly wish to talk to her about that necessitated absolute secrecy? Panic gripped her when she realised she would have to find her own way to the centre of the maze. Alone. She couldn't possibly.

Except, of course, she could. The old, helpless Anne had briefly reared her head, but Anne pushed her feeble objections aside. There were few things the new Miss de Bourgh would not attempt, especially if there was the remotest possibility of her actions earning Pierce's approval. Just keep turning right, she reminded herself as she snatched up a flimsy shawl and ran from her room without bothering with a bonnet. She didn't need to concern herself about Mama. Strangely, she had gone off in her carriage that morning without telling anyone where she was going.

Anne cut across the lawns at a brisk pace and reached the entrance to the maze without, as far as she could tell, being seen by anyone, not even a gardener. Taking a deep breath, she plunged between the tall beech hedges, which without Pierce's comforting presence seemed especially sinister and forbidding. Anne jumped at every sound, saw things that didn't exist in the shadowy hollows between the hedges. She swallowed down her anxiety and concentrated on turning right at each opportunity, determined to prove this simple task was well within her capabilities. She chose not to think what might happen if she took a wrong turn and became lost in the maze. The alarm would eventually be raised, she supposed, Pierce would have to admit what he had asked her to do, and his fate would then definitely be sealed.

She could not permit that to happen, but her resolve was almost immediately tested when she came upon a confusing crossroads that brought her to halting indecision. She convinced herself that the narrow right hand path was too insignificant to be an actual turn and so walked straight past it. Pierce's warning the last time they had done this together echoed through her mind, stopping her before she had advanced ten paces. *Never be tempted to deviate, and have the courage of your convictions.*

She turned back and took the narrow path, breathing a sigh of relief when it widened almost immediately. Pierce knew these traps waited to fool the unwary but had faith in her ability to tackle them alone.

Surely, it had not taken this long to find their way out of the labyrinth the last time? Once again, Anne was filled with doubts, until she remembered Pierce was waiting for her. She would walk barefoot over hot coals to reach his side, such was her total fixation with the man. Perhaps being with Pierce when they did this before and trusting his navigational skills — because there was absolutely nothing he could not do and do well — meant she had not noticed the passing of time.

She continued to walk on, more confidently now, turning right without having to think about it. It was with a small gasp of triumph that she unexpectedly emerged into the clearing with the statue of Pegaz dominating it. Pierce was already there, a lock of dark hair falling across his brow as he concentrated on the sketch he was working on, presumably of Pegaz.

He looked up when a twig snapped beneath her foot, put his pad aside and stood up, sending her an enticing smile.

'You found your way. I knew you would manage it.'

Anne felt tongue-tied and shy. She had always been that way in the past, but it was a situation that seldom happened when she was with Pierce because they always seemed to have so much to say to one another.

'Yes, I just kept turning right.' she replied, glancing at her feet because her heart was overflowing and if she looked at him she was sure she would give herself away.

'I am sorry if my invitation appeared mysterious, but I was anxious to see you, and knew if we met anywhere else, Mr. Collins would find us.'

Anne managed a brief smile. 'I expect he would.'

'Come and sit down.'

He held out a hand and Anne slipped hers into it. The moment she felt his warm skin against her un-gloved hand, his long fingers curling around her palm, her nervousness left her and she was able to meet his eye.

'Are you drawing Pegaz?' she asked.

'No.'

He seemed distracted and unsure of himself. 'Then what?'

He put the pad aside and didn't answer her. 'Colonel Fitzwilliam was successful,' he said, staring at a point somewhere beyond the silent statue.

'Yes, and I am glad for it.'

'You realise what that means?'

'Of course.' Anne shivered. 'We will perform the play tonight, and then tomorrow the colonel and I must face Mama.'

Pierce stood up and paced up and down in obvious agitation. Anne wanted to reassure him and opened her mouth to do so, but closed it without speaking. There was little she could say about his future, other than that Mama would give him a character. But would she? Now that she had wilfully disobeyed her, Anne was unsure if she would keep her word, and was unwilling to offer assurances she wasn't in a position to keep. Fidgeting, she waited for him to speak again.

'My timing is deplorable, I know that perfectly well.' He stopped directly in front of her and ran a hand through his hair. The thick, sleek locks fell directly back into place again, gleaming, unruffled. 'I am asking the impossible, but cannot seem to help asking it anyway. If, as I suspect, I am to be disappointed, I would prefer to know it now.'

To Anne's utter astonishment, he fell to one knee in front of her and took her hand. 'Will you do me the honour of becoming my wife, Anne?' he asked, his gorgeous eyes filled with uncertainty.

He looked up at her with a convincing display of adoration. Anne was too shocked, and too angry with him, to make any response. He must have sensed her feelings for him and was exploiting them to his own advantage. His cruelty took her breath away because, of course, it wasn't her he wanted, but Rosings.

Rosings, always Rosings.

She shook her head and brushed away an errant tear. She simply would not cry, or demonstrate any form of weakness before him. She was not her mother's daughter for nothing, and took refuge behind a haughty expression and her fierce personal pride.

'I know it is asking a great deal of you,' he said passionately, 'to give up everything you have been raised from the cradle to consider your own, but if I have learned nothing else in this world, at least I know that happiness is a rare and precious commodity.' Still grasping her hand, he implored her with his eyes. 'You have blossomed in the time I have known you from a shy, delicate creature into a woman in your own right with growing confidence, an enquiring mind, and lively spirit. With the restoration of your health has come a translucent beauty that is as compelling as it is precious. You have my total admiration, Anne. Even though we are poles apart in our situations in life, I feel we are also soul mates. Can you not feel it too?' He did not pause to allow her to respond. 'I have never felt this way before, and know I never will again. I cannot think what it is about you, but you have captured my heart.'

Anne knew precisely what it was. He might dress it up with pretty words and protestations of undying love, but Rosings was his ultimate goal. No one who looked like Pierce would choose her above her prettier, more confident sisters, unless he had a compelling financial incentive to do so.

Anger had filtered out his words and it took her a moment to appreciate what he had actually said.

'What do you mean, give up everything I have been raised to consider my own?' she asked.

He blinked, looking as surprised as she felt. Anne had to admire his acting skills. 'Why Rosings, of course,' he said. 'And your mother, I suppose.'

'Rosings.' Anne shook her head, totally bewildered. 'I'm sorry, did I hear you right? Are you saying you don't want me for Rosings?' Her mouth fell open in a most unladylike manner. 'I do not have the pleasure of understanding you. If you don't hanker after the estate, then what other reason could you possibly have — '

'Oh sweet love.' He gently cupped her chin with the fingers of one hand. 'I cannot bear to see how all this expectation has sapped your self-belief.'

'You make no sense, Pierce,' she replied, feeling dazed, unprepared to believe what he was actually saying.

'Then let me make myself clear. I would be lying if I said the proposition of Rosings was not attractive, but I am a realist, my love. Your mama requires you to marry a gentleman, not a plantation manager's son with barely three farthings to his name.'

'I am well aware of that,' Anne replied bitterly.

'You will soon be of age, free to do as you please. I realise I am asking you to forego your mother's love, as well as your birth right, and you will be reduced to living on what a school teacher can provide for you, but I have fallen in love with you.' He grasped her shoulders and fixed her with an intent look. 'You, Anne. Not Rosings, not your wealth and consequence but you — the real you. The lovely creature I have watched emerge like a butterfly from a chrysalis these past weeks.'

She looked up at him and knew in an instant that he was sincere. Her heart melted and happiness surged through her.

'Yes!' she cried joyously. 'Yes, yes, a thousand times yes.'

His arms closed around her and he expelled a long, expressive sigh. 'I did not mean for you to give me an answer immediately. You need time to consider. You will have to give up your fortune and most likely never know your mother again.'

'I care nothing for my fortune. I should be very sorry if my mother put pride before my happiness.' She paused, tilted her head back, and met Pierce's gaze. 'But if she forces me to choose between her and you, then I could not hesitate.'

'Your bravery leaves me speechless with admiration.'

Pierce lowered his head and kissed her deep and long, his arms holding her in a tight prison she had no wish to escape from as delicious sensations cascaded through her body. When he broke the kiss and they pulled apart they were both breathing deeply.

'I must make one stipulation,' she said.

'Name it,' he said, gently tucking a stray curl behind her ear.

'I do not require false compliments.'

He looked bemused. 'Whatever can you mean?'

'You spoke earlier of my beauty.' She laughed, wondering why the entire world was not laughing with her. Everyone deserved to be as deliriously happy as she was at that moment. 'I have never been beautiful, nor will I ever be, but if you like me the way I am then that is enough for me.'

Pierce shook his head. 'Come and see this.'

He led her to the bench and picked up his discarded sketch. 'You asked me what I was drawing when you arrived.'

Anne looked at his picture and gasped. It was a very flattering, very well executed likeness of herself. 'I do not look a bit like that.'

'You mistake the matter. When we are alone and you feel as though you can be yourself, when you ask me a particular question about some point in literature or other that has been perplexing you, that is exactly how you look. Your eyes widen, your lips . . . well, we will not talk about your lips or I will be compelled to kiss you again. And once I start that, I might never stop.'

'I feel numb with happiness,' she said simply. 'Never in my wildest dreams — '

'We have a lot of hurdles to clear before we can be together. First of all, your mother will be angry with you and the colonel. Then she will almost certainly dismiss me. Even if Sir Marius convinces her that I am not the rogue she takes me for, she will separate us as a punishment.'

'Yes, I know.'

'There are six months before you come of age. I wanted to speak to you today because I don't know how much more time we have together before I am cast out. Your mother will start looking for another husband for you immediately. If you are serious in your love for me, which, by the way, you have not put into words, then we ought to make plans for our future together, while we have the chance.'

She laughed, stood on her toes and placed a gentle kiss on his lips. 'How could you ever doubt my feelings? I love you, Pierce. If I did not, I would not find the courage to stand up to Mama. But I will stand up to her. Never doubt it. No man she tries to push on me will find favour.' She smiled up at him and reached up to touch his face. 'Only you, my love. Always you.'

'I shall take myself off once I lose my position. Hard as it will be to part from you, I shall endeavour to find something else, and I will be at Rosings on the morning of your twenty-first birthday, ready to take you away with me.'

'We could always elope.'

He looked scandalised. 'We most certainly could not. I will not marry you in a tawdry ceremony over the anvil, as though I was ashamed of you. We will marry before God and a parson in a church of your choosing.'

'Whatever you say,' Anne replied, biting her lip because all this smiling surely was not ladylike.

His arm closed around her and suddenly six months seemed more like an eternity.

17

Lizzy heartily wished Mr. Collins back in Hunsford; a place to which he seemed in no particular hurry to transport himself. One additional guest in a property as vast as Pemberley ought not to make any difference, and nor would it if that guest was anyone other than Mr. Collins. He had a happy knack of tracking her down wherever she happened to be and insisting upon bearing her company. She tolerated him and his long-winded speeches because he was her relation, and because she would not wish him upon the others.

Now Mr. Collins had nothing to do with himself, Lizzy fell over him at every turn, and could no longer call her house her own. She managed to remain civil and polite — until this morning. Mr. Collins had chosen to advise her against something trivial, and she could take no more. Unless she found a way to distract him, she would most likely say something she would later regret. Will, Fitzwilliam and Mr. Bingley had taken refuge in the billiards room, Jane was resting, glad to be relieved of her chaperone duties, most of the young people were out walking and Lizzy was stuck with Mr. Collins. Again.

That did not seem fair.

She told him the gentlemen needed him to make up the numbers. Lizzy watched him bustle away, muttering something about billiards being a perfectly acceptable pastime for gentlemen of quality provided, of course, that no wagers were struck and play did not take place on the Sabbath. She suppressed a smile, anticipating the revenge Will would extract later in the privacy of their chambers.

Giddy with relief, Lizzy headed for the gardens, looking forward to a long, solitary stroll. She had not been outside for more than five minutes before she noticed Anne and Mr. Asquith approaching from the direction of the maze. Surely they had not been . . . Lizzy grinned, thinking that they very likely had. Anne appeared flushed yet radiant. Mr. Asquith seemed quietly pleased about something. They were in deep conversation, heads close together, and were almost upon Lizzy before they noticed her.

'Mrs. Darcy.' Mr. Asquith's head jerked away from Anne's. 'Forgive me. I did not see you there.'

'We have been exploring the maze,' Anne explained, blushing crimson.

'Have you indeed. I hope you did not get

lost in it.' Although Lizzy rather thought Anne would enjoy getting lost with Mr. Asquith, and he with her.

'Pray excuse me, Mrs. Darcy,' Mr. Asquith said. 'I have a few matters to attend to regarding tonight's performance.'

'By all means.' Lizzy turned towards Anne and together they watched Mr. Asquith until he disappeared into the house. 'Walk with me, Anne, unless exploring mazes has exhausted you.'

'Not in the least. Besides, I was hoping to catch you alone.'

'Without Mr. Collins dogging my footsteps, you mean.' Lizzy rolled her eyes. 'I am seriously considering taking up residence in my private sitting room. It is about the only place in the house where he cannot intrude.'

Anne laughed. 'He can be rather tenacious.'

'That is not the word I would use to describe him, but I shall not offend your ears by using a more appropriate one.' She linked arms with Anne and together they crossed the lawns at a slow pace, taking a track that bordered the trees at the far end of the reflecting ponds. 'Now what did you wish to speak with me about?' Lizzy laughed. 'As if I couldn't guess.'

Anne chewed her lower lip, but a grin still

escaped. 'Am I so very transparent?'

'You are violently in love, and it shows.' Anne gasped but Lizzy waved a hand to prevent her from interrupting. 'Your complexion glows, your eyes sparkle, and you cannot seem to stop smiling. Colonel Fitzwilliam has not inspired such a change in you. That does not leave many other candidates.'

Anne winced. 'Colonel Fitzwilliam plans to tell Mama of our decision not to marry after the play, probably tomorrow morning.'

'And when does Mr. Asquith plan to speak with her?'

'There's no point.' Anne shook her head. 'Mama will never agree to the union.'

'No, I dare say she will not.' Lizzy felt terribly sorry for Anne. She had changed from a timid mouse into a lively, independent woman with character and determination. Lizzy didn't doubt that she would marry Asquith as soon as she was of age, regardless of her mother's feelings, forfeiting her fortune for the man she adored. Even so, it could not be an easy decision to have to make, choosing between one's mother — no matter how dictatorial — and one's heart's desire. 'Presumably the liaison in the maze was arranged by Mr. Asquith so he could propose.'

Anne's smile widened. 'Yes.' She gave her head a defiant toss. 'And I have accepted him.'

'I am very glad to hear it. I hope you will be very happy.'

'You approve?' Anne looked relieved. 'I hoped you might, but I thought you would caution me against giving up Rosings. I shall have to, and everyone will think I am out of my senses. But, to tell you the truth, it feels as though a great weight has been lifted from my shoulders. I know Mr. Asquith wants me for myself and not for Rosings, you see, because he is aware Mama will disinherit me and he doesn't care. Well, of course he would much prefer to be master of Rosings, but he is sensible enough to know that cannot be.'

Lizzy smiled. It was the longest speech she had ever heard Anne make. Being in love, and defiant, had made her loquacious.

'You never know.'

'Oh, I know. Mama hates being defied and will never tolerate it from me. Mr. Asquith declared himself now because he is convinced he will be dismissed the moment Mama learns the colonel and I do not plan to wed. He wanted to know how I felt, but can you believe this?' Anne stopped walking and turned to face Lizzy, her eyes glowing. 'He actually thought I would reject him. How silly!'

'Mr. Asquith is a fine young man. I am sure you will be very happy.'

'Yes, I am sure of that too, although I expect I shall feel guilty about Mama for a long time. She will be very lonely in that big house without me, but she would never admit it.'

'Will Mr. Asquith start looking for a new position?'

'Yes, he will have to.'

'Then I shall have a word with Mr. Darcy. He has a lot of influence around these parts, and if anyone is in need of a tutor, then I am sure he will be happy to recommend Mr. Asquith.'

'Oh, thank you. That is very kind. I should like to be close to Pemberley.' Anne looked startled. 'Who would have imagined me ever saying that?'

'Times and circumstances change.'

'That is certainly true. Speaking of which, please make sure any positions on offer allow for a wife to remain with her husband. I do not intend to cross swords with Mama, only to be separated from Mr. Asquith.'

Lizzy laughed. 'As if I could overlook anything so important.'

They strolled along the treeline. With the arrival of autumn, the leaves had started to turn glorious shades of red, russet, and brown. Because they were both looking up, they did not see a man emerge from the tree line until they almost bumped into him.

'Miss de Bourgh?' the man asked, sweeping off his hat and executing an elegant bow.

Fear trickled down Lizzy's spine. She had never met this man, but knew at once whom he must be. His nose was swollen and crooked, as though it had recently been broken. She recalled seeing scratches on Colonel Fitzwilliam's knuckles last night. It did not take a genius to put the two things together. This was Percival Sheffield, and he had sneaked onto the Pemberley estate.

Before Lizzy could turn and call for help, Anne spoke.

'Yes, I am Anne de Bourgh. Who are you and what do you want of me?'

'Anne, run!'

Anne turned to look at Lizzy with a quizzical expression, but didn't move. 'Why?'

Perdition, Anne. Just run. Anne still didn't move. What to do? With seconds to react, Lizzy could do nothing more than thrust herself between Anne and Sheffield.

'Leave this property at once,' she said. 'You are trespassing.'

'Gladly, but I won't be leaving alone. Stand aside.'

Lizzy spread her arms in a futile attempt to

hide Anne from his view, as if by not seeing her, he would forget she was there. 'Certainly not.'

'Very well then. Have it your way.'

Sheffield gave Lizzy a vicious shove, causing her to lose her balance. She gave a startled cry and fell heavily to the ground. Her head swirled, and her first thought was for the baby she carried. *Please God, don't let it be harmed*. She was conscious of Anne crouching beside her, her brow creased with concern. Lizzy wanted to tell her to flee while she still could, but it was too late now to do anything. She watched, helpless as Sheffield bent down, scooped Anne from the ground, threw her bodily over his shoulder, and disappeared into the trees.

* * *

Joshua caught Darcy's eye across the table. This was purgatory, attempting a serious game of billiards with Collins, who could barely strike the ball cleanly. Joshua could see that Darcy had reached the end of his patience. Following his example, he replaced his cue in the rack. Bingley did so too, claiming the need to check on his wife. Darcy disappeared in the direction of the estate office and Joshua made a hasty exit also, leaving Collins standing beside the table, looking rather stupid with a cue still in his hand.

Joshua strode away from the room, mentally rehearsing what he planned to say to Lady Catherine when the time came, and encountered Asquith crossing the vestibule.

'A perfectly good game of billiards was brought to an end by Collins,' he explained by way of greeting.

Asquith expressed sympathy. 'Does he know how to play?'

'Barely. His cueing was so uncoordinated that we feared for Darcy's baize.'

Joshua glanced out the window and smiled at the sight of Mrs. Darcy and Anne arm in arm on the farthest edge of the lawn. His smile turned into a frown when it occurred to him that something wasn't quite right. The ladies were talking to a man who approached them from the trees. At first he thought it might be one of the estate's keepers, but soon realised his mistake when the rogue knocked Mrs. Darcy violently to the ground.

'Asquith, look!'

Asquith did so, and paled. 'Quick! That's Sheffield and he has Anne. We must do something.'

Both men headed for the door at a run. Joshua paused to tell a footman to summon

Darcy from the estate office. They raced across the expanse of grass, not wasting breath by speaking. How the devil had Sheffield come to be on Pemberley land? Cox had put him on the London coach, but he had obviously got off at the first stop and doubled back, bent on revenge. Deuce take it, Joshua should have considered that possibility.

They reached Mrs. Darcy, who was attempting to sit up.

'He took Anne,' she said, gasping. 'Someone has to stop him.'

'Stay with Mrs. Darcy, Asquith.'

'No, you stay. I shall get Anne back.' Asquith's tone brooked no argument. 'Which is the most likely direction for him to have taken?'

'There's a path directly through the woods to the perimeter of the estate,' Joshua replied. 'He probably has a horse tethered there. Go! I shall send others after you as soon as they get here.'

'You go too, Colonel. You know the estate. I shall be fine.'

Asquith disappeared but Joshua could not leave Mrs. Darcy. She was in a delicate condition, and Darcy would crucify him when he saw what had happened to her. And so he should. This was all Joshua's fault. He had been told Sheffield was both devious and intelligent. When such a man lost all expectation, it stood to reason he would become unpredictable.

Darcy came racing across the lawn, several footmen in his wake.

'Lizzy!' he cried, crouching down and cradling his wife's head. 'Are you hurt?'

★ ★ ★

Anne could not believe her own stupidity. This oaf had no business being on the Pemberley estate, springing out of the woods and accosting them. She ought to have heeded Lizzy's warning and taken to her heels instead of standing there like a fool. But even if she had reacted quicker and understood the danger, she still would not have done that and left Lizzy to face this brute alone. She was in a delicate condition and could not run. Lord above, the man knocked her down! If she or the baby were hurt, Mr. Darcy's fury would know no bounds.

Don't think about that now, she told herself. There was nothing she could do to help Lizzy. Instead, she concentrated on her own situation. Her head bumped repeatedly against the man's back as he clutched her legs and moved through the trees at a rapid pace. She was unable to kick him because he had too tight a hold on her calves, but she refused to be kidnapped without making a fight of it. She tried wriggling around. If Sheffield — for she realised now that was whom he must be — was inconvenienced by her movements, it didn't slow him down. She didn't weigh very much, and he appeared to be discouragingly strong.

There must be something she could do to help herself, or at least delay him until reinforcements arrived.

'Where are you taking me?'

'Be quiet or it will be the worse for you.'

Nothing could be worse than this. This had proven to be the very best morning of her entire life, and the very worst. She had accepted a proposal of marriage from a man who had demonstrated his absolute love for her in the most romantic fashion imaginable, and then was careless enough to allow herself to be kidnapped by a desperate fiend. She had once thought her life dull and tedious. At that particular moment, she would not complain about a little tedium.

He would have a horse somewhere, she thought. She could not allow him to get her on its back and take her off the estate. If that happened, she might never be found. Either way, her reputation would be in tatters. In some respects, that might work in her favour since it would be social suicide. All her money and position would be insufficient to restore her to society's good graces, and Mama could hardly object to her marrying Mr. Asquith. Even so, she would infinitely prefer to be rescued before Mama returned from her mysterious outing, then she need know nothing about it.

Her hopes improved when her abductor turned off the path and took a narrow fork, reminding her of her earlier journey through the maze. Was that only an hour or so ago? Clearly, he meant to hide her on the estate until the search went wider. Anne tugged one of the yellow ribbons from her hair and dropped it at the juncture of the main path and the fork Sheffield had taken. It would be impossible for her pursuers to miss. Impossible for Sheffield to miss as well if he happened to look back. Fortunately that did not happen. He seemed too intent upon reaching his destination before anyone caught up with him.

They reached a ramshackle building. Anne thought it was probably an abandoned woodsman's cottage. Even from her undignified upside down position over Sheffield's shoulder she could see the roof had collapsed and the entire structure looked on the point of falling in on itself. This man had chosen well, especially given how little time he must have had to reconnoitre. But for her ribbon, she doubted whether anyone would think to look in this direction.

Sheffield ducked his head as he carried her through the crooked doorway and threw her, none too gently, onto some foul-smelling sacking. She sent him a murderous glare as she rubbed her sore limbs, but he didn't appear to notice. Satisfied that she was uninjured, Anne took a good look around the place. It exuded an aroma of damp and decay, and had only one way in and out through the doorway Sheffield was blocking with his bulk. The walls were of flimsy timber, and looked as though a strong male shoulder would be able to knock them down. Unfortunately, one as feeble as her own would never do the job.

She looked up at her abductor, adopting one of her mother's most aloof expressions.

'What do you want with me?' she asked imperiously, furious rather than afraid.

'Blame your friend Fitzwilliam.' Sheffield's voice was nasal thanks to his broken nose. 'He took what was mine, and I'm returning the favour.'

'If you think you will get away with this

then you are deluded.'

'I got you this far, didn't I?'

'And they will find you.'

'Nah, they'll go straight for the perimeter. Thanks to Fitzwilliam, I knew you was likely to leave here tomorrow, once your Mama realised the two of you ain't set on marrying. Still, Percival Sheffield don't need long to make plans. I have an accomplice who will collect us at nightfall and take us somewhere safe. That will give Mama time to get really worried. Then, when I make my demands tomorrow, she will fall over herself to pay me. From what I hear, she will hardly notice the loss.'

'They know who you are. It is hard to disguise oneself with a broken nose.'

Sheffield snarled at her. 'I shall be long gone, back to Jamaica, by the time they think to hunt me down. Besides, they won't make a fuss for fear of damaging your precious reputation.'

Very likely, but Anne remained silent rather than giving the odious man the satisfaction of knowing he was right.

* * *

'Is Mrs. Darcy all right?' Asquith asked when Joshua and two footmen caught up with him.

Joshua's lips tightened. 'She says she is. Darcy is not so sure. Any sign of Sheffield?'

'Not so far, but he must have taken this path.'

'There is no profit in stealth,' Joshua said. 'We must stop him taking her off the estate at all costs.'

Asquith led the way, moving fast as they all kept a close eye on the ground. It had rained heavily a few days ago, and footprints made by a man bearing the weight of a young lady over his shoulder had sunk into the loamy leaf mould. Joshua continuously glanced ahead but saw no movement, heard no unnatural sounds. Why wasn't Anne screaming as loud as she could? She must know they would be immediately on her trail. Although perhaps she did not. She and Mrs. Darcy had been some distance from the house, and it was pure chance that he and Asquith happened to observe the abduction.

'If anything happens to Miss de Bourgh, if Sheffield harms so much as one hair on her head, I will not be held responsible for my actions,' Asquith muttered, his expression murderous.

Joshua slapped his shoulder. 'She is too important to him to risk harming her.'

'That had damned well better be the case.' He ground his jaw. 'She is my responsibility but I was not there to protect her when she needed me the most. I am a miserable failure.'

'Don't waste time on regrets,' Joshua replied. 'It does no good.'

'Here, what's this?'

Asquith stopped abruptly, and Joshua almost cannoned into his back. He held a finger to his lips, advising caution.

'This is the ribbon Anne had in her hair earlier,' he whispered, glancing further along the main path. 'The footsteps end here. They only go one way, which is towards Pemberley, so Sheffield must have taken this path to try and fool us. Miss de Bourgh kept her wits about her. I told her leaving signs was a good way not to get lost in a maze. Do we know what's down here?'

'There used to be a woodsman's cottage, but it was abandoned years ago when I was still a boy,' Joshua whispered back.

'A perfect hiding place,' Asquith said softly. 'We never would have thought to look there.'

'How did he find it?' Joshua mused.

'He must have an accomplice, someone he met at the inn. I can't think how else he can have done it. He would not risk trying to get back to the perimeter in case we caught up with him. Besides, being mounted on a horse in broad daylight with an unwilling lady

310

would attract attention.'

'Right, this is what we ought to do.' Joshua took control because he was a soldier accustomed to doing so. 'There are four of us against one, but we don't know if Sheffield is armed. If he is, you can be sure he will hurt Miss de Bourgh if that's what it takes to get away. He won't be expecting us to find him, but he will still be alert.'

'What do you have in mind, sir?' Asquith asked.

'A ruse,' Joshua replied. 'He knows me and wants his revenge. I suggest I walk right up to the door, without using any stealth. I will tell him others are searching farther into the woods, but I plan to take Anne back from him then and there.'

'And in the meantime, we will have crept to all sides of the building,' Asquith said. 'While you two argue, we swoop in and get Anne.'

'Precisely, but only when I give you the signal. Are we ready?'

Everyone nodded, and Joshua, his expression grim, strode purposefully up the path.

★ ★ ★

Anne thought Sheffield had probably been a handsome man before the colonel broke his nose, but there was also a petulance about

311

him. He was the sort who assumed life owed him a living simply because he had looks and charm. Anne could well understand why Mrs. Sheffield wanted nothing to do with him. Unfortunately, Anne currently had a great deal to do with him. She didn't think he would actually kill her. If he did that, his financial expectations would die with her. She suppressed a shudder when she considered there were worse things he could do to her.

He stared at her, his expression cruel and calculating, unnerving her, but she refused to show any reaction whatsoever. She occupied her mind by wondering instead if she and Lizzy had been missed yet. Most likely not, but she refused to be discouraged. The hour for luncheon was approaching, and the alarm would then be raised. Pierce knew they were walking together, and she was sure they had been seen at one point by at least one gardener. Her ribbon would be found and then . . . and then what? Sheffield would not let her go without putting up a fight, would he?

She received her answer when she heard someone approaching — someone who was making no effort to do so quietly. Sheffield tensed, but Anne's heart lifted.

'What the devil?' Sheffield peered through the doorway and an evil grin spread across his face. 'Morning, Colonel. You should not have come, but I am very glad you did. You and I have unfinished business.'

'I am hardly likely to let you kidnap my cousin and do nothing about it.'

Anne wanted to cry with relief when the colonel peered past Sheffield's shoulder to ensure she was unharmed. She had never been more pleased to see anyone in her life. She smiled at him and nodded once, which appeared to satisfy him.

'The way I see it, you'll do nothing about it now 'cause you have to get past me to get to her, and I won't let you catch me unawares a second time.'

'You are still on Pemberley land, Sheffield, and will not be allowed to leave it with Miss de Bourgh. If you try to harm her in any way then you will lose your only bargaining tool and swing for your crime.'

'It might almost be worth hurting her,' he snarled, 'because I know you will be blamed for pulling her into your scheme.'

'I volunteered,' Anne said sweetly.

Sheffield turned to glance briefly at her. His eyes widened, and she took satisfaction from having shocked him. 'You knew what they were doing?'

Anne shrugged. 'The colonel would not do something like that without my permission.'

'So, Sheffield, what is it to be?'

Anne's sight of the colonel was impaired by Sheffield's body, but she was sure her rescuer had his hands behind his back, making some sort of signal with them. She understood the colonel's plan now, or thought she did. He was taunting Sheffield into fighting with him, aware that Sheffield couldn't fight and keep her from running. In his haste to abduct her, he had overlooked the very obvious need for rope to restrain her. Perhaps he was not so intelligent after all. What self-respecting kidnapper went about his business without a way to keep his captive subdued?

She would not like to see Colonel Fitzwilliam come to any harm in a fight, but was fairly sure he would be able to overcome Sheffield. Sheffield clearly thought the same thing because instead of standing to face the colonel, he moved back into the hut, pulled Anne to her feet, and thrust her in front of him, a dagger at her throat.

'Very brave,' the colonel said in an indolent tone. 'Hiding behind a lady's petticoats.'

'A change of plan,' Sheffield replied. 'Miss de Bourgh and I are leaving the estate, and if you attempt to prevent us then she will suffer the consequences.'

A crystalline stillness filled the hovel, broken only by the sound of Sheffield's rapid breathing and the beating of Anne's heart. She felt the cold steel of the dagger nicking the skin at her throat, and sensed a wild desperation about Sheffield's behaviour. Truly afraid now, she implored the colonel with her eyes to do something to help her. She dare not move her head for fear of the dagger actually penetrating her skin. The colonel nodded just once and definitely made a signal behind his back this time. Now that she was standing in front of Sheffield she saw it quite plainly.

The next second a thunderous noise came from the back of the small hut. The crumbling wooden wall crashed in, and Pierce stood there, glowering at Sheffield, magnificent in his anger. Sheffield himself had turned to see what was happening, loosening his hold on Anne just enough for her to dip beneath his arms and flee straight into the colonel's arms. He swept her from the ground, and they watched Pierce as he floored Sheffield with two massive punches, adding more damage to his nose and, unless Anne was mistaken, relieving him of several teeth.

'It's all over,' the colonel said. 'Are you all right?'

She nodded. 'Yes, he didn't actually hurt me, just scared me half to death.'

'That is as well for him,' Pierce said, taking her from the colonel and swinging her effortlessly into his arms. 'Come along. I shall take you back to the house while the colonel deals with the mess here.'

18

'Are you absolutely sure that you are both all right?' Will asked for the tenth time, sitting beside Lizzy in the small salon and holding her hand, mindless of the fact Anne, Mr. Asquith, and the colonel were also in the room. 'You look fearsome pale.'

'Yes,' Lizzy replied. 'Please stop fussing.'

'The doctor has been sent for,' Will said. 'I want his reassurance. I do not trust you to tell me the truth.'

'I am so very sorry this happened,' the colonel said. 'I underestimated Sheffield.'

'Well, he is locked safely away in the cellars for the time being,' Will replied, scowling, 'until we decide what to do with him.'

Lizzy blinked. 'Surely, he must answer for his crimes?'

'Not if we wish to protect Anne's reputation and keep this business secret from Lady Catherine,' Will said.

'Ah yes.' Lizzy nodded. 'I had not considered that.'

'It is fortunate Mama is not here today,' Anne said. 'I have a great curiosity to know where she has gone, but would infinitely prefer her not to know what happened.'

'I'm glad you found a reason to send Mr. Collins into Lambton,' Lizzy said to her husband. 'He knew something was not quite right, and he is perfectly capable of listening at doors.'

'Especially if he thought he might overhear something to my detriment,' Mr. Asquith said. 'And he would have done too. This is as much my fault as it is yours, Colonel. I ought to have taken better care of Miss de Bourgh.'

Unlike Will, Mr. Asquith was not actually free to touch his beloved, but that did not prevent him from fixing her with a look of such total adoration that no one in the room could have misinterpreted its true meaning.

'We should not waste time castigating blame,' Will said. 'Instead we must decide what to do about Sheffield.'

'He could be put on a ship back to Jamaica,' Anne suggested. 'That is where he planned to go once he extracted money for my release.'

'We could,' Will agreed. 'But that would hardly be punishment, and what is to stop him from returning to England and trying something even more desperate?'

'Surely he could be prosecuted for trying to

steal Mrs. Sheffield's estate,' Lizzy said. 'That would not implicate anyone.'

'Yes, that might be the best thing to do,' Will agreed. 'If he starts making accusations about Anne, no one will believe him because no one but those of us in this room knows about it. My servants will not say a word. You had best warn Mrs. Sheffield and obtain her agreement first, Fitzwilliam.'

The colonel nodded. 'Very well. I shall speak to her this evening when they come to dinner.'

'What about Sheffield's accomplice?' Lizzy pointed out. 'Do we know who it was?'

'Oh yes, we had a frank discussion about that,' the colonel replied, flexing his grazed knuckles. Lizzy was sure there were fresh cuts on them. 'A groom was dismissed by your steward for pilfering, Darcy, and bears a grudge. Sheffield heard him grumbling about Pemberley while in the taproom and fell into conversation with him. Sheffield knew where the man lived and looked him up as soon as he got back to Lambton. He only went five miles out of the village, by the way, had the coach stop on some pretence, and made his way directly back.'

'What is this accomplice's name?' Will asked. The colonel provided it. 'Right, I shall make sure he says nothing about his part in all of this. It will be the worse for him if he does.'

'Good,' the colonel replied. 'Then we are agreed on our course of action.'

Everyone confirmed that to be the case.

'We can now put the matter behind us and look forward to the play this evening, 'Anne said.

'Are you sure you should participate, Anne?' Will asked. 'You have had a shock.'

'I would not think of letting the others down. Besides, if I do not take my part we shall have to cancel and explain why. Mama would then know.'

Before the matter could be discussed further, the door opened and Lady Catherine sailed through it, an unknown gentleman beside her. Unknown to everyone in the room except Mr. Asquith, it appeared.

'Sir Marius,' he said, looking astounded.

★ ★ ★

So that is where Mama has been all day, Anne thought incredulously. She had received a reply to her letter to Sir Marius and had gone to meet him somewhere in private. How extraordinary. Mama looked different too. Animated, younger, less disapproving. Anne studied Sir Marius as she waited her turn to

320

be introduced, intrigued by Pierce's mentor. He was perhaps fifty years old, with thick grey hair and whiskers, a deeply tanned face etched with lines and a tall, upright stance. He must have once been very handsome. He was still elegant and commanded one's attention.

She watched as he greeted Pierce by clasping his shoulder and shaking his hand for a prolonged time.

'It is a pleasure to see you again, my boy,' Sir Marius said.

'As it is you, sir. I trust I see you well.'

'Fit as a flea,' Sir Marius replied cheerfully.

Anne breathed an inaudible sigh of relief. If there were any truth in Mr. Collins's accusations, Sir Marius and Pierce would not be on such congenial terms.

'Ah, so you are Miss de Bourgh,' Sir Marius said when Anne made her curtsey. 'I have heard a great deal about you, and it is a pleasure to make your acquaintance.'

When everyone was seated and refreshments had been served, it was Sir Marius who broke the silence.

'I dare say you all wonder what brought me here uninvited, and where Lady Catherine and I have been all day.'

'You are very welcome here, sir,' Lizzy said.

'Thank you, Mrs. Darcy. I would not have

dreamed of intruding, had I not received Lady Catherine's letter. When I heard of the accusations my daughter levelled against Asquith, I knew a visit in person was necessary to set the record straight.'

Everyone probably felt as uncomfortable as Anne did about having the subject discussed so openly. But no one could feel greater curiosity than she did.

'I came to England because I plan to return here permanently. My wife died a year ago, during rioting by slaves from an adjoining plantation, so there's nothing left in Jamaica for me.'

'I am sure we are all very sorry for your loss,' Mr. Darcy said.

'Thank you, sir.' Sir Marius rubbed the back of his neck. 'Now, where was I? Ah yes, I was explaining about Jamaica. The place ain't what it once was. I have seen the best of it, made my fortune, and want to end my days on British soil. All of my children are either married, or at school over here. Miranda is the only one still living beneath my roof, and there's a reason for that.' This time he rubbed his bristled jaw and took a sip of his tea. 'She's a charming chit, but not quite right in the head. We all knew it the moment she came into the world. Asquith here took especial care with her schooling, showing devilish patience because she was slow, you see. She mistook Asquith's patience as something more and got quite fixated on him.'

'Ah,' Colonel Fitzwilliam said softly.

'Quite so,' Sir Marius replied. 'That was one of the reasons why I suggested he return to England. Her memory isn't all that, and she was bound to forget him. But the moment we got here she found out where he was, waited until I was out of the way, and took off after him.' Sir Marius shook his head. 'I never would have credited her with that much guile. Anyway, Asquith is blameless in the entire affair.'

'And yet kept silent when accused in order to protect the lady's reputation,' Lizzy said. 'I applaud your conduct, Mr. Asquith.'

Pierce inclined his head. 'Thank you. I am grateful to Lady Catherine for not accepting Mr. Collins's account at face value.'

'I was acquainted with Sir Marius when I was a girl,' she replied. 'I knew he would not recommend a man unworthy of his endorsement.'

'Well, Sir Marius, I do hope you will stay tonight and watch the play Mr. Asquith is putting on for our entertainment,' Mrs. Darcy said.

'Are you taking part in it, Miss de Bourgh?'

'Yes, sir, I am.'

'Then I shall stay with pleasure. Thank you very much.' He turned towards Pierce. 'Dolores, Daphne and . . . er — '

'That's the one, sir. I had no notice to prepare anything else.'

Sir Marius laughed. 'Asquith wrote that himself. Don't suppose he told you that.'

'No,' Anne replied. 'He did not.'

'Wrote it and put it on in Jamaica with half my brood participating in it. Best entertainment we had in years.'

'Well then,' Mrs. Darcy replied. 'I now have an even greater desire to see it.'

Simpson was summoned to show Sir Marius to his chamber and Anne took the opportunity to escape to her own. She had had a very full day, and it was far from over. She had no wish to see the doctor because there was absolutely nothing wrong with her, although she was very glad he had been called to attend Lizzy. She would never forgive herself if anything happened to the baby.

★ ★ ★

Joshua slid his arms into the coat Cox held out for him. He was nervous and on edge. The Briars and Celia would be arriving momentarily. When the play was over, he would be seated at table with her and knew it would be a living hell. He wanted her more than ever. The passion that burned inside of him could not be suppressed and so had to be endured with fortitude.

Celia was at her loveliest that evening. She wore a shimmering turquoise gown with delicate lace bows running from bosom to hem, its small capped sleeves trimmed with similar lace, drawing one's attention to her fine figure. Her eyes sought out Joshua the moment she entered the drawing room, and he was powerless to look away from her.

There was no time for them to converse in private before they were ushered into the music room. The gentlemen helped the ladies into chairs and took the ones behind them. Joshua did his damnedest not to sit behind Celia, but somehow that was how it turned out, and he was tortured by the sight of her lovely profile for the entire production. Her laughter rang in his ears, and every so often she looked back to share her pleasure with him. *Ye gods, this is purgatory!*

The play itself was light-hearted, funny in places, and surprisingly well acted given the limited amount of time they had had to prepare. The girls threw themselves whole-heartedly into their parts, and Captain Turner did not once stutter over his lines. The scenery the girls had agonised over appeared natural enough with the lights lowered, but even if it had not, no one was of a mind to criticise.

Lady Catherine and Sir Marius sat together, slightly apart from the rest of the audience. Joshua's aunt appeared to enjoy herself and actually laughed aloud in places. Joshua was astonished. He could not recall ever hearing her laughing aloud before. She considered such conduct unladylike. She had been heard to mutter disapproving comments all week about the play itself. Had anyone but Asquith suggested it, Joshua was sure Anne would not have been permitted to participate. He was filled with curiosity regarding her tolerance for Asquith, which obviously had something to do with Sir Marius, who certainly had a beneficial effect upon her temperament.

When the play ended, the applause was loud and prolonged. The players, flushed with success, mingled with the audience to accept individual congratulation — his cousin Anne included. He was probably not the only person to notice she never strayed far from Asquith's side, or the long probing glances they shared.

Joshua had the pleasure of escorting Celia into dinner, which was a rowdy affair and presented no opportunity for them to speak in private. And speak in private they must since Joshua had been charged with securing her agreement to prosecute Sheffield. The gentlemen did not linger over their port, and Joshua knew he must now find an opportunity to see her alone. He would obtain her consent and never see her again after tonight.

He was the last to leave the dining room. He followed the other gentlemen towards the drawing room but was waylaid by the feel of a feminine hand reaching out to rest on his arm. He did not need to look down to know who owned that hand.

'If I did not know better,' said the melodic voice that haunted his dreams, 'I would say you were avoiding me, Colonel.'

Joshua sent her a raffish grin, he simply couldn't help himself, and steered her into the vacant small sitting room. 'We have been in one another's company the entire evening.'

'But there has been no opportunity for me to thank you for your kindness.'

'No thanks are necessary. It was entirely my pleasure.'

'I did not know quite what to think when the will and Percival's written recantation regarding his claim to my property arrived and you did not accompany them.'

'There was no need for me to push myself

upon you,' he said, looking everywhere except at her. Perhaps that way she would understand she was under no obligation to him.

'I might have been anxious to be pushed upon, as you so charmingly put it.'

'Celia, don't.' He turned away from her. 'I rejoin my regiment in a few days' time, and I dare say you are anxious to return to Buckinghamshire.'

'That is a miserable excuse for your neglect.' Still turned away from her, he heard the condemnation in her tone. 'I thought we knew one another better than that.'

Dear lord, she was not making this easy for him. 'Something happened today that you need to be aware of,' he replied in a deliberate change of subject.

Succinctly, he outlined the events of the day. Celia clapped a hand over her mouth, rightly appalled, her eyes luminous with shock.

'This is my fault. I should never have involved you. When I think what could have happened to Miss de Bourgh, and to Mrs. Darcy as well.'

'Everyone involved is anxious to take the blame, but in actual fact the only person culpable is Sheffield.'

'I don't see it that way.'

'Mrs. Darcy has been seen by the doctor and suffered no harm to herself or her baby.'

'Thank goodness.'

Joshua smiled. 'Precisely. Darcy would have ripped me apart with his bare hands had it been otherwise.'

'What have you done with Percival?'

'He is secured in the cellars here. We cannot charge him with abduction without Lady Catherine discovering what happened. And so we hoped you would agree for him to be charged with attempted fraud, otherwise he will escape punishment.'

'We cannot allow that to happen. Certainly you may charge him with wrongfully claiming my property, forging a will, and anything else you think might help.'

'Thank you. Darcy will be pleased to hear it.'

'And so, Joshua,' she said after several tension-filled seconds of silence between them, 'we come to the real reason why you are avoiding me.'

'I am not avoiding you, Celia.'

'Liar!'

Joshua's body jerked. He was not accustomed to being addressed in such a fashion, even if it happened to be true. 'Excuse me?'

'Was I wrong to assume you admired me?' she asked, looking down at her hands.

'How could any man fail to admire you?'

'That is not precisely the answer I was hoping for.'

The wounded look in her lovely eyes crushed Joshua's resolve. She deserved to hear the truth.

'I do admire you, Celia. More than that, so very much more, but I have nothing to offer you.'

Her clouded expression cleared. 'Oh, is that all. Your silly pride stands in the way. I ought to have foreseen as much.'

'It is not pride, but plain economic fact. I live on a colonel's pay and very little else. You have not long been widowed, and have had to battle to obtain your rightful inheritance. You do not need me complicating matters by stifling your freedom and independence.'

'You treat me like a green girl rather than a woman of experience.' She sent him a smouldering look. 'I was attracted to you the first moment I saw you, as I believe you were to me. We were drawn together in a way I had long since stopped believing existed. It was as though we had been waiting to find one another our entire adult lives.' She placed her hands on her hips and glared at him. 'Deny it if you can.'

Joshua shook his head. He could lie to her, but she would know it immediately. 'In all

330

conscience, I cannot.'

Her smile was triumphant. 'Then be a gentleman and propose to me, rather than leaving the matter to me.'

He pulled her into his arms, unable to resist a moment longer. 'Are you absolutely sure, Celia? I would not have the world think I married you for your money.'

'What do I care for the world's opinion? Besides, men marry for money all the time. Your aunt certainly expected you to, and the fact that you turned down those riches, when they would have seen you comfortably settled for life, is to your credit.'

'How could I smile upon Anne after meeting you?'

'You will be far less wealthy with me. My property is very modest, as is my fortune.'

'What you offer me is beyond price.'

He kissed her then because the urge to do so was too powerful to resist. He pulled her closer and her arms wound their way around his neck as though it was the most natural thing in the world.

'I love you, Celia,' he said softly, whispering the words against her moist lips. 'Please say you will be my wife.'

'That depends,' she replied playfully.

'Upon what?' He kissed the end of her nose.

'Upon whether you know anything about managing estates.'

'A very great deal. And what I don't know, I can learn.'

'Very well then, Colonel Fitzwilliam. It sounds as if you could be very useful to me.'

He growled in her ear. 'You have absolutely no idea just how useful I can make myself.'

'But I have every expectation of finding out.'

This was all happening the wrong way around, he thought as he claimed another kiss. He still had to inform his aunt he didn't intend to marry Anne and weather the fall-out. He should have done that first, but it didn't matter. Nothing mattered. He was the happiest, the most privileged man on God's earth, and would spend the rest of his life proving it to his beloved Celia.

19

'Have you been summoned too?' Anne asked as she met her cousin outside the sitting room her mother occupied.

'I was planning to break the news. I assume Lady Catherine has asked to see you.'

'Yes.'

'Then I shall come back later.'

'No, as you are here, we might as well tell her together.'

'I don't want you to have to shoulder any blame. Let me tell her alone and allow her to vent her anger on me first.'

Anne laughed. 'That is very gallant of you, but I insist. Come along, Colonel, I am sure you have faced worse situations during the course of your career.'

'At this precise moment I cannot think of a single one.'

He opened the door and stood back to allow Anne to pass through it in front of him. Anne blinked back her surprise when she discovered Sir Marius was also there. They really would have to delay telling Mama now. It was not a subject that could be broached in front of a stranger.

'I beg your pardon, Aunt,' the colonel said politely. 'I did not realise you had company.'

'Close the door, Fitzwilliam, and sit down. What we have to discuss can be said in front of Sir Marius.'

The colonel flexed his brows. 'It can?'

'Certainly.' Mama straightened her spine, even though it wouldn't dare to be anything other than rigidly upright. Subconsciously, Anne found herself sitting a little straighter too, fingers laced together in nervous anticipation of the storm to come. 'I assume all those long afternoon drives have given the two of you ample opportunity to reach a decision.'

'Indeed, ma'am.' Colonel Fitzwilliam cleared his throat. 'I am very sorry to disappoint you, but the plain fact of the matter is that Anne and I have decided we will not suit.'

Anne's anxiety increased when Mama frowned, pursed her lips, but did not immediately respond. She had expected loud objections, insults, a diatribe about undutiful relations, or downright insistence that she do as she was told. Instead, the stillness was absolute.

'I thought as much,' she said, having drawn out the silence to its lengthiest extreme. 'I already told Sir Marius you would not do the sensible thing.'

Anne was confounded. 'You anticipated this, Mama, but do not mind?'

'Of course I mind, but what do you expect me to do about it? If it was only you being foolish it would be one thing, but I believe Fitzwilliam has fixed his interest elsewhere. It's as plain as a pikestaff.' Mama scowled at her nephew. 'Why the male members of this family will insist upon marrying for love is beyond my comprehension.'

'Now, Catherine,' Sir Marius chided.

Catherine? Anne and the colonel exchanged a glance. Neither of them had ever heard her addressed so informally before.

'Well then, miss, I suppose I had better find someone else for you.'

Anne took a deep breath. She had not intended to say anything about Pierce until Mama had recovered from her disappointment. But Sir Marius being in the room appeared to wield some influence with Mama, and he had Pierce's best interests at heart. She might never have a better opportunity.

'Mama,' she said, lifting her head and finding the courage to meet her mother's gaze. 'I have already decided upon my future husband.'

'You have what!'

Colonel Fitzwilliam stood. 'Perhaps I

should leave you to discuss this matter in private.'

'Stay, Fitzwilliam,' Mama commanded. 'Someone will need to talk sense into my silly daughter. I blame you for this,' she added, turning to Sir Marius.

'Me? What have I done?'

'I took on Mr. Asquith on your recommendation, even though the decision caused many raised eyebrows. Now see where it has landed us.'

'You have fixed your interest upon Asquith?' Sir Marius asked Anne in a kindly voice.

'Yes.' Anne elevated her chin another notch. 'He has proposed and I have accepted him.'

'You are not of age,' Mama said.

'No, but I soon will be.'

'Asquith has no money. He could never support you in the style to which you are accustomed, and I will not have him at Rosings.'

'He knows that. He does not want me for my money.'

'That's what he has told you, I have no doubt.'

'Mama!'

'Be sensible, Anne. You know nothing of the ways of the world, or men like Asquith. Of course he says he is not interested in your wealth, but that cannot possibly be the case.'

'You are quite wrong. He will get another teaching position, and I will go wherever he is.'

Mama snorted. 'You would not last a month. It is easy to say you do not care about living in luxury when you have never experienced anything else.'

'Since you asked me to remain, Lady Catherine, presumably I am permitted to express my view,' Colonel Fitzwilliam said.

'If you think you can talk some sense into her. The first attractive young man she meets and he has quite turned her head.' Mama shuddered. 'I must have been out of my senses, agreeing to take him on. At first, I thought it was a good thing he had brought Anne out of herself. I can see now he has done rather too good a job of it.'

'Actually, ma'am,' the colonel said, 'I wanted to enquire what your objections are to the match.'

'What they are?' Mama's glower was shared equally between the colonel and Anne. 'How can you be so obtuse? The man is a fortune hunter, the son of a Jamaican plantation manager looking to feather his own nest. He is intelligent and personable, I'll grant you that. But he is still a fortune hunter. Would

337

you see Rosings passed to such a man? A man of no family or consequence? It would make us a laughing stock. Well, I won't have it. Do you hear me, miss?' Mama fixed Anne with the determined gaze that had always reduced her to silence on the few previous occasions when she had dared to disagree with her. This time it would not work, because Anne was equally determined to have her way. 'If you insist upon this foolish action, I cannot prevent it once you reach your majority. But hear this, and hear it well, I shall disinherit you, and there's an end to the matter.'

'I know that, Mama, and so does Mr. Asquith,' Anne said, fighting to retain her dignity, determined not to cry. 'It grieves me that we shall be estranged, but there is no help for that.'

'When he discovers I am serious, I think you will find his desire to marry you will wither on the vine. He will give you some charming excuse for breaking off the engagement and move on to another vulnerable young lady of fortune.'

Sir Marius, who had listened to this exchange without speaking, did so now. 'Before you absolutely refuse your consent, Catherine, you should know a little more about Asquith's history.'

'You also?' Mama turned to Sir Marius,

but her expression softened. 'Does everyone think I enjoy denying my daughter her heart's desire? It is only that I know what is best for her, and she will thank me in years to come.'

'I take no sides, Catherine. I only ask you to hear me out. And since what I am about to tell you will come as news to Asquith as well, perhaps he ought to be present to hear it.'

'Very well.' Anne could see that Mama's interest was piqued every bit as much as her own was. 'Ring the bell, Fitzwilliam. We will settle this matter now, this morning, once and for all.'

The footman who answered the bell was despatched to find Pierce. No one spoke while they waited for him to respond, but mercifully the wait was a short one. The moment Pierce walked into the room, bowed to Mama and Sir Marius then treated Anne to one of the slow, curling smiles he seemed to reserve exclusively for her, all her concerns about disappointing Mama evaporated. With Pierce beside her, she could achieve anything she set her mind to. Anything at all.

'Asquith, my daughter has just told me some preposterous story about the two of you marrying. Quite apart from the fact you ought to have had the good manners to speak to me on the matter first, you must realise it is impossible. However, Sir Marius has something to say on the subject and wanted you to be here while he says it.' Mama transferred her attention to Sir Marius. 'We are all ears, Marius.'

Pierce took a seat beside Anne, curiosity forming the bedrock of his expression.

'I went to Jamaica as a young man.' Sir Marius's voice was firm and controlled, almost as though he had rehearsed what he planned to say. 'I had acceded to the baronetcy upon my father's death and also assumed his debts, which were substantial. Ergo, I had little other than my title, a few pounds in my pocket and a great disappointment to put behind me.' He stared at Mama as he said those words, increasing Anne's curiosity about their history, especially when Mama's face coloured and she looked away. 'I will admit I was reckless, and Jamaica was the right place for a young man to be reckless in those days. The more risks one was willing to take, the greater the rewards on offer. I also . . . pardon me for mentioning such delicate matters, but I did not behave well. Or perhaps I should say, I behaved as many a young man would, once let loose to make his own way in the world and with a grudge to bear against it. Looking back, I regret some of the things I did — the corners I cut to make a start. But I hope I have atoned for those mistakes since growing older and wiser.'

'Speaking as one well acquainted with your plantation, sir,' Pierce replied, 'I think you certainly achieved that ambition.'

'Thank you, Pierce, but you do not know it all yet. When you do, you might not think so well of me. I will not offend your ears, ladies, by going into the particulars. Suffice it to say I sowed my wild oats.' He paused to rub his whiskered chin, looking embarrassed as he faced Pierce and spoke directly to him. 'The result of one such liaison is you.'

Anne's gasp was the only sound to break though the stultifying silence this admittance engendered.

'I . . . you are my father?'

'I have that honour, and it is one of the reasons why I have taken such an interest in you.'

Mama fanned herself rather violently, but didn't look nearly as surprised as Anne felt, nor did she express her outrage. Instead, she looked thoughtful.

'There is so much I don't understand,' Pierce replied, shaking his head. 'How could I not have known? Why did you not say before now? Were you ashamed of me?'

'If you think I did not take you into my house for that reason, you are quite wrong. As Lady Catherine will tell you, I have never been one to shirk my responsibilities, but your mama would not hear of it. She wanted to keep you with her, and I could hardly refuse.'

'My father, I mean the man I always thought of as my father, was married to my mother when you . . . er — '

'Quite so. It was not my finest hour, but I cannot regret I have you to remind me of it. I had sent him to England to act for me on plantation business, and he was gone for a year.' Sir Marius cleared his throat. 'There is no doubt whatsoever about your being my son.'

'And my father, when he returned, just accepted what had happened?' Pierce widened his eyes. 'He did not care?'

'Oh, he cared. He loved your mother very much, just as he loved you. It was your mama's most ardent wish to have a child and . . . well, he was unable to — '

'We understand, Marius,' Mama said briskly, with a significant glance in Anne's direction. 'We do not require all the particulars.'

Anne thought that was a great pity. She would very much like to know what the unfortunate man was unable to achieve. No matter, she would make Pierce tell her when they were next alone.

'Quite so.' Sir Marius took a sip of water. 'When the man you thought was your father died, you were just three years old. Your Mama needed you more than ever, since she had no other children. But at least she then allowed me to take more of an active interest in your welfare, which is why you spent so much time with my children and why — '

'And why I enjoyed such a fine education. Thank you, at least, for that.'

'I never told you the truth because I promised your mother I would not. It took me a long time to establish my fortune, and she did not wish you to think yourself a gentleman's son and have expectations I was not in a position to fulfil. Now she is gone, and so is my own dear wife, which means I can publicly acknowledge you as mine and see you financially secure.'

Anne could see it was too much for Pierce to take in. She longed to reach for his hand and reassure him this was good news, but she dare not do so with her mother in the room.

'Are you against me too, Marius?' Mama asked. Anne was astonished to see tears in her eyes.

'They are in love, Catherine,' Sir Marius replied softly. 'Any fool can see that.'

'Love, bah!'

'That is not what you once thought.'

'What is it, Mama?' Anne asked, unable to contain her curiosity. 'Were you once in love with Sir Marius?'

When Mama, who appeared to be lost in the past, made no response, it was Sir Marius's deep voice that intruded upon the silence. 'That, Catherine, is a very good question. I wonder what answer you will give.'

'Don't do this, Marius,' she snapped.

'You might as well tell us, Mama,' Anne said gently. 'Otherwise we will make up our own minds.'

'Oh, very well. If you must know, when I was younger than you are now, I met Sir Marius and Sir Lewis at a ball. They were childhood friends, and ... oh botheration, this is so difficult to talk about.'

'I flatter myself that Lady Catherine preferred me, but I was penniless, whereas Sir Lewis was not. Pressure was brought upon Catherine to do the sensible thing, which she did. To this day, I have no idea if she regrets that decision.'

'And you cannot possibly expect me to tell you,' Mama replied with asperity and a slight smile.

'That is why you went to Jamaica, and Mama was your great disappointment,' Anne said, her soft heart melting in sympathy.

'Quite right, my dear.' He turned to look at

Mama. 'Well, Catherine, will you force history to repeat itself?'

Mama looked up at him. 'For history to repeat itself, I would have had to have been in love with you, much as you claim my daughter loves your son.'

'Were you?'

Sir Marius fixed Mama with a steady gaze she failed to meet, which was an answer in itself. Mama in love. Who would have thought it? Colonel Fitzwilliam sent Anne a probing glance. No wonder Mama was such a stickler for duty if she had been forced to give up the man she loved for its sake.

'I am not giving my permission for this marriage,' Mama said. 'But I will not dismiss Mr. Asquith either. He may return to Rosings with us, and we will see how matters progress.'

Anne's heart swelled. This was more than she had dared to expect, even in her wildest dreams. She felt Pierce smiling through his confusion and could easily imagine how his head must be reeling after Sir Marius's extraordinary revelations. He and that gentleman were now shaking hands, talking quietly together. Anne assumed they would need to talk for many hours more before Pierce learned everything he wished to know. She felt his glance repeatedly returning to her and knew he was desperate to hold her in his arms and celebrate their good fortune.

But it could wait. They had the rest of their lives to love one another.

20

Lizzy and Will were alone in the drawing room, enjoying a little solitude after the vicissitudes of the past few days. Jane and Bingley had left first thing that morning. Kitty and Georgiana had taken themselves off somewhere to get over the loss of Major Halstead and Captain Turner, who had returned to their regiment. And now Will and Lizzy had just waved off Lady Catherine and her entourage including, thankfully, Mr. Collins.

'You are to be congratulated, Mrs. Darcy,' Will said, stroking her hair. 'Your guests were here for less than two weeks, but in that time you have managed to engineer two betrothals and keep Lady Catherine happy.'

'Just one betrothal,' Lizzy replied. 'Lady Catherine has not agreed to Anne's marriage.'

'No, but she will. There is little she will not do for Sir Marius, I think.'

'Yes, isn't it remarkable? I could scarce believe it when Colonel Fitzwilliam told me the particulars of their history. Perhaps it explains why Lady Catherine has always seemed so severe. She was disappointed in love, and never recovered from that disappointment.'

'She seems quite rejuvenated now that Sir Marius is back in England.'

'He intends to purchase a small estate close to Rosings,' Lizzy replied mischievously.

'I know that smile, Mrs. Darcy. Surely you do not expect my aunt to conduct herself with anything other than the utmost propriety?'

'I would like to imagine her behaving irresponsibly, but even I am not that much of an optimist. Still, I am glad Sir Marius's company pleases her so much. He can make her laugh, and I thought that was an achievement beyond anybody.'

'I am pleased Sir Marius has acknowledged Asquith as his own. I like the young man tremendously, and he is very good for Anne. I have never seen anyone so altered.'

'Never underestimate the power of love, Mr. Darcy.'

'I, of all people, ought to respect its potency,' he replied, placing a protective hand on the swell of Lizzy's belly. 'But I fear it has all been too much for you.'

'Nonsense, I enjoyed playing the part of matchmaker. Not that there was much for me to do, other than listen to the afflicted parties singing the praises of their loved ones.'

'You speak of Fitzwilliam.'

'And Anne, too. Your cousin is at Briar Hall, making arrangements with his Mrs. Sheffield to bring charges against her former brother-in-law.'

'Is that what they are calling it this week?'

Lizzy laughed. 'Well, at least Sheffield is no longer in our cellar but safely locked up in Newcastle gaol. For that I am very grateful.'

'Fitzwilliam is to sell his commission, you know, and settle down to being a man of property the moment he and Mrs. Sheffield are married, which is to be as soon as the arrangements can be made.'

'I am very pleased to hear it. The colonel deserves to be happy, and Mrs. Sheffield will make him so. I like her very much.'

'Mr. Collins has a great deal of ground to make up with Asquith. He made no attempt to hide his disdain for him and now, if things turn out the way we expect them to, he will eventually be the owner of Rosings, with Collins's fate in his hands.'

'If anyone can grovel his way out of trouble, it is Mr. Collins. However, Mr. Asquith will suffer no interference from him, nor will he put up with false flattery.'

'Then life at Rosings will be very interesting.' Will massaged Lizzy's shoulders, causing her to moan and close her eyes. 'Where are the girls?'

'I have no idea. In one of their rooms, I expect, discussing their paramours.'

Will frowned. 'Don't say that.'

Lizzy examined Will's face. 'You don't like Major Halstead very much, do you?'

'I don't think he is right for Georgiana, if that is what you are asking me.' Will removed one hand from her shoulders and waved it about. 'I know you think I am overprotective, but there is just something about him that worries me. Don't ask me what it is because I couldn't tell you.'

'If it puts your mind at rest, Kitty seems as keen as ever on Captain Turner, but I think Georgiana's interest in the major is on the wane.'

'Why do you say that?'

'I've noticed she no longer actively seeks his company.' Lizzy touched his face. 'You can stop worrying. Georgie has a great deal more sense than you give her credit for.'

'Then I shall take your advice, stop worrying about my sister, and concentrate my concerns on you instead. You do too much, Lizzy. But from now until your confinement you will not move a muscle unnecessarily, or you will have me to answer to.'

Lizzy slid onto her husband's knee and

wrapped her arms around his neck. 'For the sake of your sanity, my dear, I will do as you ask.'

Will grunted. 'Excuse me if I do not believe you.'

Lizzy laughed as she lowered her head in anticipation of his kiss. She counted her blessings, well aware how fortunate she was, even if her mother was threatening to come north for Jane's confinement and remain for Lizzy's.

'You should believe me,' Lizzy said, breathless when Will stopped kissing her. 'Because you are my life, my love, my entire reason for being and I would never knowingly do anything to cause you anxiety.'

We do hope that you have enjoyed reading this large print book.

Did you know that all of our titles are available for purchase?

We publish a wide range of high quality large print books including:
Romances, Mysteries, Classics
General Fiction
Non Fiction and Westerns

Special interest titles available in large print are:
The Little Oxford Dictionary
Music Book
Song Book
Hymn Book
Service Book

Also available from us courtesy of Oxford University Press:
Young Readers' Dictionary
(large print edition)
Young Readers' Thesaurus
(large print edition)

For further information or a free brochure, please contact us at:
Ulverscroft Large Print Books Ltd.,
The Green, Bradgate Road, Anstey,
Leicester, LE7 7FU, England.
Tel: (00 44) 0116 236 4325
Fax: (00 44) 0116 234 0205

Other titles published by Ulverscroft:

MISS BINGLEY'S REVENGE

Wendy Soliman

Elizabeth Darcy is determined not to be found wanting when she and her new husband throw their first house party at Pemberley. Of course, Miss Bingley will be there, but Lizzy has nothing to fear from her old nemesis — or so she thinks. Miss Bingley has convinced herself that Mr. Darcy made a mistake in his hasty marriage to Lizzy, and is determined to save him from his own folly. When Lydia Wickham puts in an unexpected appearance, and Miss Bingley learns that Wickham himself is also in the neighbourhood, an unlikely alliance is formed between two people with very different reasons for wanting the Darcy marriage to fail.

TO DEFY A DUKE

Wendy Soliman

Elias Shelton, the Duke of Winsdale, has a duty to produce an heir. Completely indifferent, he leaves his mother to invite the most suitable candidates to a house party at Winsdale Park, promising to choose one of them as his duchess. Returning home after several days of pre-nuptial carousing, he falls from his horse and badly injures his head. His life is saved by a mysterious woman who fascinates and enthrals him: Athena Defoe, who along with her young twin sisters is hiding from her past in a tumbledown cottage on Eli's estate. Can Eli help his new love escape her pursuers before it is too late?